THE F-WORD

MITA KAPUR runs Siyahi, a literary agency based in Jaipur, which also conceptualizes and directs literary events. She writes for various newspapers and magazines on subjects ranging from women's rights to lifestyle and food.

Praise for the Book

'A fascinating culinary trail from Lucknow to Minneapolis that takes in a variety of recipes and the history behind them.... The blending of fast foods with traditional recipes is hugely imaginative.... The book has to be read if only for the wealth of recipes and culinary information. *The F-Word* is a valuable addition to the bookshelf' – *The Hindu*

'The recipes included in *The F-Word* are a wonderful mash-up.... What's most compelling, however, is Mita Kapur's candour about herself and her family. Kapur distills her memories and experiences with relish, and she has an eye for the rituals and intricacies surrounding food that belongs only to the most passionate, involved kind of cook' – *TimeOut*, New Delhi

'Not unlike *Like Water for Chocolate*, the recipes pepper a warm narrative.... Kapur is an entertaining writer, but perhaps more importantly she tells an engaging story, one that is bound to touch any mother, wife or child. She has done a good job of reinventing a genre...and has given it a quintessential Indian makeover – one that you must read' – *Tehelka*

'Kapur combines recipes of all kinds with pithy wisdom... [This is] a delectable addition to the feast of books that present food as memoir, politics and history' – *Open*

'Mita Kapur has written a deliriously funny book.... A chaotic culinary romp with unexpected tender moments, *The F-Word* is packed with seriously good recipes to suit every taste...' – *Mail Today*

'*The F-Word* is an assemblage of some fun recipes put together in a part-autobiographical and part-historical manner, and a rather refreshing way of pursuing the F-subject' – *Hindustan Times*

'*The F-Word*, like its author, is multifaceted – a food book, a memoir, and even a travelogue. [This is] a genre-defying work. Kapur is almost romantic in her approach to cooking' – *The Hindu*

'In *The F-Word*, Mita Kapur regales her readers with family anecdotes.... The book is a breezy read. Foodies will lap this one up' – *The Times of India*

'Don't look at *The F-Word* as a cookbook or even a collection of essays or a memoir. Just don't label it, enjoy it the way it comes. And I promise you, it will be worth every ladle of it' – *The Asian Age*

THE F-WORD

Mita Kapur

Illustrations by
Prabha Mallya

HarperCollins *Publishers* India

First published in India by
HarperCollins *Publishers* in 2010

Building 10, Tower A, 4th Floor, DLF Cyber City, Phase II,
Gurugram Haryana – 122002, India
www.harpercollins.co.in

2 4 6 8 10 9 7 5 3

P-ISBN: 978-93-5116-053-3
E-ISBN: 978-93-5029-248-8

Typeset in 12/15 Adobe Jenson Pro
Jojy Philip New Delhi 110 015

Printed and bound at
MicroPrints India, New Delhi

For Bunny
for all that shines from his eyes,
for giving of himself without measure.

Contents

Introduction

When I decided to write this book, I wanted to write about food, not just cooking. To me, food and more good food has always been symbolic of a celebration of life. Whether it's a delicately served seven-course meal in gold-plated Venetian glassware with beluga caviar served on melons or roast chicken stuffed with truffles and lemon ginger sorbet or just a simple ande ki bhurji with teen kone wali paranthi placed on the table for all of us to eat out of one dish, the only flavour that remains is that of togetherness, of shared laughter and a final contented hand on the stomach: 'Oh, I've overeaten yet again.'

Over the years, my gastronomic quest has taken me to strange and exciting places. The recipes in this book, which are an eclectic mix of Indian, Thai, European and other cuisines, have been collected over the last two decades. Some recipes bear the stamp of the army lifestyle, some have been carried back from travels to various cities around the world and some are the legacy of my mother-in-law's visits to small-town India, from Jammu to Jhansi, Nasirabad to Secunderabad. Some of the recipes came to me like half remembered songs from my childhood and some I learnt from kind chefs in their restaurant kitchens.

All along, my guiding principle has been the simple hands-on method of trial and error. I've learnt not just by observation but by following all my senses – taste, touch, smell, hearing. I've learnt by watching how the gifts of the earth are brought, prepared and set on the table. I've learnt how our dreams drink coffee with us as they put their arms around our children. Perhaps the world will end at the dining table, with us laughing and crying and polishing off that last sweet bite.

Cooking, for me, has always been a very emotional exercise. I've found euphoria staring at me from the orange zest curling delicately on a chocolate velvet mousse. I've faced anger when a burnt cake looked at me defiantly from the oven. I have squared my shoulders at the gelatine rebelling against swinging temperatures, carving layers into my caramel soufflé. I have had cricket-ball sized gulab jamuns cheekily chuckling at me. Even after so many years, it is a moment of triumph when I rustle up a dish perfectly. For a recent wedding anniversary celebration, I created a five-layered cake, with vanilla sponge, profiteroles, honey mousse, almond praline and chocolate sauce. Before this came a seven-course meal. The rule has always been that no rules are followed. I started with a kebab, threw in a Lebanese salad, Vietnamese laksa, Thai chicken curry, Indianized stir-fry, watermelon sorbet and Goan fish. All served with noodles and boiled rice. The evening turned into a cherished memory for Mom and Dad.

But forget the special dinners and lunches, the everyday meal plan for a family needs thought and caution. Equal consideration has to be given to the current obesity index, staff statistics, hormonal vagaries, the senility quotient. The success of a meal also depends on multiple moods. How did the boss treat the meal-maker that day? Is the daughter depressed about not being able to go for a party because of an extra SAT class? The son is pleading for a mobike and being refused. Everyone has to be brought together and appeased through the subtle influence of good food.

Yet, these recipes are only themes for the reader to improvise upon as mood and appetite demand. I have done away with the proverbial 'preparation time'. The quantities of cooking oil, spices, chillies also have to be varied according to taste. Cooking for a family that is crazy about chillies, chocolate, cheese and chicken means that some proportions are rather exaggerated, but they can be easily adjusted to suit specific taste buds. I've left it to the readers to set the pace and to use their common sense. Where you read experiment, innovate, recreate, you also read substitute, repair, camouflage. If the coffee custard on the double boiler gets over-cooked into coagulated shreds, don't sob over the lost soufflé. Retrieve the shreds. Let them cool while you garner the courage to reinvent. Whip up fresh cream to soft glistening peaks. Melt dark chocolate over the double boiler. Mix the two ever so gently. Add spring and foam with frothy egg whites. Pour a portion into a soufflé dish; add a layer of the coffee shreds. Chill and set. Repeat. Friends who came to dine that night still can't forget the lingering taste of 'that coffee toffee you put in your sinful mousse'.

Smoked charcoal lends mystery to a kebab. The tangy sweetness of honey teases the chunky flesh of dates in ice cream. A sunny yellow moong ki dal, with the bite of ginger and the aroma of fresh coriander, is a delight. The only condition is that it has to be 'khilwa'. Each grain of dal has to be visible, tangible, yet whole bodied. And no, it's not tough at all. You have to merely fine-tune your instincts. The pressure in the cooker should be released when your mind says, 'Okay, it's time to let go.'

Living in a small city like Jaipur, with any exotic ingredient having to be carted home from Delhi or from elsewhere in the world, it became a challenge for me to recreate the best of international cuisine in the confines of my kitchen. But perseverance, as always, has been the key, and these words by Robert Frost: 'There is only one thing more exasperating than a wife who can cook and won't, and that's a wife who can't cook and will.'

1

Papad, Peanuts or Pepperoni

Papad, peanuts or pepperoni, what will it be for starters today? Every evening begins with a verbal duel. We converge in the lounge for the ceremony of the day – a drink together before dinner is served. Old army traditions don't change.

We know it's time to emerge from our corners when we hear the signature tune – 'Bahadur, trolley lao.' The black trolley is wheeled in every evening, its edges chipped, the metal showing through long years of use. I've grown up seeing similar trolleys, in various sizes, on the pavements of Delhi's Panchkuiyan Road, and although this one is a misfit amidst the Queen Anne furniture and Rosenthal birds, it has resolutely stuck on as a part in the routine – so stay it must.

Mummy is seated on her throne – the roche bobois sofa – in her favourite corner. The cushion has given way under her and is tilted. And, as always, she grumbles: ' Look at those nuts. Why have you filled the bowl to the brim? They will not eat dinner properly.' So off goes Bahadur to empty half of it out. The men walk in, briefcases in hand. There is a general shout for all the kids: 'Papas have come, come down!'

'Where is the whisky?' Mummy's voice rings with gentle authority. She is rotund, as all grandmothers should be, although saved somewhat by her 5' 6" frame. She always has her lipstick on, no matter what time of the day it is, and her hair is streaked with dignified white strands in an uncanny resemblance to Indira Gandhi's white streak – but the similarity ends right there. Mummy grew up in Calcutta, when it was the hot seat of propah British ways, and she takes great pride in announcing, 'I grew up in a big city, having high tea at Flurys and watching Shakespeare's plays. The nuns at our school made us walk demurely. We were the Nat King Cole and Frank Sinatra generation. No junk in *our* lives.'

I stand before the bar – Laphroaig, Glenlivet 18 years, Glenfiddich, Gold Label for daily use – and make my pick for the day. There is a general cacophony as all sizes of human beings troop in. Mummy's voice rises above them all: 'Bunty, no more peanuts! You won't eat dinner properly. It's just junk.' Bunty, her elder son, indulges her by saying, 'Yes, yes, mamma, whatever you say,' and quickly shoves a handful of nuts into his mouth.

Everyone is tall in this family. Bunty is a good 6' 1", has the build of an army officer, and served as one for five years. He has a perpetual twinkle in his eyes and a mind that works multilaterally. His dream is to write a book on an island – his own. His growing middle-aged girth and fast-receding hairline, with curly tufts of hair behind the ears, draw a look of disapproval from his wife. 'If you don't get a haircut by tomorrow, I'm not going to that party with you,' she threatens. Bunty strikes a pose, drawing himself to his full height, and running his hands through his hair with an exaggerated swagger, replies, 'I think I look distinguished.' His infectious smile spreads ripples of laughter.

'Ah, we have cheese and crackers today!' he gleefully exclaims. 'Mits, are they left over from last night's dinner you had for your friends? Why would we get this honour otherwise?' I grin back at him, pointing to his slight paunch, and say, 'Yes, and we don't need to eat cheese every day.'

'Arre Mits, ek hi toh zindagi hai, jee lene de, yaar. Thoda jaldi hi to marenge, par kha pee kar na,' he says, reaching for another fistful of peanuts. With a deft move of her hand, Mummy slides the bowl out of his reach. It's always the same – day after day, year after year. The men nurse their whisky and talk shop – 'Ajmer Road is going berserk!' 'Did you see the new Murano, what artistry!' The conversation swings from real estate to the new lights catalogue from Milan.

Resham ambles in, surreptitiously sneaking her hand into the ice bucket. She fields my dirty look with a sunny smile and murmurs, 'Bas last one, Mamma.' Sigh. Resham is my younger daughter. Our Meena Kumari incarnate – a dreamer who plays little mummy with unflinching devotion to my third-born, Rehan. Her stride is like that of a model on a constant catwalk, and her hands move like a dancer's. A friend who has studied the Shekhawati School of Art says, 'She has the same large melting eyes as the women in those old miniature paintings.' I suppress my chuckle, but I know that combined with her lost-pup look and long hair (for which she was named), Resham wins over the hearts of the sternest. The smile is a family trait – it comes from my father – sweet, winsome and refreshingly innocent.

Tanay the hulk, 6' 2", lumbers in, wearing barely-there-on-the-flat-hips jeans. Looking down at me, he says, 'Hey, shorty.' I have to crane my neck to meet his eyes. Tanay is Bunty's eldest. A simple, kindhearted eighteen-year-old who comes home with six-year-olds, casually shrugging and saying, 'They're my friends,' while I look askance at the difference in size as well as age. His favourite one-liner whenever he sees me cooking is, 'CM, you are not meant to be behind the fire, you are meant to be in it.' (CM is short for Chhoti Mamma.)

The year he was head boy of his school, Raj Kumar Hirani, who was chief guest at the annual day, began his speech with, 'I'm very happy to have been invited to a school where the head boy has long hair and looks like a rock star.' Tanay's hair was a hot topic in the schools of Jaipur, where students are expected to be miraculously neat and tidy.

Tanay has a subtle way of endearing himself to his elders and getting away with a lot of nonsense. 'Aur, Siyahi ka kya haal hai, CM? Aap paise nahin kama sakte, chhod do yeh sab!' he ribs me. Tanay's taste in food bears the simplicity of his nature. He grew from a chubby baby to being huge 'just on CM's cheesy potatoes'. I have to admit guilt in this case. Tanay loves creating his own omelettes, replete with herbs, cheese and chilli flakes. He focuses on making fruit smoothies after serious consultation with me on how to balance the sugar content if bananas are being used, and how many Oreo cookies should be added for one glass of chocolate milk shake. While our intense discussion is on, Smriti, his mother and my bhabhi, glares at us, adding to the gravitas of the flavours and measurements being discussed.

Starters begin the journey to the dinner table. The men are hungry at the end of the day. The kids – well, they are forever hungry. I often insist on salad sticks with a garlic and spring onion dip. But health food doesn't appear, even as a footnote, in the family's fondness-for-food manual. On the nights when a vegetarian meal is planned, I put out chicken salami rolls with green chilli and coriander to give the 'pure' non-veg souls some succour. My own favourite thing to do is to use starter time for a huge bowl of fruit salad.

The nights we have matar paneer, khili gobi, mixed raita for dinner, I tear apart a packet of nachos, crumble some feta cheese, plop caramelized onions on top, and present it as a snappy starter – just to prepare a hungry family for the emotional upheaval of a vegetarian meal. More so, since they pride themselves on being staunchly, religiously, non-vegetarian. In case the cheese is missing, it's easy to throw together a mango-kiwi salsa with the nachos. And if there is spaghetti bolognese for dinner – well, it works as a starter, first course, second course and a midnight snack. When Resham stands in the middle of the kitchen protesting, 'I am not eating rasse wala matar paneer,' with an air of suffering that would put Bimal Roy's heroines to shame, I quickly roast some garlic and tomatoes, douse them in olive oil, sprinkle basil and sea salt, and make them sit cheekily on toasted squares of regular white bread.

We are a part of the kele amrud ki chaat, aloo pakoda, bread pakoda generation, when hunger before meal times was assuaged by these. I wonder if they would qualify as starters in any household now. The pakodas resurface only on rainy days and the kele amrud ki chaat seems to have vanished from our minds. I can still taste the sharp red chillies doing the jig with sugar crystals that defiantly resisted melting into the tang of lemon power. It's just one of the many things on my 'simple pleasures of life' list.

Chaat reminds me of the trip we took to Lucknow for a wedding. Sakshi, my first-born, is a prime example of a bigdi hui aulaad. Her first night on this earth was marked by an earthquake – which is a rare occurence in Jaipur. High ceilings, grey walls, iron beds and the smell of spirit kept me awake as I watched Metrogyl slide down the tube into my thin veins. My eyes rested on her tiny head peeping out of the pink blanket that kept her body snug. Despite the drugs and anesthesia, I was on full alert. Lying on the bed next to me, Sakshi made my mind brim with questions – what will she be like when she grows up, will she be a strong, self-willed girl, or will she be a tempestuous cracker? And I am still dealing with these.

Sakshi is the official stand-up comedian of the family. Her chubby cheeks and sparkling eyes are the same as in her baby days, although they sit on an elongated frame, which is happily heavy. She walks in from her SAT class, dumps her books on the sofa with a loud thump, and declares, 'Okay,

you guys, you know that Tushar is such a motherfuckingasshole, he took my Math file… and that other chutiyawithapenishangingbetweenhislegs stared at my freshly waxed legs… bloody assholes all men are…' The tirade continues, enveloping the whole world. Each one is hierarchically granted choice abuses according to the sins committed that day. The list of sinners changes daily and each one is given a treatment specific to the torture inflicted on her delicate female sensibilities. Her favourite abuse is, 'Oh, he can't help it, he's only a boy!' Deeply into reading women's literature, she looks down on all men as severely handicapped by their own sex.

We listen and watch, and wait for her energies to subside. 'What's for dinner, Ma?' she demands.

'Fish kebabs and corn salad.'

'I thought you said kebabs are meant to be starters. Ah-haan, lady, who's confused here, huh?' She clicks her fingers at me. 'Remember when we went to Lucknow for that blessed wedding in April, and that too by second class on the Marudhar Express – sheesh, Mom, how could you do that to me? Imagine Dadu's princess travelling in such appalling conditions, yuck!'

Resham and I cackle at the memory of that afternoon on the railway platform. The crowds and the smell of human sweat, mingled with sweet tea and pakodas fried in suspect cooking oil. Side-stepping blackened, cracked heels, which warned that the rest of the body was sleeping on the ground. Sakshi climbed into the compartment rather quietly. The rest of us spotted a tiny mouse that was scampering merrily between our suitcases, and instinctively, our eyes met and necks tilted to one side. A silent pact of understanding was signed: 'Don't tell Sakshi we have the honour of rodent company to spice up the journey.' She would have simply dived out of the moving train's window, had she seen the happy creature.

'And yes, that's when you dragged us around all the galis of Lucknow on a journey of culinary discovery – trying to lure Resham and me into becoming cooks – Gawd…!' she reminds me.

I sigh dramatically. It is evident that she is suffering from vocabulary diarrhoea – SAT class does that to her.

'The fish was sitting in the deep freeze, I decided to use it before it got smelly, Saksh, so just beat it and eat,' I say.

'But kebabs are meant to be made of mutton mince, Ma,' she protests.

I launch into lesson mode and soon realize that only Aman the foodie, Bunty's second son, is listening to me.

'Kebabs are simply meat-on-a-stick. Japanese yakitori, French brochettes, Malaysian satays, Peruvian anticuchos, Spanish pinchos morunos, Armenian shashlik are the different versions of the basic preparation. The Turkish kuftas, patties of ground meat, are what anyone from Baghdad would think of as kebabs. Local cultures naturally shape the flavour and texture of food.

'Kebabs reached India with the Muslim infiltration into the subcontinent. It was the marauding Turks who roasted meat over open-pit fires. We Indians transformed the spit-roasted barbeques of the Turks into delicacies, by using a combination of exotic spices and marinades. The Mughals introduced lavish culinary tastes and cooking styles. But it was the Nawabs of Awadh who had their cooks transform cooking into a realm of high art.'

Sakshi rolls her eyes and waves her hand in supreme dismissal before retreating to the confines of her Shah Rukh Khan-plastered room.

I once chanced upon Robert Rodriguez on YouTube in his Ten Minute Cooking School, telling people about the slow-roasted meat he craves and could sometimes kill for! For Robert, director of *Sin City*, 'not knowing how to cook is not knowing how to fuck!' As he deftly lines a tin with banana leaves to cook the meat in, he says, 'If you've got to eat for the rest of your life, you've got to know how…' Sitting in Sakhawat's small dhaba, in a by-lane next to the Gymkhana Club, Lucknow, my mind wandered back to Robert's video, as my conversation with Mushtaq Ali, the owner and chef, took its winding course back into an era of epicurean decadence. Mushtaq would baulk at the slow-roasting meat in banana leaves that Robert so proudly boasted of. And he would shudder if he saw Robert dry grind annatto seeds with cumin, cloves and black pepper in a coffee grinder.

I was visiting the genteel city of Lucknow after thirty-two years. The smell of kebabs sizzling silently on the huge tawas with upturned rims – placed alongside the ulta tawa on which rotis were deftly flipped to bake – in the bustling yet laid-back lanes of Chowk hadn't quite left me. Nor had the sweet sensation of gulkand-filled paan slowly melting and filling my mouth. Ali sahib captured my attention by saying, 'We're in food buzzyness since 1911. My son will also stand behind that tawa and fry galaavat… this is not readymade food. We actually cook. We don't just boil the rice, boil the meat, dissolve the gravies jaldi se, tad pad nahin banta hai khana… if twenty items have to be made, twenty fires are lit and each is cooked in copper vessels with silver "kalai".'

I was slowly beginning to understand what a friend had wisely told me – 'Lucknow ki nazaaqat, tehzeeb, is a delicacy in itself.' The food here had a subtle way of conquering you with its sensual appeal, just as Lucknowi tehzeeb, commonly joked about as the 'pehle aap, pehle aap' culture, charms you with its sophisticated politeness – something that most north Indian cities sorely lack these days.

'Kebab woh hota hai jo muh mein rakha aur slip ho jaaye' – you shouldn't have to chew on a kebab, it should simply melt on your tongue and slip down your throat. To make the finest of galaavati kebab, they beat it fine in a handi, add the galaavat (tenderizer of unripe papaya) and grind it on the sil batta. This implement is vital to every Indian kitchen, not only because it has probably been handed down from generation to generation, but because it symbolizes the escaping of aromas, flavours and textures of any ingredient that is put on its ridged stone surface (sil) and subjected to the pressures of the rounded roller (batta) which is made to work back and forth. For me it means a release of sensations; for my cook it means he has to labour hard over the grinding process, muttering about why I can't be satisfied with the mixer-grinder.

The mince is tenderized to coat the tongue seductively. Charcoal and wood not only provide the heat but also the flavours. The aromas that so arrest your senses come from rose, saffron and meetha itr. Herbs like sangal and jarrakesh root have a special fragrance and are sourced from shops that sell ingredients for pujas.

For Ali sahib, cooking is as sacred as his religion. It is not about eating, it is a philosophy. Awadhi food is just that. The nawabs of Awadh transposed all sensory experiences to the realm of art. The ordinary act of cooking a humble dal was rarified into an artistic process. In the eighteenth century, a certain chef was paid five hundred rupees to cook arhar dal by Nawab Shuja-ud-Daula. One day, the nawab didn't sit down to eat as soon as the dal was served. The chef left in a huff, pouring the dal down the trunk of a dead tree. Predictably, the story has it that the tree sprouted healthy green leaves.

In this country, cooking has always been considered an act of reverence. Bawarchi khanas were epicentres of research and innovation. Highly paid cooks were given the freedom to create new dishes and could lay down working conditions to suit their temperament. A unique culture existed within the bawarchi khanas. Culinary hierarchy was strictly defined and there were three categories of cooks – raqabdars who were gourmet cooks and presented delicately garnished dishes in small quantities; bawarchis who cooked food in bulk; and nanfus who made the roti, naan and sheermal. The masalchi would grind the spices and the mehri would carry the food trays. The kitchen was supervised by the daroga-e-bawarchi-khana. No wonder Ali sahib said, 'Purani cheez toh apni jagah hoti hai.'

It takes Ali sahib two days to prepare a biryani. 'Aajkal, biryani ko khichdi bana diya hai. I boil the paye ki yakhni for twenty-four hours. When the bones become white, we sieve it, temper it with cloves, cardamom and ghee, and that is mixed in the marinade. This way of cooking is called "kushta" – kuwat deta hai, taakat deta hai.'

But it's a different experience entirely to be standing on the road, waiting for a shammi or galaavat kebab, served with a parantha. The noise and clutter of the street, cars and rickshaws dodging in and out of corners to get past cycles and cows, is like being in a Formula One race in slow motion – the risks are the same! Sakhawat's menu changes every day. On a Monday, I tried boti and kakori kebab, and looked longingly at the menu for the rest of the week. How I wished my stay in Lucknow could be stretched like dough and flipped around just the way a parantha is before it settles down on the rough surface of the tawa to be cooked through.

I watched the cook Abdullah's face as he spoke about kakori being created for a nawab who had lost his teeth but not his love for food. 'This is my family recipe,' he said. 'The mutton has to be very soft. It has to be consistently thin around the skewer. Raw papaya, cloves and black pepper aid in making the mince velvety soft.' Kakori kebabs are gently spiced with elaichi, javitri, kali mirch, badi elaichi, laung, zaffran, and are made of mince from the hind leg of a young eight- or nine-month-old kid. Cashew paste, malai and onions give strength to the flavours. Proportions play an important role – the delicate aromas that each spice releases, when smoked, should not be overpowered by too much of any single ingredient. Grinding by hand, smoking the mince on charcoal, and using wood from either a tamarind, babul or mango tree to cook biryani, korma and yakhni are fixed rules of Awadhi cuisine. Spending time with chefs in this city, I realized that their sensibilities would be easily hurt by even the suggestion of using a mixer-grinder – complete blasphemy!

The charms of antiquity were visible all over the city. As my driver meandered his way about with expert nonchalance, I took in the sights of various maqbaras, the Imambara and Bhool Bhulaiya. Any question related to 'How to do *this* in Lucknow' was answered in meethi shudh Hindi – 'Ab hum kaise batayen aapko, yeh toh aap ki soch pe nirbhar hai.' Lucknowis philosophize as they speak, I thought. The driver parked with a flourish at Tundey Kebab's doorstep and led me inside as if I were a begum. If you wish to relish moments of social harmony, visit Tundey Miya, where you can see a rickshaw-walla, truck driver, peon, bureaucrat, small trader in a Maruti or a tycoon with his Mercedes parked outside, eating the same galaavat or shammi with parantha at twenty rupees per plate. A whole new world springs up, the buzz infects you, with waiters shouting over the owner's head: Ek biryani aur ek kebab roll lagana... Food links everyone, and for those few minutes, a bond is shared.

Tundey Miya's eatery is hundred and eight years old. The present owner is Mohammad Usman, whose ancestors cooked for the nawabs. His grandfather, who set up this shop, had only one arm, hence the moniker Tundey. Usman explains to me, 'Our masalas are our heritage. Dil aur dimaag dono ko durust rakhte hain. These are Unani masalas. Kebabs don't affect your health as much as plain red meat does because of the way they are fine-ground and tenderized – and the spices help in digestion. You can spend Rs 250 on pizza at Pizza Hut but there is no flavour – tripti nahin hoti. You can have Lucknowi khaana cold and you'll still be content.' I can vouch for that. Breakfast on the train journey back to Jaipur was kakori and galaavat kebabs. The scent of kewra and saffron filled the compartment. Both the girls protested, 'Ma, we've lived on kebabs this whole week.' And the driver's voice echoed in my mind: 'Yeh Lucknow ki pehchaan hai.'

Kebabs and tikkas have created a niche for themselves the world over. Far away, in Toronto, I discovered the tastiest Kissan tandoori masala. I would equate it to one of God's little make-life-easy miracles, made in Canada! Irony be ignored, this masala is the perfect blend of spices – it cooks up the most delicious chicken tikkas. The instructions for use are given in French too!

There is something deeply sensuous about the aromas that rise as masalas roast. I always inhale deeply as cloves combined with nutmeg send out their warm woody vapours, clearing the nostrils. Cardamom smoke gently curling around wisps of delicate javitri, seducing and teasing... besan turning shades of gold on the black tawa as you swiftly stir to keep it from burning into a chocolate hue.

Mix the flavours with your hands. Your fingers must touch the moist granular softness of raw mince. I have a love-hate relationship with all things deep-fried. But some kebabs, like galaavat, have to be dunked into sizzling hot ghee for the mince to acquire the tenderness that fills your mouth.

Galaavat ke Kebab

500 g keema
2 tbsp raw papaya paste
1 tsp ground ginger
1 tsp ground garlic
2 tbsp sliced onions fried brown
2 tbsp roasted chana powder
4 green chillies finely chopped
2 tbsp green coriander finely chopped
1 tsp kewra water
1 tbsp ghee
Salt to taste

Garam masala mix:
5 cloves
5 green cardamoms
1 blade of javitri
2 cinnamon sticks
1 tbsp khus khus
½ tsp saunth
15 black peppers
3 red chillies
1 bay leaf
1 tsp cumin

Roast all the garam masala ingredients on a tawa and grind together. Add 1 tsp kewra water, cover for 2 minutes. Mix papaya, salt, ginger, garlic in the keema, leave for an hour. Mix all the remaining ingredients into the keema, leave for another hour. Pat the mixture into small balls and shallow-fry in ghee till done.

The Lucknow-walas were amused to see a lady bedecked in meena kundan jhumkas and a red zari sari, pleats hitched up, holding a recorder behind the kebab counter at a wedding. Both the girls stayed far away with a look that said, 'We don't even know who you are!' and tense facial muscles that declared, 'Gosh, you are so embarrassing!' But I revelled in the little discoveries, and talking to the cooks from Chowk and Aminabad was like opening new windows in my culinary life.

The next time I made kebabs, Aman's friend was over for lunch. He was a Marwari just learning to eat meat. The spices and kewra assaulted his tongue. He swallowed quietly but couldn't resist asking, 'Is there something wrong with these kebabs?' Aman's reply surprised and delighted me. 'No, silly,' he said, 'you have to learn to pick up the delicate flavours. A kebab doesn't mean eating a chunk of minced meat. CM blends in a balance, and that weird taste is of kewra. It's exotic, an almost royal experience.' Phew, I was relieved, amused and proud in one moment.

The word kebab is of Mesopotamian origin. In Akkadian, the language of ancient Iraq, 'kababu' meant to burn or char. The earliest recipe for kebab was found in a tenth-century Baghdadi cookbook, *Kitab al-Tabeekh* by Ibn Sayyar al Warraq, which deals with cooking techniques. The tikka, as they say, is the Hindi version of the original kebab.

My eldest sister, Nita, was my first teacher. Eight years older, Didi has mothered me more than my mother has. I grew up not having to pour a glass of water for myself and was tucked into bed every night by her. When Ma suffered her first angina attack, Didi and she were alone at home. Preeti and I had tagged along with our father on a tour to Kota. Didi arranged for Ma to be admitted to the hospital and calmly made all the phone calls. In her eleventh grade, she took over running the house when Ma was advised complete bed rest. During this period, she made sure that none of us felt neglected. Our tiffins were packed on time and Ma got her special diet of clear soups and steamed veggies, dressed in different flavours, every day.

Didi has this 'always-in-control-of-the-situation' look, much to Preeti's chagrin. Suffering from the typical middle child syndrome, Preeti describes it as the 'Nita-puts-us-all-in-trouble-look'. Both of us grew up with our relatives telling us, 'Ooh-look-at-Nita-she-is-so-good-at-everything!' I would sit on the window-sill of our kitchen, watching Didi work silently and deftly through recipes of Welsh rarebit, yam curry, clear soups, cakes, chicken gol mirchi, cheese cakes, chocolate fudge. My first lessons were only through observation. I waited patiently for her to pour the fudge out to set on a thali so that I could pounce on the bowl to scrape the remains with my fingers. The joy of wiping the bowl clean of every little smudge of chocolate was sinful.

Didi's kebabs sit on the tawa with such calm. No spluttering in protest, the green chillies never threatening to fling themselves out of the confines of the soft mince. She always insists on grinding the mince mixture on the sil batta to keep the grain of the keema. 'Pulse it in the electric blender just for a few seconds to get that tinge of fineness.' I grew up on ounces of such snappy cooking wisdom. Didi would never put a knife to the slender stems of coriander, but break off the fresh stems delicately and run her fingertips under my nose: 'Can you get the whiff of its aroma? It is so gentle and fresh – you chop it, you kill the soul of coriander.'

My cook, Chander Bahadur, whom we call CB, hates making shikampuris. He can never manage to keep the stuffing from spilling out the moment the kebabs are slipped into ghee for frying. What he hates more is my amused look at his sense of frustrated helplessness. A common error is to fry the kebab over high heat for the entire time it is being cooked. Once the kebab takes on a golden hue, reduce the flame and let it sizzle along with the bubbles of fat. I remember spluttering as much as the kebabs when Bahadur cheekily mixed the filling with the mince and rolled them into flattened rounds like any other kebab. 'Bhabhiji, aap toh...' was his only defence when I demanded an explanation.

Kebab Shikampuri

500 g keema
½ cup chana dal
5 cloves garlic
5 cloves
5 peppercorns
5 big cardamoms
10 green cardamoms
2 sticks cinnamon
2 bay leaves
2 tsp chopped coriander
1 onion sliced
2 whole red chillies
10–12 mint leaves
2 green chillies
2 eggs for binding (optional)
Oil for deep-frying

Roast and grind:

1 tbsp chironji
15 almonds

Filling:

2 boiled egg whites mashed
Coriander and mint chopped
Juice of two lemons
Salt to taste

Mix the first batch of ingredients in a dekchi, add 1 cup water and simmer till tender. Grind into a fine paste. Add the ground chironji and almonds to the mince mixture. Two eggs may be mixed into the mince to keep the kebabs from breaking.

Mix all the ingredients for the filling. Divide the mince mixture into even balls. Make a depression, fill with ¼ tsp filling, close the opening and shape each kebab into a flattened round. Deep-fry the kebabs.

The first time I sampled shikampuri kebab was at Jaigarh Fort. It had been made by an old Rajput cook who worked in the kitchen of the royal family of Jaipur. He was a typical native of the land, from his curled-up moustache to his up-curled jootis, his red turban and the macho glint in his eyes – straight out of a Satish Gupta painting. Maybe he had modelled for the picture, I thought to myself and giggled. The filling of the shikampuri is crucial – it is like the heart of the kebab. This cook had added chopped raisins, the soft sweet texture set off by the sharpness of green chillies. Each bite turned out to be a play on the senses!

Hyderabad and Lucknow are the two cities in India where the kebab evolved and was refined with the infusion of local spices and changing social norms. One of the best examples of this is the cuisine of the Nizams of Hyderabad. Here the Mughul love for meat is blended with the fiery spices of Andhra Pradesh, to create what is truly one of the greatest cuisines of India. The Hyderabadi likes his meat in large chunks and heavily spiced, unlike the delicate kebabs of Lucknow, for which the meat is ground so fine that a child can eat it. Also, the subtle fragrances and flavours used in Avadhi cuisine are not to be found in Hyderabad, where the meats are spiced with fiery chillies tempered by the sourness of raw mangoes, tamarind, lemon or yoghurt.

In my earlier years, Indian food brought to mind drama and high emotion. But one bite into an unassuming kakori kebab made me change my opinion. I could now think only of subtlety – gossamer silken threads of flavour that would melt like the morning dew; the elegance of fine dining in a kebab named after a village, defying all reason. Kakori was specially created for a toothless nawab – thank god there were no dentists at his service. Imagine never savouring heaven in a mouthful. Another version of the kebab's origins is that a British officer disliked the coarse texture of the nawabi kitchen's seekh kebabs, and so the nawab instructed his cooks to come up with a more refined variety. They used the tendon of the leg of mutton, animal fat, a new mix of powdered spices – and marinated the meat with papaya paste in hollowed out pineapples. Papaya is a miracle tenderizer. But the tenderness of the kakori is difficult to get right. Professionals will tell you that you have to have the right proportion of meat with fat from lamb kidney, along with the right amount of just-beginning-to-ripen papaya. I have a slightly modified recipe that is easier to make at home.

Kakori Kebab

1 kg keema
100 g onion
20 g black peppercorn
20 g mace
15 g cloves
20 g black cardamom
20 g green cardamom
60 g khus khus paste
100 g flour
3 g saffron
salt to taste
150–200 g raw papaya grated
75 g cashew nut paste
125 g ghee

Grind mince on a sil batta, after first pounding it in a mortar and pestle. Chop onions, fry till brown and grind to a fine paste. Grind garam masala to a fine powder. Add all the ingredients (except last three) to the mince, mix well. Add the raw papaya and leave it for an hour. Add cashew nut paste and ghee to the mince. Divide into 16 equal portions and make balls. Using a wet hand, spread the balls by pressing each along the length of a skewer. Roast on a charcoal grill on high heat to cook them through quickly, basting with butter while turning. Serve with onion rings, coriander-mint chutney and sheermal.

Kebab Awadhi

500 g keema
8–9 cloves
1 blade of javitri
4 dry red chillies
8–9 green cardamoms
pinch of nutmeg powder
2 tsp khus khus
4 tbsp roasted besan
1 tsp raw papaya paste
1 tsp ginger paste
1 tsp garlic paste
salt to taste

Roast all the spices and grind with a little water. Add the besan, papaya, ginger and garlic pastes and the ground spices to the keema. Shape into round balls and shallow-fry. Serve with green coriander chutney.

Here the game is played between khus khus and javitri, both gentle on the senses and delicate. Basics like ginger and garlic hang around like old faithfuls. I somehow feel reassured, holding a piece of dusty ginger in my hand. Its 'no-shape' existence combined with its sharp zing is a symbol of life itself. Whereas, a clove of garlic is like a quiet smile that welcomes you into the world of flavours, textures and aromas. Garlic is where the heart is, while ginger is where the hearth is.

Each home reinterprets recipes to suit the tastes of the family. Mummy is wary of raw mince, she prefers it pressure cooked and then ground. No harm – after all, the people you are going to feed have to be happy. So even if it means sacrificing the authenticity of the rich Awadhi textures, do not hesitate to improvise. And there are always accidents that lead to a new dish being created. The first time I tried making seekh kebabs, the mince acted up and the seekhs refused to bind themselves into the 'tube with a hole', as Sakshi calls them. So I shaped them like round flat kebabs, filled her parantha with two instead of one and said, 'Be happy, kiddo, it's a case of break one and get one free!'

Can I ever forget the sight of Sakshi holding a still-hot-from-the-tawa parantha to her nose, breathing in the scent of baked wheat and exclaiming, 'Hmmm, nirmal anand.'

Kebab Surajmukhi

600 g keema
60 g raw papaya paste
60 g roasted chana flour
15 g fried onion paste
6 boiled eggs
ghee for frying

Masala:

5 g saffron
10 g black pepper
5 g green cardamom
5 g fennel seeds
5 sticks of cinnamon
5 g shahi jeera
5 g saunth
4 blades of mace
5 g dried mint
5 bay leaves
1 nutmeg
10 g jeera
5 g black cardamom
5 g sabut dhania
5 g amchur
5 g chandan powder
5 g cloves
10 g dried rose petals
5 g pathar ke phool
10 g garlic powder
10 g kasoori methi
5 g star anise

Smoking:

4 green cardamom
1 tbsp ghee

Sun dry all the spices (except saffron) for a day. Pound the dried spices in a mortar and pestle to a powder. Add the saffron to the spice mix and store in a jar.

Put the mince in a bowl, add papaya paste and salt. Mix well and keep for 30 minutes. Add 2 tsp spice mix, roasted chana flour and fried onion paste to the mince. Crush the green cardamom. Heat the ghee in a pan, add the cardamom and stir over low heat till brown, remove and keep aside. Put a few small pieces of live charcoal in a small metal bowl, place the bowl in a large pan and spread the mince around the bowl. Sprinkle the charcoal with the fried cardamom and ghee, cover with a lid and let the mince smoke for 30 minutes. Uncover, remove the bowl of charcoal, divide the mince into eight equal portions, make balls and then flatten between the palms into ¾" round patties. Shallow-fry in ghee. Serve with slices of boiled eggs and coriander chutney.

'Exotic! Mysterious!' were my first reactions when I chanced upon this recipe of kebab surajmukhi in the *Saturday Times* some nine or ten years ago. I recall eagerly waiting for Saturday mornings to get my hands on recipes by Jiggs Kalra – a chef who appears to be as emotionally involved with the ingredients he works with, as a mother is with bringing up her child.

This kebab is as sensual as a salsa dance. It cavorts, glides and swirls, balancing its mystery with quiet grace. The pathar ke phool, star anise and dried rose petals create aromas that conjure up the velvety softness of a rose and the sandalwood leaves its lingering scent on your hands. Smoking the mince with cardamom is fascinating. Each time I make surajmukhi, I stare at the glowing orange tips of live charcoal pieces, the slow intensity of the flames eating into the heart of the black lumps, the smell of ghee and cardamom rising with a soft sizzle. The coal protests the final seduction, its warm breath escaping as if against its wishes. Its reluctance slowly vanishes as it fills the trapped air with its soul – a flavour that is infused in the mince so subtly, it makes it seem magical. The taste of smoke on the tongue, the smoothness of saffron in the body of the mince – the spirit is rarefied and the senses filled with wonder.

Maas ke Sooley

24 sooley (4" x 1½" boneless chunks of mutton)
Ghee
45 g raw papaya paste
2 tsp red chilli powder
120 g onions
30 g garlic paste
2 tbsp ghee
15 g ginger
2 tbsp kachri powder
½ tsp clove powder
½ tsp black cardamom powder
½ tsp nutmeg powder
½ tsp cinnamon powder
150 g hung yoghurt
Butter for basting
Salt to taste

Smoking:
5 cloves
1 tsp ghee

Masala (mix and store):
½ tsp dried mango powder
½ black salt
½ tsp black pepper powder
½ green cardamom powder
¼ tsp nutmeg powder

Evenly rub each mutton piece with the papaya and leave for two hours. Rub salt, red chilli, and keep aside for another hour. Fry the sliced onions and garlic separately in ghee, over medium heat, till golden brown. Put all the spices, with kachri, onion, garlic, ginger in a blender; add a little bit of water if required, and make a smooth paste. Transfer to a bowl, add the hung yoghurt and again evenly rub each piece with this second marinade. Leave for 2 hours.

Put a few small pieces of live charcoal in a small metal bowl and place in the centre of a large pan. Spread the mutton pieces around. Place the cloves on the coal, pour on the ghee, cover and leave for 30 minutes. Uncover the bowl; carefully impale the soolas on thin skewers in convenient batches, penetrating the meat twice to ensure minimum curling. Roast on a grill for 15 minutes, preferably a charcoal one, but an oven will do as well. Then remove, baste with butter and roast again for 5 minutes. Take sooley off the skewer, arrange on a platter, sprinkle with masala mix and serve.

Sooley are mutton tikkas that are synonymous with Mewari Rajasthan. The cuisine of this state was greatly influenced by the austere lifestyle and limited availability of food in the desert. The topography and weather conditions led to a preference for food that could last for days. Scarcity of water and fresh green vegetables were also major factors in determining the flavours of Rajasthani cuisine. A long history of the maharajas' love for shikaar made game cooking a respected art form, Pathani invasions brought barbequing traditions to Rajasthan's sands, and the soola was born.

No one can escape a soola, whether you are a tourist or you live here. You just have to love them. Somehow, sooley – they can be prepared in eleven different ways – are equated with chivalry, majesty and masculinity to such a degree that they instantly bring to the tongue a taste of regal repasts. Images of swords drawn in honour fights, the glint of sunlight on a metal shield, of a queen peeping from a jharokha with her heart in her mouth as her menfolk plunge into battle.

Reshmi Kebab

12 boneless chicken breasts
2 tbsp ginger paste
4 tbsp garlic paste
60 ml vinegar
30 ml white wine
260 g hung curd
60 g processed cheese
½ tsp coriander powder
½ tsp red chilli powder
½ tsp fennel powder
½ tsp cinnamon powder
¼ tsp mace powder
¼ tsp nutmeg powder
1 tsp green cardamom powder
1 tbsp green coriander chopped
120 ml cream
1 tsp saffron (soaked in 1 tbsp milk)
Salt to taste

Clean and cut each chicken breast into three equal-sized tikkas, wash and pat dry. Mix ginger and garlic paste, white wine and vinegar, leave for 30 minutes. Whisk the hung curd. Mix grated cheese, spices and fresh coriander with the curd, stir in the cream and saffron soaked in milk. Leave the marinated chicken in the fridge for at least 2 hours. Thread three tikkas on a skewer. Roast in a moderately hot tandoor for approximately 8–10 minutes. If cooking in an oven, keep a tray underneath to collect the drippings. Preheat oven to 200°C, cook kebabs for approximately 15 minutes, basting with butter regularly.

2

Barmy Beginnings

We were at Rick's for our twentieth anniversary. This quiet evening was a transit stop, before we went on a surprise holiday that Bunny had planned. I watched a young couple seated on the bar stools, newly in love, or so it seemed. Her hand was on his thigh and he kissed her on the lips. I was watching the exuberance of youth, the first flush of romance. This was a different kind of fire, all consuming, shaping destinies and lives.

'Did I tell you how Rehan was being *almost* poetic last night – for once I felt he is truly my child and not just a copy of you,' I jibed at Bunny, who raised his eyebrows enquiringly at me. The night before, Rehan and I had watched the night sky from his room. My eight year old found lightning scary and his eyes stared out into the stormy skies, flinching each time a streak of lightning lacerated the deep grey. I pointed to the glistening leaves that trembled with the gusts of wind and asked him, 'Isn't it beautiful?' Relaxing, Rehan noticed how the weeping willow bent down, as if bowing in respect to the pealing sounds of thunder. His fear left him, and smelling the rain on dry earth, he became one with the elements. The lights went off – predictably. We lit candles and he caught me gazing into the flame, lost. 'Why do you like fire so much, Mom?' he asked.

'It's beautiful,' I replied. 'It's magical.' I want to catch the core of the flame, trap it in my palm, feel what it is to hold fire and shape it... but it wins each time. I can't hold it, much like life... random, merry, sort of shapeless and defiant. I told Rehan that smoke gives flavours, different ones from different woods. Much like life, again.

Listening to my story, Bunny stared at me and said, 'You must be mad, giving him such heavy stuff to think about. He's only eight, let him be.'

I didn't want to get into reasoning with Bunny, considering that April and May are months when we tend to fight a lot more than usual. Our attention turned back to the drink resting on the table.

Bunny smiled. 'Smoke flavours a couple o' mean martinis as well.'

Roast pineapple on maple wood charcoal. Let the smoke from it seep into the succulent flesh and simply dunk it into white rum or vodka, to let loose its swirling fragrance into the liquid. The Smoky Lotus Martini is as subtle as a look exchanged in a crowded room.

The bartender got me a shot of vodka with roasted pineapple sitting in it. The smoke filled my mouth and slid down my chest. A heady fix! I kept the liquid in my mouth, my tongue tingled, urging the sip to make its journey down my throat.

'So, have you guessed where we are off to finally?' Bunny asked. He loves giving me surprises. After surprising me with a trip to Mashobra, he had been like a gleeful child, running around with a secret tucked under his belt. I shook my head and said, 'As long as I know I'm not landing up in a beach resort with winter clothes, I'm fine with wherever we go! I'll never let you forget that you packed backless dresses for chilly Mashobra!'

A wicked cackle later, we trooped down to Wasabi – recalling a friend's grumble: 'It's too expensive,' but in a mood to indulge. We were soon polishing off sake served on a bed of crushed ice and orchids. A couple seated behind our table was the next source of amusement. The wife was heavily pregnant, her tummy almost touching the table. But there were no signs of full-term lethargy. She was charging head-on at her seemingly defenceless husband, with – 'How the fuck could you do that?' He made a move to serve her and she slapped his hand down, saying, 'Rakh do, I can serve myself.' We laughed at the all-too familiar situation, with a 'nice-to-know-it's-the-same-story-everywhere' feeling.

Had Sakshi been here, she would have gloated and probably walked up to the lady to applaud her for bashing up the poor guy, and I would have nodded in full agreement. We lapsed into silence, watching the Japanese chefs work over the smoke and sizzle of their hot plates, deftly wielding knives and spatulas, while the pregnant lady continued her slicing up of the poor human in front of her.

Starting with oyster foie gras on reduced soya, sugar and herbs, we tried the yama momo, a Japanese mountain peach. It served as a palate cleanser before the soup was brought in. A dobin mushi soup, followed by a Chilean sea bass with ginger and scallions. The epice lobster had the chilli just right and the inaniwa wheat noodles from the teppenyaki section, flavoured by seven spices, made the red lights from across the lobby glow like stars. A wasabi sorbet, topped with orange zest and wine, and a chocolate tart, served with passion fruit sauce, were in competition. The sorbet won. The bite of wasabi, tinged with the zest, couldn't take on the chocolate tart. Bunny took off, grinning and tipsy: 'Tarts are always nice...' only to receive a withering 'Oh, please spare me the clichéd male crap!' from me.

'Hmm, maybe the wasabi could have more bite,' I mused. It did. I simply had to wait for it, then reach out for the flavour.

Bunny had to take off his glasses to read the fine print on the bill, eyebrows raised and eyes rounded, which prompted an 'Old man, huh!' from me. Back at Rick's, we did a flaming Lamborghini again. The couple sitting nearby, on bar stools, laughed along with us. 'It's been quite a journey, hasn't it?' We nodded, each slipping back into the past for a fraction of a second. Yes, it's been quite a trip!

We kept sitting there, each lost in thought. It's a sign of age coming on, when silence is preferred and reminiscing becomes a frequent pastime.

'I miss the kids, we could have brought them along.'

'We can't take Rehan to a pub. Who told you to have a baby so late in life?' was Bunny's prompt response.

April and May are certainly bad months. 'It was an accident, if you remember. I didn't want to have another baby.' I withdrew into myself, hating the memory of my third pregnancy.

'You were crazy, you tried everything possible to have a miscarriage – you jogged, skipped, cycled, swam and did all those steep water slides at that water park in Mehsana, even the one that had you going down head first.'

'I'd always wanted two girls and I had them. This didn't quite fit into my plan. I'm not much of a mom anyway.'

At thirty-five, with Sakshi and Resham ten and nine years old, I had been revolted at the thought of plunging back into the mess of sleepless nights, colds, fevers, loose motions and nappies. Friends rallied around, knowing how disturbed I was. That month I experienced multiple shades of contempt, frustration and revulsion – my head still hurts when I think about it. Somebody close suggested that I should have a sonography to figure out whether it was a boy this time, and only then go ahead. Bunny needs an heir to his business, I was told. A friend turned around and said, 'Mita, what if you abort the baby and it's a girl, will you be able to live with yourself?'

That nailed me. I steeled myself, gritted my teeth, and monitored my pregnancy strictly. This meant an hour of brisk walking every morning and an hour of swimming every evening. It meant lots of fruits, salad, and a Hitlerish no to desserts, non-veg and fried food. It meant not giving in to the craving for French fries that came upon me every morning. Starters became the main meal. Khandvi and sevpuri became a staple diet, with the papdi baked in the oven especially for me. Once a week, I allowed myself to gorge on gol gappas – piquant and sharp flavours were all that I wanted.

Sakshi and Resham were told only when I was six months up and had begun to show. They were amused at first, and then the excitement of having a baby to play with set in. They kept praying for a baby sister and that was the only delightful thought that made me smile as well.

Despite my diet control and just seven-and-half-kilo increase in weight, Rehan was born a chubby seven-and-half-pounder – his cheeks were the size of table-tennis balls, which amazed me. I may sound like a conventional mom when I say this, but I felt for Rehan something I hadn't felt for the girls. From day one, I don't think I treated him like a baby. We bonded kind of differently. By the time he was three, he had perfected the art of walking into the drawing room, when people were

MAR
APR

over, to loudly announce, 'Inko bolo na ghar jaane ko, mere ko aapke saath cuddle time chahiye.' Post-dinner is cuddle time for both of us. It's sacrosanct. That time and space can't be invaded by anyone.

Rehan's connection with food is strange. It's not every day that an eight-year-old watches Kylie Kwong and Nigella Lawson on Travel and Living, giving involved comments and asking all sorts of questions. I feel at rest – at least I can be assured that there is an alternative profession awaiting him, just in case he doesn't get to be a truck driver. Born as a millennium baby, he is a favoured child with all my friends. One of them can never stop saying, 'In spite of having both of you as his parents, I see a lot of potential in him.' Judgement passed.

It's an old wives' tale, but a pregnant lady's food choices probably do stay with the child forever. That explains why Resham still eats ice cubes, as if it's a dish, and Rehan loves hot and sour flavours. In fact, all that focus on a controlled intake has turned Rehan into a confirmed foodie. He watches all the food shows on TV with me and observes keenly when I cook or bake.

Rehan is my 'soogla'. Averse to even the slightest suggestion of personal hygiene, he has to be reminded to have a soap bath every day. My favourite line to him is, 'Go wash your face and hands with soap – I want to smell them,' and Sunday means a vigorous 'mommy scrub'. That is the only day he looks humanly clean and his original skin colour shows. Back from school, his 'hello' means a stinky, sweaty rub of his head against my cheek and a hug with grubby, muddy arms. The minute I suggest 'it's time for homework,' he flees to Dadi's room with an 'oh, I haven't met her yet.'

Mummy and Rehan exchange hi-fives the moment I announce my travel plans. I know that for those few days, McDonald's burgers and Domino's pizzas will be on the menu for lunch and dinner for both of them.

Sev Puri

8–10 papdis
2 boiled potatoes sliced
2 onions finely chopped
¾ tsp green coriander chutney for each papdi
1 tsp tamarind chutney for each papdi
Lemon juice
Salt to taste
Fresh coriander leaves to garnish
Sev to garnish

Arrange papdis in a serving plate. Place a slice of boiled potato on each. Top with chopped onions. Place coriander chutney on top of the onions. Top it up with tamarind chutney. Sprinkle salt and lemon juice and top it with a generous covering of sev. Finish with fresh coriander.

Khandvi

1 cup gram flour	**Tempering:**
1 cup curd	1 tbsp oil
2 cups water	1 tsp mustard seeds
2 tbsp ginger-green chilli paste	2–3 green chillies split
½ tsp salt	2 sprigs curry leaves
¼ tsp turmeric powder	Coriander leaves chopped
	2 tbsp coconut grated (optional)

Add all ingredients (except tempering) in a large, heavy bottom pan and whisk well. Place pan over high flame and bring to a boil. Stir vigorously till a semi thick consistency forms. Oil three flat steel thalis and spread equal quantities of the mix with a flat spoon. Allow it to cool and gently roll each layer of khandvi tightly to a tube. Slice with a sharp knife to 2" pieces. Heat oil in a small pan, crackle mustard seeds, curry leaves and chillies; sprinkle, along with coriander and coconut, over the khandvis.

It is strange, but the same actions, repeated every day, never fail to amuse. Is it the comfort of the familiar, or is it only good old family bonding? But certain refrains like 'Aman, your skin is going to rip at the seams of your cheeks – all that gross flesh will come spilling out!' feature like old-time hits on MTV.

Aman was born the same year as Sakshi. And I can tell you, it doesn't really help to have two sixteen-year-old 'we-know-our-mind-and-you-are-a-fool' characters around. With Aman, I can never figure out where his face ends and his body begins. His neck is tucked away under the folds of his chin and his knuckles can't be seen or felt. He is at peace only when he is eating.

Aman is my honest critic. I find myself instinctively gauging his reactions to what I cook. If he likes it, I know I've done well. His birthday, in September, translates into three days of eating. I must cook authentic pasta with white wine on day one, a Thai meal on day two, and a layered fudge cake for the final day. Both of us go berserk over food when we eat out, willing as we are to experiment with new flavours. His refrain is, 'CM, whenever you are in Delhi next and plan to eat Thai, take me with you, please.' We get into grave consultation over the menu card, keeping everyone else at the table waiting with varying degrees of irritation. We agonize over whether fish cakes will start the meal better, or should we order crab instead, only to get snapped at by Sakshi. 'Oh, just see the two food afficianodos at work, such pretentious buffoons!'

It is obvious that a cuisine is more than a sum of its parts. It indigenizes foreign influences, adapts to seasonal variations and, of course, shapes itself according to geographical conditions. For instance, coconut milk, lemon grass, shrimp paste, galangal, kaffir lime leaves are integral to Southeast Asian cooking because they are abundantly available there. Satay started off as a version of the kebab, introduced to Java by Arab traders, and is now the favourite street food of the region.

Chinese traders added their own contributions to the cooking pot of Southeast Asia. Malaysian, Indonesian and Thai food cannot be divorced from woks, stir-fry and soya bean products. The Dutch brought cloves and nutmeg from the Spice Islands, chilli peppers from Mexico and peanuts from the Americas to add to the spectrum of flavours.

I grill satays in an oven or use the combination cooking mode in a microwave oven. More than the satay, the peanut sauce does me in. I use it as a dip with salad sticks – crunchy baby carrots and spring onions get a spicy exuberance with this sauce. Slather it on slices of bread, and a sandwich never tasted better. Have it with a parat wali roti – it beats all pickles – and later, agonize over the calories like I always do. The peanuts clash with the red chillies, texture pitted against taste. All the taste buds get their fair share – sweet, salty, sour, or as fiery as you want to make it.

A couple of times, I have sautéed satays on a high flame in a wok, left them covered for ten minutes, and served them on a bed of shredded cabbage. The peanut sauce is poured over and I leave the wooden sticks on the side of the platter for everyone to pick up the satays with this one authentic touch. The many ways in which short cuts can be camouflaged never fail to amuse me. You just need to have a dash of style to get away with it. Smart packaging and suave marketing works everywhere, including in the kitchen.

Chicken Satay with Peanut Sauce

500 g boneless chicken breast or thigh cut into thin 3" strips
1 small onion chopped fine
1 tbsp ginger grated
2 tbsp garlic chopped
2 tbsp soya sauce
2 tsp red chilli powder
1 tsp coriander powder
2 tbsp oil
1 tbsp brown sugar
2 tbsp lemon juice

Peanut Sauce:
300 ml coconut milk
4 tbsp crunchy peanut butter
4 dried red chillies ground
1 tbsp fish sauce
1 tsp lemon juice
1 tsp brown sugar
Salt and pepper to taste

Place all the ingredients for the marinade in a shallow dish and mix well. Add the chicken pieces and coat evenly. Leave for two hours, or overnight, for best results. Thread the pieces onto bamboo satay sticks. Grill the chicken for 8–10 minutes in a preheated oven at about 180°C – turning and brushing occasionally with the marinade – till cooked through.

To make the sauce, mix all the ingredients together and bring to a boil – serve with the satays.

(Fine bamboo or wooden sticks are traditionally used for cooking satays. Soak in cold water for at least one hour to prevent scorching during cooking.)

Oriental Chicken Cakes

500 g chicken mince
5 chopped spring onions
½ pod chopped garlic
25 g chopped ginger
3 chopped green chillies
Pinch of thyme
Pinch of rosemary
½ tsp turmeric
15 g chopped coriander
3 egg yolks
Salt, pepper to taste

Sauce:
500 g peanut paste
10 dry red chillies
1 tbsp coriander seeds
1 tbsp cumin seeds
20 g lemon grass
10 g garlic
20 g jaggery
1 cup coconut milk
Salt, pepper to taste
2 tbsp oil

Heat oil and sauté the spring onions, ginger, garlic and green chillies. Add thyme, rosemary and turmeric and take off the fire immediately. Cool to lukewarm and add to the chicken mince along with the yolks, salt and pepper. Mix well; divide the mixture into small balls and shape them into flattened cakes. Grill or bake until cooked to a light brown.

To make the sauce, grind to a thick paste the coriander and cumin seeds, red chillies, garlic and lemon grass. Heat the oil, add the mix and the peanut paste, and sauté for 5 minutes. Add the jaggery, coconut milk, salt and pepper and simmer for 5 minutes. Serve the chicken cakes on this sauce.

Stuffed Chicken Rolls

250 g chicken mince
1 cup spinach chopped
1 tsp red chilli paste
1 tsp green chilli paste
2 tbsp ginger paste
2 tbsp garlic paste
Salt to taste
1 cup cornflakes
2 tbsp flour
1 egg
Oil for deep-frying

Add the red chilli paste (reserving ¼ tsp) to the chicken mince and keep aside. Heat oil in a pan, sauté the spinach till soft, and then add the salt, green chilli, ginger and garlic pastes. Remove excess water from the spinach. Make an oval of spinach and then coat it with a layer of mince to create a cigar-shaped roll. Make 10–15 such rolls. Wrap each roll with a piece of foil, twisting both ends as in a toffee, and poach them in boiling water for 10 minutes.

Next beat the flour, ¼ tsp red chilli paste, a little water and egg to make a batter. Coat the poached rolls in the batter and then roll in the cornflakes. Shallow-fry till golden brown and serve hot with tomato–chilli sauce.

This recipe may sound tedious, but a calm, systematic approach will help you glide through all the stages. When the kids were younger, they were fascinated by the toffee-like appearance of these rolls – a wonderful camouflage that got them to willingly swallow the spinach stuffed inside.

Grilled Spiced Chicken

4 chicken breasts cut into strips
1 tbsp tomato sauce
1 tsp soya sauce
2 tsp garlic paste
2 green capsicums diced
2 red capsicums diced
2 tomatoes diced
2 dry red chillies
1 tbsp coriander leaves chopped
1 tbsp honey
1 tbsp lemon juice
Salt, pepper to taste

Marinate chicken in tomato sauce, soya sauce, garlic paste, salt and pepper for 30 minutes. Skewer the chicken and grill in a preheated oven (180° C) till done. Heat oil in a wok; add red chillies, diced capsicums and toss for 1 minute. Add tomatoes, coriander leaves and lime juice. Adjust seasoning and toss for another minute. Place the vegetable mix in the centre of a platter and arrange chicken strips around it. Sprinkle more lemon juice if required and garnish with sprigs of fresh coriander.

I have used this starter as a main course too. Chicken strips can be mixed with julienned vegetables and slivers of blanched almonds. Sprinkle some fresh mint or basil and toss them all together with some sea salt, pepper and lemon juice. I avoid adding any sauce, however, to keep it simple and basic. Serve the dish with cold cucumber soup, churned in a blender with mint and lemon. To add sharpness, strain some garlic paste into the soup for that perfect taste.

The Indian genius squeezes several flavours out of the same spice, by roasting, grinding, popping it whole in hot ghee, and combining it with other seasonings. Mustard seeds team up with curry leaves, ground roasted cumin with mint, ginger and garlic with green chillies. A lot of this is absorbed knowledge. As they say, collective learning is always more successful and after a few years, it becomes engrained in our consciousness. I follow my instinct much more than a recipe, and memory more than a list of instructions – much like how our mothers make kadhi, casually ladling besan into the chach, instinctively knowing when to stop.

We all learn by stumbling – the way Preeti did when she made kadhi for the first time, when she was newly married, in her Saket flat. Preeti was always a misfit in the kitchen. She kept adding besan to the curd mixture, waiting for it to turn yellow. Fed up with the yellow not showing up, she thought the heat would force the reticent colour out. Alas! The kadhi turned into a congealed blob in minutes, while our science student (MSc) dissolved into liquid shame. Back from my journalism classes at IIMC, I found her moaning, 'I hate cooking!' Till then I had not ventured into curry land, but common sense made me ask her, 'Did you add haldi or not?' Move over Archimedes, my brainy sister just made a 'besic' discovery!

Now, Preeti single-handedly lays out a feast for sixty in Sydney.

'Without an army of Bahadurs to help me,' she says scornfully, adding, 'I've started baking too, y'know!' I watch her as she pulls out a tray of perfectly flaky, golden bite-sized puff pastries. She moves with confidence towards the fridge and reveals a bowl of chopped salami, celery and green onions coated with mayonnaise. It is my turn to be impressed. 'You actually baked these?' I ask, trying to keep the disbelief out of my voice, as she deftly fills each puff with the filling. Another don't-ask-obvious-questions-look comes my way and I resort to calm surrender with a shrug. We spend the evening over wine and lots of laughter. Clearing up in the kitchen later, I see a bag with the words, 'Pre-baked puff pastry, ready to eat; thaw and heat for forty-five seconds,' staring at me from the giant garbage can.

Chicken Puffs

2 tbsp butter

¼ cup flour

1 egg

¼ cup grated processed cheese

Filling

1 cup boiled chicken finely chopped

¼ cup celery finely chopped

2 tbsp red bell pepper finely chopped

¼ cup mayonnaise

Salt to taste

Melt the butter in ¼ cup boiling water. Add the flour and a dash of salt, and stir vigorously. Cook, stirring, until the mixture forms a ball that does not fall apart. Remove from heat, cool slightly. Add the egg, beat till smooth, and then stir in the cheese. Drop 1 level teaspoon of dough in evenly spaced rows onto a baking sheet. Bake at 250° C, for about 20 minutes. Remove the puffs, cool and split.

Combine the ingredients for the filling and sandwich each puff with 2 teaspoons of the mix. Alternately, serve each half as an open bite with the filling spread on top.

These puffs can be made a day before and stored at room temperature. Versatility can swing into action with the fillings. Stir-fried vegetables, with Indian or Chinese flavours, is a good choice for vegetarians. I often flavour the mayonnaise differently, using blue cheese dressing or a thousand island dressing, with goes with veggies and chicken. Ham or chicken salami diced into fine bits can also be used. I once used mango-kiwi salsa as a topping!

Stuffed Mushrooms

180 g button mushrooms

1 tsp oil

1 tbsp chopped onion

¼ cup chopped salami

¼ cup cheese spread

Fine soft breadcrumbs

Remove the stalks of the mushrooms and hollow out the caps. Chop the scooped out portions finely. Cook the chopped mushrooms with the onion, salami and cheese spread. Stuff the mushroom crowns, with this filling and sprinkle over with bread crumbs. Bake at 250°C, for 6–8 minutes.

You can use canned mushrooms as well. The cheese can be replaced by bell peppers, green onions or chives. Use olive oil to add a distinctive flavour.

Sesame Mushrooms

16 whole button mushrooms

50 g flour

50 g cornflour

1 egg beaten

Salt and pepper to taste

1 carrot chopped, blanched

1 onion chopped

2 tsp garlic chopped

15 g sesame seeds

Remove the stems from the mushrooms and chop finely. Sauté them along with the onions, garlic and carrot. Sandwich two mushroom caps together with the filling inbetween. Insert a toothpick to hold firmly. Next, sift both the flours and beat in the egg, salt, pepper and a little water to make a smooth batter. Dip the mushrooms in the batter, roll in sesame seeds and deep-fry. Serve with a sweet chilli sauce.

We were inseparable, Tina, Anamika and I. Known in school as the terrible trio, it seemed like destiny's gift when we joined the same college in 1984. Papa and I lived in a small house at C-248 Defence Colony. Tina and Anamika were wait-listed for hostel accommodation at Lady Shri Ram College (LSR) and had managed to bully their way into the hostel of the girls' polytechnic at Defence Colony. The three of us used to walk back from college at 3 p.m., past the then notorious Vikram Hotel, building up our appetites for the huge mixed-cuisine meals that awaited us in my kitchen.

Tina was as fat then as she is now, and short. Although she has the girth of Saturn's rings, she is beautiful, and her face vibrates energy and goodness. And she is forever hungry. Anamika can pass off as a twenty-year-old even today, with her slender frame and black-rimmed spectacles that shade her intense eyes. She gives the impression of belonging to another world – her own. Nothing ever ruffles her. She has a wicked sense of humour that makes her eyes light up with an evil glint, and a grin that shows off her two overlapping front teeth. She still buys her jeans from the kiddies' section – at age forty-four.

Anamika and I would saunter into Diana Stores in the Defence Colony market to buy chunks of chicken salami, only to polish it off while walking back home. The vegetable shop owner never concealed his amusement at a pair of young girls buying two packets of mushrooms every couple of days. He finally couldn't resist and asked us, 'Aap sirf mushroom khaate hain? Aur kuch nahin? Aapko banana aata hai?' In response, Anamika passed an imaginary mike to me, saying, 'Ab yeh aapko batayengi mushroom ki special recipe.' In my most serious voice, I explained to the hapless chap how I simply tossed them in a dollop of butter, salt and red chillies. Tina, on the other hand, hated mushrooms – I think she willed herself to hate them the moment I told her that they were healthy.

Tina was fully awake only while eating or trying to make herself something to eat. I remember struggling to make her read through *Richard II* just before our board exams. She had to be poked sharply with a pencil every five minutes, with me screaming, 'Tina, don't you dare doze off on me. How will you pass?'

Tina loved pottering around in my kitchen, which was one place I let her be by herself. Refusing to fall victim to Tina in action, I conveniently let Chanchal, our Bengali cook, silently clean up the spilt ketchup, sprinkles of bhujiya and raw egg droppings while she rustled up her favourite – French toast sandwiched with a layer of Kissan mixed fruit jam that threatened to ooze out because there was just so much of it. This was her way to begin a meal while we gazed at Yul Brynner in *King and I*, or Clint Eastwood on horseback, in a racy Western. The perfect ending came when Papa would return from work, take one look at Tina and say, 'You look weak, haven't you eaten?'

My love for salami has gone far beyond any teenage fancy. I like it for being so versatile as a starter. Chop it to make an impromptu salad with cucumber, bell peppers, onions, fresh mint or chives. Serve it with cheese and bran crackers. Whip up hung curd with lemon juice, white pepper, coriander leaves and green chillies, then place a small dollop on a slice of salami, roll and secure with a toothpick. Looks good, tastes great – you can make it in advance and fridge it.

I've always loved walking into the kitchen with that create-something-to-eat-with-whatever-you-find-in-the-fridge feeling. Tied down by just cucumber in your fridge? Cut into one and a half inch slices – each thick enough to stand alone as a piece. Scoop out the seeds. Mix whatever fresh veggies you have – finely-chopped spring onion, carrot, capsicum – with crumbled paneer or hung curd. Season it with salt, a dash of garlic, pepper, even Tabasco, and stuff the hollow of the cucumber. I do the same with mushrooms. Combine finely-chopped spring onion, crushed peanuts, green chillies, coriander and a pinch of Thai red curry paste to stuff the mushrooms and lightly turn them around on a frying pan. I have seen lah-di-dah ladies go into a swoon over such starters – tasty and not a challenge to their waistline.

Vegetable Tikki (Baked)

500 g boiled potatoes grated
½ cup onion chopped
1–2 green chillies chopped
2 tsp mint leaves
2 tsp coriander leaves
Salt to taste
½ cup peas mashed
½ cup carrots grated
½ cup French beans chopped
Chaat masala to taste
½ cup roasted crushed peanuts

Add onion, green chillies, mint and coriander to the potatoes. Next, mix in all the vegetables and seasoning. Form into tikkis and roll them in the crushed peanuts. Place on an oiled baking tray, bake for 15 minutes till golden brown.

As a newly engaged, not-shy girl, I was packed into a Maruti 800 with Bunty, my new-found jeth, Smriti, my sister-in-law, and Bunny, my husband-to-be, and we skidded off to Niros for dinner. The order was, 'Three chicken chowmein, three chicken chilli dry, three shredded lamb, green and red peppers, two garlic chicken, two chicken fried rice – but we'll start with four butter naan and reshmi kebab, and bring four hot and sour chicken soups also.' Phew. If I was a fish, I would have swallowed five gallons of water. 'Who's going to eat all that?' I asked. It was their turn to stare, puzzled at my question, before answering with a casual shrug and a matter-of-fact 'We, who else?' I went through the evening in a stupor. Amused, scared, stricken, my mind was buzzing with a zillion thoughts. 'Gosh, how much do these folks eat?' 'Typical Punjus – they can't see beyond food.' 'How much will I have to cook?' 'Wait till I tell Ma and Papa, they'll be shocked.' An hour later, a very quiet, bemused me took in the empty dishes. No wastage here. Oh, did I miss out listing the knickerbocker glory and vanilla ice cream with chocolate sauce?

We were three girls at home, all small eaters. When we were out for a meal, the order went like this: one rogan josh, one chicken chowmein, one chicken chilli, one fried rice, two rotis for Papa – a complete meal for the five of us. We went home and shared two mangoes amongst us for dessert. Clearly, I was in for a culture shock.

The dinner that night was the start of multiple shocks in cookery land for me. I was used to cooking full meals; it was never an issue at home. Ma, with her travelling job, had made sure we could dish out decent vegetarian fare. I recall making shraadh ka khaana – mirchoni, aloo rassewale, gobi, mooli baingan ki sabji, dahi pakodi and kheer for the pandits when I was in my second year at college.

And here I was now, dressed in a sari, with two gold chains around my neck and dangling earrings, in my new kitchen. How my arms ached as I stirred a huge kadhai full of boiled potatoes soaking in oil, coated with a spicy mix of sukha dhaniya, lal mirchi, garam masala, jeera, amchur. I didn't tire at the thought of cooking as much as the handling of large quantities. At the end of the first six months of married life, I had developed strong biceps and a graceful equanimity – nothing that happened in the kitchen shocked me any more. I took it all in my stride.

The obsession with potatoes in a household dominated by males is quite natural, but using it as a chaat before the meal reduces the mania for this starchy vegetable. Potatoes cut to bite-sized pieces, tossed in a little oil, with generous amounts of coriander leaves, mint, green chillies, chaat masala, lemon juice, salt and garam masala to taste, saw me wean the family away from a sinful consumption of aloo at every meal. Kill them softly, slowly with their own medicine.

The humble aloo ka tikki has so many avatars. From the chaat corners on the streets to a regular kitchen, it has created a niche for itself. In Jaipur, the tikki is served with urad dal stuffed inside, doused generously with coriander chutney and imli ki saunth. At home, I like to give it a healthy twist. When the kids were younger, potato-soya rolls was one of the devious ways I had of making sure protein went into their junk-food-lined stomachs. Most moms would read this as the story of their lives, planning obsessively to give their kids a balanced diet. Mutton mince replaced by black chana to be ground into kebabs, soya nuggets exalted to work as boneless mutton, and much more...

Potato-Soya Rolls

500 g potatoes boiled

¾ cup soya granules

1 onion chopped

1 tbsp ginger chopped

1 tbsp green chillies chopped

1 tbsp fresh coriander leaves

1 tbsp cornflour

Chaat masala to taste

Lemon juice to taste

Salt to taste

Grate the potatoes. Soak the soya granules for an hour in water. Heat oil in a pan and sauté the onions, ginger, green chillies, coriander, salt and soya granules for about 6–8 minutes. Cool, add lemon juice and grind in a mixer. Add salt, chaat masala and cornflour to the potatoes. Stuff the soya mixture into portions of potato and shape into flat balls. Shallow-fry and serve with coriander chutney.

My heart lets out a silent, yet joyful whoop of triumph – it does a war dance on the side – while I watch my family devour the tikkis with

unsuspecting relish. There is nothing like the taste of silent victory. My acting skills are put to the test – I must keep a straight face when one of the kids remarks, 'Not bad, Mum, I don't mind the potatoes, as long as the keema inside tastes good. Thank God you haven't mixed veggies with it!'

Savoury Cheesecake

1½ cup tortilla chips finely crushed
2 tbsp olive oil
2 (8 ounce) packets cream cheese
2 eggs
240 g soft, flavoured cheese
½ cup jalapenos chopped
½ cup spring onion greens chopped
1 cup yellow and red bell peppers chopped
¼ cup black olives chopped
⅓ cup tomatoes chopped
½ cup sour cream

Preheat oven to 200° C. Stir together chips and olive oil, press into a 9" spring form pan. Bake for 15 minutes. Keep aside ¼ cup each of red and yellow pepper, olives and onion greens as toppings. Beat cream cheese and eggs at medium speed till well blended. Pour into baking pan. Mix the cheese, jalapeno and remaining peppers, sprinkle over the surface. Bake for 30 minutes. Cool completely. Spread sour cream over cheesecake and sprinkle the toppings. Chill for two hours. Remove from pan after chilling. Let it sit out for a while or the base may break. Serve on a platter surrounded by tortilla chips and celery sticks.

Cream cheese is usually available in stores. If not, substitute with curd that has been hung overnight. To add flavour, I use any soft, flavoured cheese, garlic-pepper or apricot-walnut, or simply Amul cheese spread. If sour cream is not available, make it by mixing fresh cream, curd and a little lemon juice. If you don't want to bake an entire cheesecake, just bake the base. Then blend in the body, minus the egg yolks, add gelatine and chill until the cheesecake sets; it works beautifully that way too.

Cooking is not a mundane activity – you move the soul and spirit of the people you feed. It is a sensuous communication, which should speak of love and caring. When you cook, you touch the ingredients with love, with a gentleness that is also powerful. I have noticed that the day I cook mechanically, without immersing myself in what I am doing, without really touching the flour or the tomatoes, or inhaling the heeng jeera ka tadka, the dishes just don't taste right. It is an out and out case of being totally there. Don't cook because you have to, cook because you want to. It is an act of deep respect. Be gentle, fluid, and tender, if you want the ingredients to give of their flavours. A simple dal can go wrong just because you ignored the cumin seeds that demanded attention at the exact moment they crackled. The 'tempering' is always important, as they say.

Like the blurring of boundaries in the mind, there is a barely visible line between salads and starters. I happily skip sides as and when I feel like it. In a climate like ours that remains hot for most of the year, salads and dips are the best way to begin a meal, which is precisely what I have been harping on about as a mother – 'Please grab a carrot or cucumber every time you feel like snacking. It's good for you, your skin will glow, you will never wear spectacles, blah, blah, blah…' And that's precisely the kids' reaction – the blah bit.

Four months after Sakshi left for her undergraduate studies to the US, we were on our usual Skype spree, and before her camera sparkled alive, I heard a comforting crunch. I smiled to myself. 'Ah, see, finally, I knew she'd realize she's putting on weight and should resort to snacking on celery sticks.' I had always known that some day, all my carping would manifest itself into practice. Alas, tucked into her progesteronely-pink candy-striped duvet, she was reaching into a bag of fried Spicy Ranch pita chips and crrunncching a mouthful gleefully. 'Shai shaven shad sshhdinner!' she mumbled, quickly swallowing, 'I lost track of time while studying.'

'Was that supposed to soften the blow of the pita chips, babe?'

'No, Mommy…'

'Well, I almost thought you'd be biting into a carrot or a celery stick, considering you've put on some of the weight you lost before leaving India.'

'Duh!'

The petulant mommy tone continued. 'And that isn't your T-shirt – it's five sizes too big for you.'

Sakshi's face cracked up like a Halloween pumpkin as she swooned, 'Ooohhh, isn't it just sooo cool?' She vanished inside the neck of the T-shirt, bobbing her head in and out like a jubilant duck dipping into a placid lake to find fish at her webbed feet. 'It's Terrel's shirt and he smells soo good.' Her head went in once more. The smile grew evil by the millisecond.

'And what exactly is his shirt doing in your room, on your person?'

'I'm wearing it.'

'I can see that.'

Her eyes glinted naughtily.

'He left it here last time... we were watching a movie together. He'd come straight from the gym and changed here.'

'Why did he leave the shirt behind? And did he go to the loo to change?'

Her voice was bursting with laughter, annoying me further.

'No, Mommy, he changed here. I simply turned my back and he gave me a hug too.'

Short of visibly spluttering, I went through the trembling shivers of being a mother, for the nth time, and bit my tongue. 'Wouldn't it be wiser if you joined the gym with him instead? Hasn't the thought ever crossed your mind?'

'I love you too.' She bit into another chip.

'Stop eating that rubbish. Why don't you keep some carrots in your room? And I asked you to buy oranges, didn't I?'

'Well, if you wanna know, I haven't really done anything I shouldn't be doing... according to you,' she said, her grin widening.

'Y'know the rules, babe, always fill yourself with salad before a meal.

Your dietician said the same thing and it's common knowledge, isn't it? It gets the juices flowing, activates the appetite and fills you partially so that you don't pig out over the main course.' I enunciated gravely.

I couldn't sustain the feigned seriousness any further. We both exploded into peals of laughter that left us in tears.

We looked at each other; a fleeting few seconds of 'I trust you' passed between us.

'Please, please get into eating lots of salad and lose weight before you come back for your winter break or I'll put you on a diet of boiled vegetables.'

She scoffed, 'Oh, your usual drama. Keep at it, Mommy. Good luck.

But don't you remember your so-called cardinal rules about food and cooking?'

'Which ones are you talking about?'

'One, that there are no rules, that a recipe is a theme and an intelligent cook will swing it differently each time. Two, you always talk about some James Beard who said, "I don't like gourmet cooking, *this* cooking or *that* cooking. I like good cooking." Huh, Mom?'

3

Sultans of Swing

Cruising down the highway at 140 km per hour, eyes scanning the stark, black boulders, the strains of *Sultans of Swing,* chilled Pepsi and *Catcher in the Rye* in my hands. The road snaked through the rugged terrain, rocks loomed over us, cactus flowers merged into stretches of sun burnt grass, the brown earth blushed purple under my gaze. All that was needed was for John Wayne to come galloping from behind on a magnificent horse. The landscape set the mood for Deogarh.

Deogarh was the stronghold of one of the sixteen Umraos (Rawats) of Mewar. Here the gold of the desert sand continues to climb up the stone-and-lime walls of the three-hundred-year-old palace. Stone stairs, smoothened by centuries of use, took us up to the Sheesh Mahal, our suite. Belgian glass, framed within the windowpanes, burst into myriad hues, making the sunlight dance in the room. Bunches of grapes glowed from a Murano glass chandelier hanging from the ceiling, and an old cradle, lined with royal maroon velvet, served as a centre table.

The wind lifted sunlight in its palms, waking up the shy sun. The only sound that could be heard was the gentle clip-clop of hooves, as the mare took us cautiously through the narrow lanes into the sunset. Serenity lived here. Peace cast its transparent veil, despite the chirping crickets. I smelt tranquillity in the wild 'palash' blossoms. A ride in the gig that dated back to British times, circling the auburn fields. Our valet 'Mithu' chivalrously helped me off and into the open four-wheel drive.

Then the pace of the evening changed from a quiet swish of the breeze to the thrill of throttling up the rocky hills in an open jeep. The four-wheel drive gripped the rough serrations of the rocks, enforcing control over their rough contours. We hurtled along, the speed, the incline rising ahead, the daunting hillside giving us a wild rush of adrenalin. We drove up to the summit which laid bare the raw beauty of nature, dressed in twilight, and I lay down on the black rocks, my back sensing the warm welcome of mother earth. I took in the vastness, creation's patchwork in gold and green. A train rumbled past, its faraway lights glowing like the beaded necklace around a queen's neck. I could see Venus winking down at us. Our host, Shatrunjay, scion of the Deogarh family, quipped, 'See, I ordered moonshine for you,' as he heard me gasp at the full moon. Champagne was served 'on the rocks'. We sipped in bliss, beaded bubbles glittering all around the brim.

The next morning, we walked into the village lanes and found ourselves amidst shops selling embroidered jeans, antique locks, large ghungroos, silver bracelets, bright saris, sukha dhaniya and sacks of red chillies. The smell of dhaniya teased my nostrils and the vapours from the red chillies made me sneeze.

A metre-gauge train took us from the Kamlighati station through the hills, ravines and valley. Steep cliffs suddenly appeared under our feet. We were sitting on the floor of the luggage van, our legs dangling, breathing in with our eyes the shades that changed from burnt sienna to borrowed gold. A man carrying a chapri on his head hopped on as I beckoned. He was selling fresh chana chaat, salad in its raw, earthy avatar. The package deal included an army of hungry monkeys to feed. Bunny was his usual self. 'His knife can't be clean,' he grumbled, for which he got an exasperated stare. I watched as the man deftly cut up onions, tomatoes, cucumber, green chillies and raw mango, mixing them with chana, then squeezed some lemon juice and added a generous chutki of masala. He served it to us on a newspaper. The train meandered through tunnels, then into bursts of light. Barren trees stared bravely at the proud sun, a whiff of neem flowers and a dash of green peeked cheekily around the corner – eight rupees per ride. For those few moments, I didn't wish for anything more from life.

On days when you think you're seeing a mirage at every four feet on the melting roads, long, thin, crisp cucumber, split halfway along its length, is thrust under your nose at each crossing. This is salad for the man on the road. Succulent tomatoes, cucumber and papaya, piled high in patterns and sold on paper plates outside colleges and government offices in Jaipur are the only means of keeping cool in the summer heat. With an Indian meal, a kachumbar salad or a boiled chickpea salad, sprinkled with sprouted lentils, are regulars. Or boiled potatoes in mint-coriander chutney, with raw mangoes added generously to give that extra tang and take away the sting of summer. For the turbaned farmer, wrinkled as if fried by the sun, a 'mukkewala pyaz' and hari mirch is the salad to his main course of thick roti.

Just salads for dinner is a frequent 'to do' on my list. Rustling up a salad is like painting, playing around with splashes of colour, mixing textures, balancing flavours. To be able to make a good salad is to be a brilliant diplomat – the problem is entirely the same in both cases: to know how much oil to put with one's vinegar. There is a new challenge each time, a mystery to unravel, a story waiting to be told. The taste buds savour crispness, a burst of juice, a tanginess, a creaminess, a bite, a crunch, filling the mouth with sensations. Hot, warm, cold, sweet, sour, salty, peppery, piquant – I call them the building blocks of the kitchen world.

I think God's creations form a classic conundrum when the sea, land and air mate in a bowl of salad. The whole universe appears in front of you, in its very basic form, and the human hand is ready to mix it all up. Preparing a salad can offer unlimited possibilities. It's not only the raw ingredients that make up a salad, it's a game played with pulses, nuts, grains, herbs, spices, poultry, fish, meats, fruits and vegetables. Use them as starters, as accompaniments, as the main course – salads are forever versatile. Perhaps a salad's most defining feature is the dressing. Typically, it is either oil or vinegar based, with a host of other ingredients added. However, the purpose is always the same – to unite all the separate elements of the salad into a glorious whole.

It was April, and mangoes had just started to show up. I was battling a series of deadlines. On one of those mornings, as I stared down at my computer, willing it to unleash Potterisms so that I could connect my mind to the keyboard, Smriti called out from downstairs, 'I want us to do a different menu this time, for dinner on Wednesday.' Smriti, my silent sister-in-law! She loves her job – taking care of our home. She is the queen and her subjects the hapless kitchen and ground staff. Even the drivers are steered by her. They all flock together, forming one big circus of Nepali, Rajasthani, Bengali humanoids, walking the tight rope, juggling duties and holidays, under her sharp eye. She is the proverbial caring, giving Punjabi bahu. The two of us are contrary in our beliefs and ways, and our lifestyles occupy two extremes of the spectrum. I guess that's why we give each other enough space to do our own thing, but at the same time, share common quips about Mummy, our favourite observation being, 'She's lost it!' Tall, and now slim, after years of struggling in the gym, Smriti is at her happiest when she's eating junk – a bun omelette at a thela while shopping.

I grinned; the devil was dancing around the fresh greens, ripe tomatoes, vinegar and lemon juice. 'Yes, let's not do the typical butter chicken, dal makhani, sukhe matar bit. We'll only do salads, what say?'

Smriti replied, 'Good idea, but you'll have to do everything then,' happily stepping away from the prospect of sweating over cuts, cubes and juliennes of an array of raw food. Images of a certain unhappy creature flashed through my mind – a typical dal makhani and parantha loving friend, who would experience third-degree torture on seeing my salads-only menu for dinner. He publicly announces, 'I eat at home when I'm invited to the Kapurs for dinner.' Call me a pervert, but just the thought of his proclamation inspired a complete line-up of twelve salads, in which I brought the world together. Europe, Middle East and Asia sat next to one another in their near-authentic flavours and textures.

The trick here is to plan the salads in such a way that they are balanced not only in terms of colours, flavours and textures, but also to make sure that the spread is filling enough. Rolls and hot buns do suffice, but to appeal to a typical Indian palette, I decided to go for a tandoori chicken salad and then offset it with a Thai chicken mince salad. I left the table bare, save for a small arrangement in the centre with red candles and red Bohemian bud vases placed horizontally. The flames flickered, spreading a red glow like a halo around the table. It helped to create an interesting aura around the muted colours of the potato salad and rice salad. Fruits in honey-cream salad were placed next to corn niblets in ginger and soya sauce. Cabbage and carrot in coconut milk and tabbouleh were given a corner with the mango and onion salad, and the spinach, red bell peppers and chilli salad. Lettuce and cherry tomatoes, dunked in orange juice, orange marmalade and red chilli flakes, were placed next to the shredded mixed greens, piled carelessly in a bowl, topped with dates, almonds and walnuts. A cold platter with salami rolls, assorted cheeses, sour cream and chive-flavoured crackers completed the table.

Vineet, the parantha guy, asked aghast, 'Roti kahan hai?'

I looked at him and said with flourish, 'Aaj roti ki chutti hai. Aaj gas par tawa nahin rakha jayega.'

He grumbled and muttered something under his breath. His wife scolded him, saying, 'She has put in so much effort to give you a taste of something different, why don't you ever want to be adventurous?'

Everyone laughed; they had eaten several plates of salads and yet felt light. There was a general feeling of well-being around the table, which spread with the golden glow of the candles. Profiteroles, Bailey's mousse cake and a simple lemon soufflé provided an airy ending to the evening.

Summer Tuna Salad

10–15 red radishes cut in halves	3 tbsp olive oil
1 cucumber cubed	Salt and pepper to taste
3 celery sticks cubed	200 g canned tuna flaked
1 yellow pepper diced small	2 tbsp parsley
10–15 cherry tomatoes halved	Lettuce leaves to serve
4 spring onions sliced	Juice and rind of 2 lemons

Stir salt and lemon juice together in a bowl until dissolved. Pour this over the vegetable mixture. Add oil and pepper. Toss to coat the mixture well, then cover and chill for an hour. Add parsley to the drained tuna, toss gently with the vegetables. Arrange lettuce leaves on a platter, spoon the salad in the centre. Garnish with strips of lemon rind.

Mango, Tomato, Onion Salad

2 large mangoes peeled and sliced in semi-circles
4 large, firm tomatoes sliced round
1 large onion sliced round
1 cucumber sliced round

Dressing:

2 tbsp oil
3 tbsp lemon juice
2–3 tbsp hot pepper sauce
Sugar, salt, pepper to taste
Chives/cilantro/celery to garnish

Arrange the tomatoes, onions, cucumber, mangoes, in the same order, in concentric circles. Mix all the ingredients for the dressing, shake vigorously. Pour the dressing over the salad just before serving.

The luscious sweetness of mango, the raw smell of onions, and the alluring red of tomatoes might startle people, but this is one of the tastiest salads I've put on my table. The sharpness of the onion matches my tongue when I rap Sakshi's knuckles for picking up only the mango slices. 'I don't want to die so young, tomatoes are poisonous,' she mumbles.

Water Chestnut Salad

500 g fresh water chestnuts
2 tbsp chopped spring onions
Juice of 2 lemons
Red chilli flakes
2 tsp lemon grass chopped
Fish sauce (optional)
Salt to taste
1 tsp brown sugar
4–5 whole dried red chillies for garnish

Peel, wash and thinly slice the chestnuts. Mix all the ingredients well and serve on a plate. Garnish with red chillies.

It was one of those stand-in-front-of-the-fridge-staring-at-it-blankly evenings. What do you do with such immediate demands? 'They are coming to see some lights for their new house. Quickly, get something ready.' It had started as a hobby, lights procured from top-of-the-line design houses in Italy, Spain and Germany, to be supplied by us to large corporate houses and mansions. I grew to understand how a wrought-iron modern Murano centrepiece with eight lamps, or a wooden chandelier, could be looked upon as a work of art. And how significant a role light can play in shaping the aesthetics of a room or changing its very character. But right now, the more pressing issue was that 'they' had to be served something. And then my mind said, 'Duh! Singhare!' I agree they don't look very appetizing in their coats, but they were the only choice I had. Undressing them helped.

The salad simply came together. Slightly sweet, because of the carb content; nutty, smooth and crisp, water chestnuts are a versatile aquatic vegetable. The Chinese use them in their stir-fries, to make stuffing, and for salads with fish sauce. Rich in calcium, potassium, iron and zinc, high in water content, they make for perfect diet food. Dried and ground into flour, they're also used as a thickening agent for sauces. On Janmasthami, this flour is kneaded together with boiled potatoes; the resultant puris are sinfully tasty, though they sit heavy on the stomach. In India, it's safest to serve this salad without the fish sauce, or you run into the danger of a CBI interrogation by the vegetarian squad. Crunchy and lemony, the chilli flakes lift up the natural sweetness of water chestnuts; spring onions add a dash of colour.

The lady in the 'they' called up next morning to ask for the recipe. They didn't order any lights, though.

Cabbage, Spinach and Carrot Salad

1 head of cabbage shredded

8–10 baby carrots grated

Spinach chopped (same quantity as cabbage)

1 onion grated

1 hard-boiled egg sliced

1 cup mayonnaise

Toss all the vegetables in a salad bowl, pour over the mayonnaise and garnish with slices of boiled egg.

Cabbage, Apple and Orange Salad

1 head of cabbage

2 oranges, peeled and cut into small sections

1 apple grated

2 tbsp lemon juice

1 cup mayonnaise

1 cucumber sliced round

1 tomato sliced round

Mix the cabbage, apple and oranges with lemon juice. Arrange in a salad bowl, pour mayonnaise over it. Garnish with cucumber and tomato slices.

'Bunny went "baaaalllllkkkk" the first time he tasted a chicken mayonnaise salad,' said Mummy. He was only ten years old, on his first ever visit to Pot Pourri at Nirula's, the newly opened salad bar at Connaught Place. He stuffed himself with buns and rolls instead. Dad piped up, 'Aur itne saare salad sirf solah rupaye mein!' I laughed and thought, how come it's always Dad who remembers the price, whether it's a twenty-rupee haircut or the four thousand he paid at 360 for a lunch. I remember him grumbling when he came back to Jaipur, 'Mits, you always send me to the most expensive places.'

Mummy still guffaws heartily when she sees her younger son nibble his way through a spinach or corn salad. 'Look what a wife can reduce a virile, meat-eating hunk to!' she says.

When we were young, Delhi meant Janpath and Connaught Circus – shopping for the latest in street fashion, and then lounging in Nirula's. Pot Pourri opened on the first floor of Hot Shoppe Nirula's. It was a Mecca for food-starved people like us from Jaipur, where eateries in the seventies and eighties did not go beyond the usual Indian vegetarian fare. A Hot Shoppe burger and a hot chocolate fudge were looked forward to in the same way as I look forward to sushi now. Lettuce was exotica then. Asparagus was as unthinkable as caviar. Thousand island dressing on pasta salad, with an extra dash of Tabasco, was a special treat.

butter
cheese
eggs
OJ
Cola
milk
tap
tap

If we were lucky, Papa would take us to Gaylord for sizzlers and buy us chocolates from Wenger's, which in those days, at Rs 100 for eight pieces, were horrifyingly expensive. Just behind Wenger's, in A-Block, is Keventers. I still love their strawberry-flavoured milk served in bottles. The smell of milk with strawberry essence, pistachio, coffee and chocolate, all fuddled together, wraps itself around me like a warm blanket – those old, worn-out, faded ones that you carry over as remnants of your childhood.

Thai Melon Salad

1 white melon	1 tbsp lemon juice
1 musk melon	2 tsp garlic chopped
½ watermelon	1 tsp peanuts toasted
Dressing:	2 green chillies chopped
2 tbsp fish sauce	Fresh coriander
1 tsp brown sugar	Lemon zest

Peel and dice the melons. Crush the peanuts. Mix all dressing ingredients and add to the melons. Adjust seasoning and serve chilled.

Melons are my seasonal best friends. Castor sugar, rose water, lemon juice and mint can give them a Persian flavour. Before serving, sprinkle crushed ice on top. If you add strawberries and peaches, drizzle a bit of honey, lemon juice and chopped mint. It takes only a few seconds for melon magic to take over! I've even used ½ cup tequila, with orange juice, sugar and mint, to take it to a 'higher' level, if you know what I mean!

Lettuce, Cucumber and Ham Salad

1 crisp lettuce	1 tsp lemon juice
1 cucumber	1tsp apple juice
1 bunch watercress	1 tsp honey
4 spring onions	1 clove garlic
4 ham slices	Large pinch mustard powder
Dressing:	Salt, pepper to taste
1 tbsp olive oil	Extra virgin olive oil

Select the best lettuce leaves, wash, and pat dry. Place in a large bowl, chill. Slice cucumber, chop spring onions, and sliver ham. Mix together all the salad ingredients and add to the lettuce. Shake the dressing ingredients and pour over the salad. Drizzle with some extra virgin olive oil just before serving.

Anything green repulses the kids – at least those growing up in my home. Sometimes I feel as through my sole aim in life has been to make Sakshi eat veggies. As a baby, I fed her tindas and cauliflower, calling them miniature footballs and yellow trees. But that bliss was not meant to last. She grew up from being a cute stuffed doll to a person who knew her mind, and that too, quite well. There was a standard rule at home: 'Don't give Sakshi anything sweet to eat after dinner.' A sugar fix got her high and she'd be running along the corridors, squealing and pummelling the other kids into frantic activity, which is something no parent wants at 10 p.m., after a day's work.

We had what an uncle of ours rightly called a kukad khana, with four children born within two and a half years to Smriti and me. Home was a series of 'cluck clucks', and we spent years smelling of Cerelac, mashed banana and vomit. The sweet baby smell, as one of them nuzzled the swell of their sleepy, well-fed cheek trustingly into my neck, is a tender memory. It remains the same, even though the kids have grown up and are on their way to college. When Resham puts her head on my shoulder and cuddles up, the weight of her head is more than before, but the contentment is the same.

What is truly strange is that I find myself feeling like this in spite of my vociferous debunking of the concept of motherhood and relegation of all the associated bliss to bookish crap. 'How can you feel blissful when you are breast feeding your child or powdering her bottom, and it only means more backaches, headaches and sleepless nights?' I used to ask all my friends who gushed over their babies. Only one of them mustered up the courage to admit, 'Yes, you are right, it's hardly bliss, it's just a drab routine of diapers and milk bottles. Bliss is when you see your baby gurgle, from afar, in someone else's arms!' The others merely listened to me raving and ranting while they continued mashing potatoes, stewing apples, straining khichdi, sterilizing feeding bottles and not having the time to read.

In our house everything was bought in sets of four, from dolls, cricket bats and balls to chocolates and tricycles – just to keep our sanity intact. Even haircuts took place with all four heads aligned in a row at the salon. Sakshi, in her first grade, would lie on top of me, covering me with herself, to talk about her day at school. 'I've decided what I want to do,' she declared one afternoon, sombrely. I tousled her mop of hair and asked, 'What is that?'

'I will have five children when I grow up.'

I spluttered, shook her off, and stood up. Not a very kind thing to say, I thought, to a mother in the throes of child rearing in a joint family.

My answer was grave: 'Well, then, don't expect me to turn up each time to play nani. I'm done with bringing up the four of you, no more for me, lady!'

'You will not have to "come" anywhere. I'll have my kids here, with you.'

I was baffled. She carried on, 'I'm not going to marry and go away.'

I lost my afternoon's sleep worrying about what was going on in the child's mind. I did not know then, that as the years went by, this desire for having many children would take deep root in her mind, but rather differently. Today, I wish so much that her beliefs were grounded in something as simple as wanting to bring up her children as strong, resilient individuals.

We have different grades of battles, Sakshi and I. Food is the biggest of them all. We fence over her excessive fondness for eggs, bread, mutton,

biscuits, chocolates and sukhi roti. She shoves two rotis quickly into her mouth when no one is around to supervise her lunch. Bunny clips her nose between his fingers and drains a bowl of curd into her mouth – even now, when she is all of seventeen years old. Typically, she picks up all the chicken pieces from the salad, and all the peppers, broccoli, spring onions and carrots are left forlorn on her plate. With much relish, and a devilish glint in her oh-so-expressive-eyes, she removes that scraggly, limp lettuce from her (oh-so-repulsive) McD chicken burger, and calmly places it before me, saying, 'You eat this, you're putting on weight.' I can protest in oily anger all I want.

Last year, a summer course at Penn State University unleashed a lettuce fairy on her, and the same happened to Tanay while he was at Yale. I thought my eyes were seeing @@@ when I saw both of them pile crisp lettuce on their plates for breakfast, the morning after they landed back in Delhi. The croissant, slathered with strawberry preserve, all but slipped from my hand. 'CM, you're eating junk, man. Don't you know green is healthy? Lettuce is only water and it's so yum, huh?'

'Mom, gawd, look at all that heavy-duty stuff you're eating. Eat this – you'll know what mother earth has gifted us, how DM (downmarket) can you get!' Sakshi said, fluttering her eyelashes and flicking a 'propah' wrist at me. It was good to have them back, even if it meant having my dialogues thrown back at me.

A week later, Mummy called from her room, 'Where is that daughter of yours? I'll thrash her when I see her. You've laid down the rule that I mustn't give her my keys, so she sent Rehan saying, "Didi wants biscuits." She woke me up just when I was falling off to sleep. That too, after having a bowl of kheer and cheekily calling me mean when I refused her a second helping, and then you say I indulge her...' Mummy and I laughed together, exasperated.

The tussle between a grandmom and a mom can smell like burnt milk in a household when it comes to feeding the kids. I could devote a whole chapter to kitchen wars and tick off how many battles she won and I lost, or vice versa. We've both made our compromises – pizzas to be made only on a wheat base, dal to be served in three versions – without tadka, only with heeng-jeera, and with onions. Mayonnaise is practically banned; only curd-based dressings are used.

Tangy Chicken Salad

- 4 chicken breasts
- 2 garlic cloves crushed
- 2 tbsp soya sauce
- 2 tbsp oil
- 120 ml coconut cream
- 2 tbsp fish sauce
- 2 tbsp lemon juice
- 1 tsp sugar
- 120 g water chestnuts sliced
- 25 g cashew nuts roasted
- 4 onions sliced
- 1 stalk lemon grass chopped fine
- 1 tsp galangal chopped
- 1 large red chilli sliced
- 2 spring onions sliced
- 10–12 mint leaves
- 1 lettuce
- Coriander, red chillies to garnish

Marinate chicken in soya sauce, garlic and oil for 2 hours. Heat the coconut cream, fish sauce, lemon juice and sugar on gentle heat, till the sugar dissolves. Grill the chicken till cooked and tender. Cut the cooked chicken into strips, mix with water chestnuts, cashew nuts, onions, lemon grass, galangal, red chillies, spring onions, mint leaves. Pour coconut dressing over the chicken mixture, mix well. Spread lettuce over a large serving plate. Spoon the mixture on top, garnish with coriander sprigs and red chillies.

Spicy Szechuan Noodle Salad

- 350 g thick noodles
- 175 g cooked chicken
- 50 g roasted cashews
- 4 spring onions chopped

Dressing:

- 2 tbsp fresh coriander chopped
- 2 garlic cloves chopped
- 2 tbsp peanut butter
- 2 tbsp sweet chilli sauce
- 1 tbsp vinegar
- 2 tbsp olive oil
- 2 tbsp chicken stock
- 1 tbsp sesame oil
- 10 peppercorns ground

Cook the noodles, drain and rinse under cold water. Combine all ingredients for the dressing in a bowl, mix well. Add noodles, chicken, cashews and spring onions, toss gently to coat. Adjust seasoning to taste.

Thai Chicken Mince Salad

- 500 g chicken mince
- 1 stalk lemon grass chopped fine
- 3 kaffir lime leaves chopped
- 4 red chillies
- 4 tbsp lemon juice
- 2 tbsp fish sauce
- 2 spring onions sliced
- 2 tbsp fresh coriander chopped
- Fresh mint for garnish
- Mixed salad leaves, cucumber, tomato slices for serving

Cook chicken mince with a little water. In a large bowl, mix all the ingredients with the mince. Arrange mixed salad leaves, cucumber, tomato slices on a platter, spoon chicken mixture and garnish with sprigs of mint.

It's difficult to define a salad. Its role is ambiguous. It's a perfect accompaniment, but almost every cuisine in the world has its main course salads too. A main course salad takes centre stage in a meal. It can also stand alone as a full meal if perfectly balanced with the necessary protein, vegetables, beans, rice or pasta to provide the carbs – don't skimp on these. Rich dressings can be left out. Low-cal dressings, herbs and lemon juice add more flavour, without the calories. Thai cuisine often uses fresh salad leaves, water chestnuts, herbs and nuts, combined with spicy poultry or fish. Chicken is marinated and cooked before being sliced; coconut cream or lime dressings bring it all together in perfect harmony.

I first tasted Thai food twenty years ago. We were on our way back from our honeymoon in Europe, and were staying with my cousin in Manchester. I can't remember what we ate, but the taste still lingers. The sensations of galangal, lemon grass, chillies and coconut milk exploded on my tongue, and I was smitten. I was in Bangalore when Thai food came to Paradise Island (Taj West End). Neither Jaipur nor Delhi had a Thai restaurant then. I carried back lemon grass and the other flavours in my mind.

Experiments began in the kitchen. If Jaipur didn't give us Thai food, I would learn to make it. Over the next few months, I stirred up enough courage to convince Mummy to do a Thai dinner for sixty people. I had scoured the markets in Delhi, carried back fresh lemon grass, galangal, Thai chillies, some sauces, even bell peppers and celery, for the dinner. Planning, shopping, grinding and extracting – it took me about a week to put it all together. The drivers sat in the basement to 'do' coconut milk from heaps of coconuts – in two consistencies, thick and thin. All the starters, soup, salads and curries were systematically ticked off. Two days before the dinner, I sealed the pastes, labelled red curry, green curry, yellow curry, peanut sauce, and refrigerated them. The actual cooking was done on the day of the dinner. To dish up crisp stir-fry in three different flavours and combinations of vegetables, to serve them piping hot, with only one person cooking (my kitchen staff played audience), was like balancing between the soup and the saucepan. Though most of Mummy's friends are seasoned travellers, to get such food in Jaipur was a surprise. The grapevine was efficient as usual: at a wedding lunch the next day, where all of Jaipur was present, I didn't know where to hide my face. Whispers ran amuck. 'Oh, you should've been at the Kapurs' last night – what Thai food!' I could smell galangal, garlic, lemon grass and fish sauce in my sleep. Since then, the Thai chicken salad has remained a perennial favourite.

Thai Cabbage Salad

2 tbsp fish sauce
Rind and juice of 2 lemons
2 stalks lemon grass chopped
½ cup coconut milk
2 tbsp oil
2 red chillies cut in thin strips
6 garlic cloves sliced
3 onions sliced
1 cabbage shredded
2 tbsp roasted peanuts chopped

Combine fish sauce, lemon rind, lemon juice and lemon grass with coconut milk. Heat oil; stir-fry red chillies, garlic and onions till crisp. Blanch cabbage in boiling salted water, drain dry. Stir dressing into cabbage, sprinkle with fried onion mixture and roasted peanuts.

Curried Rice Salad

1 tsp coriander seeds
1 tsp cumin seeds
1 tsp ground cinnamon
1 tsp cloves
1 star anise
1 tsp green cardamom
1 tsp peppercorns
1 tbsp oil
6 onions chopped
6 garlic cloves chopped
2 stalks lemon grass sliced
1 tsp salt

Curry:

3 tbsp oil
1 cup tofu/paneer
125 g green beans cut into 1" pieces
6 cups rice cooked
3 onions sliced and fried
4 spring onions chopped
2 tbsp peanuts chopped
1 tbsp lemon juice

Grind the spices into a powder. Heat oil in a wok, add onions, garlic, lemon grass, cook till soft. Grind this together with the dry spices and salt. Heat oil in a wok, cook the tofu on high heat for 2 minutes, add curry paste and beans, and stir. Add the rice, using two spoons to lift and stir on high heat for about 3 minutes. Transfer to a serving dish, sprinkle the fried onions, spring onion, peanuts and lemon juice.

Mexican Mixed Salad

3 tbsp white vinegar
1 tsp Dijon mustard
2 tbsp single cream
¾ cup oil
1 garlic clove chopped
1 tsp ground cumin
1 tsp dried oregano
500 g minced chicken
1 onion
½ tsp red chilli powder
200 g corn niblets
250 g red kidney beans boiled
1 tbsp fresh coriander
1 small lettuce
3 tomatoes sliced
2 cups cheddar cheese grated
½ cup black olives
2 spring onions sliced
Salt, pepper to taste
Tortilla chips to serve

To make the dressing, mix vinegar and salt with a fork until dissolved. Stir in mustard and cream. Gradually add the oil, garlic, cumin, oregano and pepper. Heat oil; add chicken mince, onion, salt, chilli, cook for 7–10 minutes, till tender and a little brown. Leave to cool. Toss the chicken, beans, corn niblets and coriander. Shred lettuce leaves finely. Place in another bowl, tossed with 3 tbsp of dressing. Pile up the mince mixture in the centre of a plate, sprinkle over with cheese. Arrange the tomatoes around the edge. Scatter spring onions and olives, and pour remaining dressing over the salad. Garnish with coriander and serve with tortilla chips.

Fruit Salad with Honey Cream

2 oranges segmented
175 g black grapes halved
2 pears cubed
1 apple cubed
½ papaya scooped out in balls
1 banana sliced
75 g cream cheese
2 tbsp milk
2 tbsp honey
1 tsp lemon rind
150 ml cream

Soften cream cheese with wooden spoon; gradually beat in the milk, honey, lemon rind. Whip cream till thick but not stiff. Whip in the cheese mixture. Toss the fruits gently in a large bowl and serve chilled. Serve honey cream separately.

Persian Melon Salad

2 melons
1 cup strawberries
3 peaches cubed
1 bunch grapes
2 tbsp castor sugar
1 tbsp rose water
1 tbsp lemon juice
Sprigs of mint
Crushed ice

Cut melons in half, remove seeds,.scoop out the flesh with a melon scoop and reserve the shells. Reserve 4 strawberries, slice the rest. Place in a bowl with melon balls, peaches, grapes, sugar, rose water, lemon juice. Pile the fruit in the melon shells and chill. Garnish with reserved strawberries and sprigs of mint. Before serving, sprinkle over with crushed ice.

The punch in a fruit salad comes from summer fruits being dunked in a tangy dressing like fresh orange juice. When the juices meet, the medley begins. Watermelon adds grace to the luscious sweetness of mangoes, apricots mellow down the peaches, bananas weigh down the textures, melon lifts the tone, and the grapes release their juices. To feel each fruit as it teases the tongue, to taste its oneness, is to taste nectar; to taste them as they are, one bite at a time, is to understand how each one of us makes the world whole.

I've dressed fruits with ginger syrup made by boiling ginger, sugar and cloves in water. Combine this syrup with coconut milk, grated nutmeg and cinnamon, and blend with bananas into a creamy dressing. It makes a fun salad for a party. The energy that spices like nutmeg and cinnamon add to a salad is of the resilient Indian sort. You know what I mean? We absorb, we hit out, we relent, we adapt, we resist, we change, we turn corners, we walk the road on one leg, but we walk and we laugh. These salads reflect our seasons, sentiments, solutions, and the passing of time, of life. They make me connect to simplicity the way a dal chawal meal does.

Caesar Salad

1 head lettuce

4 slices of bread cubed

3 tbsp olive oil

1 garlic clove crushed

2 tbsp lemon juice

1 tsp Worcestershire sauce,

5 tbsp grated Parmesan cheese

3 ham slices chopped

½ cup olive oil

1 egg

Salt, pepper to taste

Separate, rinse and dry the lettuce leaves. Tear the outer ones, chop the heart. Mix together cubed bread, olive oil in a bowl till the bread soaks up all the oil. Place bread cubes on a baking tray, put in a hot oven till golden brown, leave to cool. Break the egg in a food processor; add garlic, lemon juice, Worcestershire sauce, 2 tbsp ham. With the motor still running, pour olive oil in a thin stream till the dressing has the consistency of single cream; season with salt and pepper. Pour dressing over the salad leaves, toss well. Add in the cheese, croutons, remaining ham and serve.

Caesar Cardini, an Italian, created the Caesar salad in the nineteen twenties, in the US, when a popular salad in that country meant boiled celery with vinaigrette. A hundred years ago, long before a salad came to be looked upon as healthy, it was thought to be an exotic European import. Waldorf, Coleslaw, Russian salad and chicken mayonnaise are what I call a 'post-colonial burden'. Mayo-driven salads gave way to the 'googly-wooglies' as Resham calls them – the aspics or veggies floating in lemon gelatine. In the seventies, salads were reinvented into robust, fulsome creations with boiled potatoes, boiled eggs or sausages, once again soaked in mayonnaise, or they were tomatoey versions of baked beans. You still find baked beans in their bland tomato sauce passed off as salad at buffet lunches in some pretentious five-star hotels.

A salad has to look good and taste good – maybe not always taste as good as it looks – but go easy on the calories. I've learnt to micro-manage salads in the way one micro-manages life itself. Indeed, to take it to a serious note, they work as socio-political statements about our lifestyle, apart from being an exercise in discipline. As Aman and Sakshi frequently demonstrate, having religiously disciplined themselves to pick out all the chicken from Caesar, or pick out all the baby corn from a Garden and leave the earthy goodness for us lesser mortals to eat. 'I'm above all this, y'know,' Sakshi says, sneering at the spinach or olives. Sigh! I'd love to order a bottle of salad pills for the kids, throw one per day in their mouths and say, 'Good girl, here's a cookie.'

Tabbouleh

1 cup fine bulgar wheat
Juice of 1 lemon
3 tbsp olive oil
40 g fresh parsley chopped
3 tbsp fresh mint
4–5 spring onions
1 capsicum sliced
2 tomatoes diced
Few black olives

Add enough water to the bulgar wheat and let it stand for at least 30 minutes to 2 hours. Then drain it and squeeze to remove excess water. It will swell to double its original size. Spread it on some paper towels to dry completely. Place it in a bowl, add lemon juice, oil, salt, pepper and let it stand for 1 or 2 hours to allow the flavours to develop. Add parsley, mint, spring onions, capsicum and mix well. Garnish with diced tomatoes and olives.

Turkish Feta Salad

1 lettuce
1 green pepper
1 red pepper
1 cucumber
4 tomatoes
1 onion
2 cups feta cheese
Black olives to garnish
3 tbsp olive oil
3 tbsp lemon juice
1 garlic clove crushed
1 tbsp parsley chopped
1 tbsp mint chopped
Salt, pepper to taste

Break lettuce into bite-size pieces. Cut peppers into juliennes. Chop cucumber, slice tomatoes and onion, scatter crumbled feta on top and toss lightly. Blend olive oil, lemon juice, garlic. Add parsley, mint and season with salt and pepper. Pour dressing over salad, toss lightly, garnish with black olives.

Avoid storing your greens next to fruits like apples and bananas. They emit ethylene gas as they ripen. This causes brown spots on the greens and shortens their life. A salad is like a layered haircut. From whole lettuce heads to fluffy, frilled edges, it has lightness and crunch. Lettuce can confuse and confound with its varieties. Lolla rossa, green tango, romaine, iceberg – of which romaine and iceberg stand up well to dressings, retaining the crucial crunch. Rocket, or arugula, and watercress have blatantly peppery flavours and are best served with light vinaigrettes. Try layering some rocket with the chicory family – endive, radicchio, escarole or dandelion.

Fragrance and flavour in salads come from soft herbs like parsley, coriander, mint, basil, dill, tarragon and chives. Rosemary, oregano, thyme have no place in a salad bowl. Milder greens, like spinach and peas, also get lost in an aggressive salad.

Salads have been around since the time of the Romans. They ate their veggies and conquered the world (Girls, are you listening?). Over the years, they have changed their identity, finding new ways to combine different ingredients.

A cookbook of the forties divided the empire of salads into eleven kingdoms – chilled, frozen, hot, bowl, decorative, platter, individual, moulded, whole meal, fruit, and chicken – they forgot edible! This is the beauty and the burden of creating a salad. No rules, no constraints – they allow a cook to express the anxieties and the fascinations of the era. There is more room to play with a bowl of mixed, dressed vegetables than with a tandoori chicken leg! But what do you do when you're just about to enter the kitchen to toss a salad and Aman remarks, 'CM, I'll eat salad for dinner, just go easy on the veggies!'

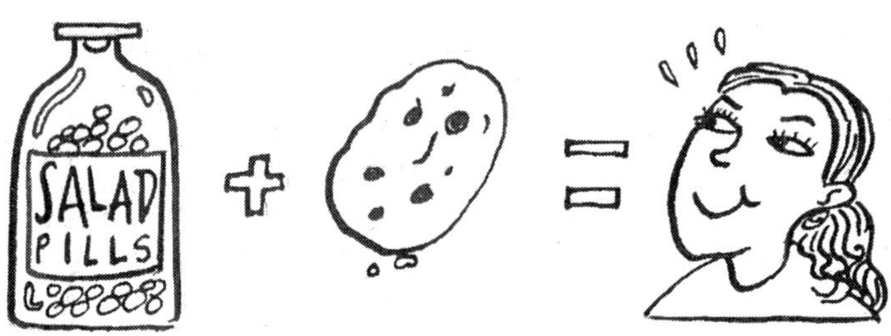

4

Spice on the Side

Resham, as a toddler, always wanted a full meal. But she was a calm baby and hardly ever yelled for food. If she was hungry, she'd crawl up to the fridge and find a small coriander leaf or whatever else was behind it, left untouched by a careless Bahadur while sweeping, grin at me and quickly shove it into her mouth. That was her way of saying, 'Give me my lunch.' At a birthday party, she surveyed the table, waddled up to me and tugged at my salwar and said, 'Tandoori chicken nahin hai, I won't eat this food.' I couldn't look my hostess in the eye.

A few months later, while driving down from Abohar in Punjab, after being part of a typical Punjabi wedding, where there was more tandoori chicken and fried fish than flowers and shahnai, we stopped to stretch our legs. Miles of barren, sandy land stretched before us, without a vestige of green in sight. Dust clouds rose as cars swished past. Even the trees were covered with sand and looked piteously scraggly, like freshly shorn sheep. Resham piped up, 'Detho Mamma, titni saari haddi.' She pointed to the bare branches, which actually did look like gnawed chicken bones. I knelt down and asked, 'Are you hungry?'

She nodded, her wide eyes turning into liquid honey. 'Haan, car mein kuch khaane ko nahin hai!' It was as if someone had cruelly squeezed my heart into pulp. I couldn't bear to see my child hungry. I had always scoffed at this mushy sentimental nonsense, but here I was... Resham was only four then and had an adorable stammer, which was the family's source of entertainment every evening. 'Tottolade laddoo dedo na,' she said now, asking for a Ferrero Rocher chocolate. I could have killed for that 'tottolade laddoo' just then. We had exhausted all our snacks for the journey, which had been prolonged by a few hours because of a series of punctures. We passed the rest of the time by telling her stories of how crocodiles attacked human beings and ate them, bones and all. Resham was most concerned. 'Totodile tabhi tabhi taatha hai na?' (Crocodiles only bite sometimes, no?)

There were times when I couldn't understand what Resham was saying. Sakshi connected with her better – perhaps because she was the elder sibling, or maybe it was just an instinctive tuning in, but she did mediate for all of us when it came to understanding Resham's special language. That is why I also found my first-born's tendency to connect with all things bizarre quite easy to accept. If I found her sitting at the dining table, cheerfully dipping and swirling the arched back of a pepperoni pizza slice into a glass of Pepsi before popping it into her mouth, I never felt surprised. She wouldn't be Sakshi if she didn't do something strange and uncommon. From eating Marie Gold biscuits sandwiched in a slice of bread, to filling gol gappas with crumbs of chocolate fudge cake and eating cabbage spewed over with tomato sauce, she has always shown an uncanny grasp of flavours in food. I have to admit that I've never indulged in absurd combinations like these. Using tomato chutney in a sandwich or dipping mathi in Kraft cheese spread or serving Thai sweet chilli sauce with chicken mince kebab, is the farthest I have gone.

Sakshi made sure that I always kept hung curd ready in the fridge, since she constantly hollered from the table, 'Koi dip-ship nahin hai to make this food go down my throat?' It took two minutes to turn hung curd into a dip of any flavour, which, of course, depended on what she felt like eating at that particular time. Fried fish with tartare sauce meant that she'd eat the tartare sauce and not the fish. Coriander and tamarind chutneys have a ubiquitous presence in almost every Indian kitchen; mixing coriander chutney with curd, adding herbs and garlic salt to it, was enough to satisfy Sakshi.

Dips are to the West what chutneys are to us in India. It doesn't take much to get a dip ready, but it can add a great deal to your meal. Some dips are versatile enough to serve as sandwich spreads. The walnut chutney I learnt from Mummy remains steady on the top of the charts. I use it to go with mince kebabs, chicken tikkas, as a dip to be served with crackers, as a sandwich spread, or simply to be left on the table to go with any meal.

Walnut Chutney

250 g walnuts
25 g green chillies chopped
50 g onion paste
750 g hung curd
Salt to taste

Soak walnuts in water for 30 minutes to soften them. Break them into pieces and grind them, adding a little water. Add the green chillies, onion paste and salt. Add the hung curd and whisk well.

Mango Salsa

1 mango (preferably alphonso) diced
2 spring onions chopped
½ cucumber diced
2 tbsp coriander leaves
1 green chilli chopped
Juice of 1 lemon
1 tbsp extra virgin olive oil
Salt to taste

Mix all the ingredients. Keep aside and chill once the juices are all out.

Herbed Cream Cheese Dip

100 g hung curd
1 tbsp extra virgin olive oil
25 g garlic crushed
25 g mint chopped
Salt and Pepper to taste

Mix all the ingredients and set in a bowl. Make a small indent in the centre, fill with a little olive oil and garnish with fresh mint.

For Bunny, all dips should be made with melted chocolate. 'I can have gol gappas filled with that,' he says. I wonder who takes after whom? Both the father and the first-born, vouch that gol gappas filled with tequila are the best starter. They are quite a pair when it comes to suggesting weird combinations of food. I can rhapsodize as much as I want about beetroot caviar or tomato mozzarella salad, served as full-bodied tomato juice with basil oil, topped with a white foam of mozzarella in a shot glass (this is what molecular cooking is coming to). All they do is look at me as though I were an alien and say, 'We'll settle for a fruity dip with tequila.'

Fruity Dip

150 ml orange juice
150 ml pineapple juice
120 ml tequila
1 tbsp fresh mint chopped
1 tbsp icing sugar

Whisk all the ingredients and chill. On a summer evening, this serves as a light dip to spoon over fresh slices of melon and mango.

Sultana scones, strawberry preserve and slices of history. Tea rooms, cobbled streets, bands playing music and quaint stores selling eclectically designed pots and pans, porcelain, Viking weapons, hats and willowy skirts, along with homemade preserves, chutneys and jams. The remains of a Roman castle, lush green stretches of meadow, wild bursts of flowers and a river flowing by, forming a canvas in front of you as you step out of the train station.

York in England, is one place I would love to be lost in. A walk through the Shambles, the oldest preserved medieval street in Europe, made me want to never find my way back, because each turn I took led me to a sight that delighted me even more than the one before. It turned out to be a magical mix of the medieval and the modern, adding up to the charm of a small town and the upbeat mood of a pulsating city. Weekend crowds had the streets abuzz, ale flowed in pubs, a group performed to African beats on the drums. Shops named '...And Give a Dog a Bone' sold Christmas angels, Bohemian artifacts and other bric-a-brac. We spent a long time browsing, inhaling the character of the city. A narrow street suddenly opened out into a small square, a café seemed to spring out of nowhere – cheerful, welcoming and replete with joyful vigour.

The mood was set. Rubbing my hands in gleeful anticipation, I gently guided my brood to the Railway Museum and the York Castle Museum – the 'must-sees.'

The thousand-year-old York Minster, standing tall

with its stained-glass windows and Gothic pinnacles stunned us into awed silence. Each step was worship. The silence, despite the crowd, was calming. Close to the Minster, Rehan spotted Ate O'Clock. 'Look, look, they've made a spelling mistake, Mumma; you always point out wrongly spelt shop names to us – Sucksess Traders yaad hai?' He was puzzled since he probably assumed that Indians have a copyright over such errors. We trooped into Ate O'Clock, ravenous for lunch. It had a warm, cosy ambience, with the soothing strains of guitar being played. Fried fish and big chips dipped in classic mayonnaise, tiger prawns served with a petri-dish of thousand island dressing, sea bass cooked to perfection with olives and sun dried tomatoes, succulent stuffed chicken breast on creamy potatoes. The chef came to our table himself, a thing pretty much unheard of, unless a celebrity is being waited upon. The meal was bribe enough to cajole the kids into agreeing to go on to the Viking Museum.

And right after that, a traditional English tea service – just the right way to wind down after such a day.

Finger sandwiches, cakes and delicate pastries were served on a three-tiered salver at Betty's, a beautifully done up tearoom. Tea was poured with quiet grace: 'Milk or lemon? Sugar? One lump or two?' After the ceremonial serving, we attacked the menu. Each pastry had to be tried, prawn and avocado sandwiches came next, and a banana toffee sundae followed the freshly baked scones with strawberry preserve and dollops of cream on the side. While the British sipped their tea daintily, we ate voraciously. York stirs up an appetite... it feeds you the past, makes you live in the present, and leaves you hungry for more.

Betty's had a counter selling preserves, dips and sauces. Cherries steeped in sherry and lemon juice, relishes sitting pretty in glass jars with chequered lids, displayed in a come-hither-pick-me-up manner. There was so much I would have loved to carry back home!

The visit to Betty's for high tea, with finger sandwiches and relishes, brought back memories of how smitten we were with Rajmata Sahiba Gayatri Devi while we were students at Maharani Gayatri Devi School (MGD) in the early seventies and eighties. Miss Lutter, our British principal, would serve high tea, with thin cucumber sandwiches and tiny, latticed lemon tarts, along with mini samosas and mint chutney, supplied by the MGD kitchen. The Rajmata's husky voice, her chiffon sari, and the ready twinkle in her eyes made us self-conscious pre-teens feel completely in awe of her.

We had Home Science as a subject in the eighth grade and the cookery exam at the end of the year was reason enough for all of us to go about quaking with fear – fear of the ladle, as Didi calls it. We were divided into groups and asked to lay the table with a thematic menu. There was a scramble to procure crockery, cutlery, lace table covers, crocheted place mats and bone china tea sets. Hand-painted menu cards were made. Our group had the maximum number of silent and sleeping spectators, who preferred a ringside seat to the entire circus, which suited me perfectly. Two friends and I rustled up some much-coveted gold-plated cutlery, a Wedgwood tea set and Venetian lace table linen. Each group guarded their cookery plans as TOP SECRET and there was a lot of hush-hush whispering in class as the day approached.

Strangely, I recall that our sandwiches and cupcakes came out perfectly, but I can't seem to remember exactly which cupcakes we made. We didn't know how to make scones, but still wanted to do the entire served-with-freshly-whipped-cream-and-strawberry-preserve thing, so the cupcakes were served like that, cream jug et al. The tour de force was a chicken mayonnaise salad right out of the *Hamlyn Cookbook*, garnished to perfection with thinly sliced tomato wedges, served on crisp, curling cabbage leaves and sprinkled over with curry powder. Our cookery teacher watched the three of us working in perfect sync, cutting our sandwiches just right and finger thin, our cupcakes rising to a warm golden crust, the oil being poured in a thin stream into the blender while it whipped up the egg yolks into mayonnaise. Then we scurried out to lay the table with forks and knives in their rightful places. She was sure we'd come first – she said so, and we were jubilant. But we had an external examiner coming in as taster, and the lady couldn't believe that gauche fourteen-year-old girls could put together such a classy presentation. I can never forget her words: 'I am sure you made half the things at home with your mothers' help.' And we were given the third place. For being perfect?

Classic Mayonnaise

2 egg yolks
2 tbsp vinegar
2 cups salad oil
2 tbsp lemon juice
1 tsp salt
½ tsp black pepper
½ tsp mustard

Blend egg yolks; add dry ingredients, vinegar, mix well. Add salad oil in a slow, steady stream, keeping the blender on. Add lemon juice.

Make sure all the ingredients for mayonnaise are at the same temperature. You can leave the egg yolks to stand for a short while with the mustard before adding the oil, experts say it works to hold the emulsion together.

Good ol' mayo has come a long way. It is strangely ironic for me to include basic mayo in this book, given the fact that I've all but banned its presence in the kitchen. A friend, who is a die-hard mayo fan, scornfully informed me of how she makes hers with organically grown basil, freshly squeezed garlic juice, free-range eggs, expeller-pressed saf-flower oil! 'You can go on about calories, cholesterol and carbs but mayonnaise has evolved,' she says.

The word mayonnaise evolved from the old French 'mayeunaise' – 'mayeu' means the yolk of an egg. Though, the French love to maintain that it was created to celebrate their victory over the British, in1756, at the port of Mahon. Put simply, it is an emulsion of egg yolk and oil, with the lecithin in the yolk acting as an emulsifying agent.

Versatile Mayonnaise

- For a piquant thousand island dressing, mix a cup of mayo with ¼ cup chilli sauce, 2 tbsp tomato sauce, 2 tbsp each of chopped capsicum and chopped celery, 1½ tbsp of finely chopped onion.
- Add ½ cup whipped cream to a cup of mayo for a creamy dressing.
- Stir in 1/3 cup cranberry juice and 2 tbsp of chopped almonds to 1 cup of mayo for a fruity tinge.
- Mix 1/3 chopped onion, ½ tsp lemon peel, 2 tbsp lemon juice, 2 cloves garlic minced, 2 tsp Worcestershire sauce and ½ tsp mixed herbs to 1 cup of mayo to make a herby dressing.

- Add ¼ cup snipped chives, or the tender green of spring onions, and 1 tbsp lemon juice to 1 cup mayo to get an onion-flavoured version.
- Mix 1½ tbsp of any spicy Indian curry to 1 cup of mayo, dash in chopped fresh coriander, spice it up with freshly ground pepper.
- Add ½ cup sour cream, 1 tbsp lemon juice, 1 tbsp orange juice and 2 tsp sugar to 1 cup of mayo.
- Mix 1 cup yoghurt with 2 tbsp mayo, 1 tsp sugar, a dash of lemon juice.

I am his eternal Laila. He'd chase me till I gave in to dancing to *Laila o Laila* with him. We grew up in the age of *Qurbani* in which Zeenat Aman created a sensation. The song was perfect in the movie, with Amjad Khan playing the drums with careless ease. In those days, we danced to Hindi music with some disdain – at least, I did. At every party, the moment this number played, I just had to get off the floor. My friend knew I detested it. But for him, I would let go and dance as if it were the last dance of my life. I'm still used to being woken up at odd hours of the night to answer his call – not a word said, but I know it's him teasing me with *Laila* playing in some vague disc or pub, wherever he is, even in the US or Australia.

A breezy 'Hi stranger' is our understood form of greeting – it doesn't matter where we are. A round face, crinkling eyes, and a never ending love for life – there is no other way to describe him. Next to Papa, if I feel safe with another man, it is him (due apologies, dear husband). His birthday falls in June, when the heat in Jaipur is unbearable. It makes you feel like your skin is melting away and you are like a sloth bear going slowly through the motions. To stir the imagination becomes a task, and when you are faced with what-to-do-for-someone-precious-on-his-birthday, some more sweat beads break out.

One particular year, I wanted to make this eternal stranger's birthday extra special. Should I send him a hand-written card every one hour with a rose, to show him how much he means to all of us? I pondered. 'That's too tacky, man,' Sakshi scoffed. In a flash, I told him to drop by for a bite, before the movie we were all going off to see. Blitzkrieg time! The entire armoury was pulled out from the cupboards.

Lion-pawed tables were laden with snacks ready to attack. I had thrown culinary caution away with the vegetable peels. If a confused medley of semi-starters could be turned into a meal, then this was one. Kathi rolls, filled with stir-fried veggies and served with a hot-n-sweet sauce; Mexican-style baked beans salad on a bed of nachos, drizzled over with sour cream, textured with onions and fresh coriander on the side; Bombay sev puri; scrambled eggs on toast; pepper fish with a tangy orange peel dip; pasta tossed in a tomato 'Mitabiatta' (read Indianized) sauce; coin-sized buns with corn and cheese topping; boiled egg and chicken salami salad; lychees and mangoes coated with raw mango and lemon marmalade dressing; a coffee mousse cake and ice cream.

The gong sounded. The door swung open noiselessly and five tentative pairs of feet came forward. Flames beckoned – some lonely, some in cheerful clusters. Nobody was visible, only voices sounding a discordant battle cry were heard: 'We love you we do, happy birthday to you!' I would like to press the replay button again and again to relive that moment. There were audible gasps and gleeful smiles playing hide and seek with dancing shadows as the candles threw their light merrily. The man in question hugged me quietly; unspoken words were replaced by ringing laughter that echoed all around.

I had forsaken a well-designed menu to ensure that everyone who was coming had something they enjoyed. Each dish had a couple of takers. The food was served on hand-painted platters, on jute mats with huge tulips embroidered on them; the candles lent their warmth to the occasion. As usual, there were accusations like, 'You are fattening us up!' 'You do it purposely, don't you?' 'You make us eat so we put on weight and you look slimmer than all of us!'

French Dressing

½ cup salad oil	1 tsp sugar
2 tbsp vinegar	¾ tsp mustard
2 tbsp lemon juice	½ tsp salt

Combine all the ingredients in a jar, close lid and shake well. Store in the refrigerator.

Variations to French Dressing

Green Herb Dressing: Add chopped coriander, chives or basil with basic dressing ingredients.

Garlic Dressing: Add 2–3 cloves of garlic to the basic ingredients before blending.

Mixed Mustard Dressing: Use Dijon mustard and flavoured mustard in equal proportions.

Fruity French Dressing: Add ¼ cup orange juice, 3 tbsp lemon juice, 1 tsp grated onion, salt and pepper to taste, and a dash of red chilli powder, to jiggle up a fruity version.

A French dressing or vinaigrette, as it is commonly called, can be made creamy by combining all the dry ingredients, beating in an egg with the vinegar and adding the oil in a slow stream, blending constantly with an electric or a rotary beater.

Using salad oil is one of those things that have been passed on to us like a culinary tradition. However, olive, sunflower and canola oils are most commonly used these days. To finish the dressing, do the jig and shake it all around your kitchen… turn up the music, tap your toes… the dressing will last for a week.

Sakshi had invited her friends over for lunch on a Sunday. They were a group of dance instructors who missed home-cooked food. They wanted 'nothing close to dal chawal', however. Coincidentally, just a day before, a friend had sent across some music with strict instructions of 'you need to unwind'. I took that rather seriously, but Sakshi stopped and gaped at me with a this-can't-be-my-mummy expression. 'You can't dance around in the kitchen. What will the servants say? And especially you, with two left feet, even that… (splutter-splutter)… whatever you're shaking up won't be able to withstand such distasteful dancing.'

For the nth time I cursed myself, thinking, 'Why did I make sure she has a vocabulary that includes words like distasteful?'

As I ambled around the kitchen, collecting all the ingredients needed to get lunch going, she turned me around ever so gently, plugged her iPod in my ears, and said, 'All your favourite numbers are in here. You can listen to '*Cigarettes and chocolate milk*' and '*Still*' – just keep calm.' She made a dignified exit.

Soulful strains of '*One*' and '*Wish you were here*' actually helped me swing right into the heart of things, feeling all the vegetables I was handling with a different energy. I got sucked into a vortex of sensations.

Culinary charades followed. Chander Bahadur (CB) had to decipher from my hand and lip movements, 'Pyaaz lamba kato,' 'Tomatoes ko cross lagakar blanch karo,' 'Carrots, spring onions, cabbage, capsicum ko jullienes mein kato' – all this conveyed in sign language.

When lunch was almost cooked, the oven decided it could suffer no more silence. The thermostat lost control, temperatures soared, and the quiche shell turned chocolate brown. CB motioned to me, clipping his nose, holding his head and pointing to the oven frantically. Off went the earplugs and the music came to a crashing halt. The quiche shell was burnt, but thankfully, only to the point that it could still be salvaged. The mixed vegetable filling for the quiche was baked with cheese in Mummy's old Belling oven, while the quiche shell went through a makeover and got converted into a choco-praline pie. I doused the shell with freshly made praline, which was chilled in the fridge till it set, to conceal the slightly burnt look and taste. Chocolate mousse was set in the shell. These are the times when I've felt someone's presence beside me, providing me with silent inspiration. With crunchy celery and lettuce arranged like wild flowers, spilling out of a Venetian handcrafted glass bowl on the table, and four summery dips, everyone kept cool. The lunch was uneventful.

Lemony Dill Dressing

¼ cup extra virgin olive oil

3 tbsp lemon juice

1 tbsp dried dill

Salt and pepper to taste.

Mix all the ingredients and shake it all about! If fresh dill is available, it adds extra zing to the dish.

Tomato Basil Dip

4 tomatoes chopped

3 tbsp extra virgin olive oil

2 tbsp fresh basil chopped

1 tbsp red wine vinegar

Salt and Pepper to taste

Shake all the ingredients and add the basil in the end.

Caramelized Ginger

Melt 4 tbsp jaggery over low heat till it's light brown in colour. Add 2 tbsp sliced ginger and stir for about 3 minutes. Sun-dry the jaggery-coated ginger till it is a crisp yellow. These bits add a bite to a salad that has a mild dressing.

Fig and Coriander Dip

280 ml curd

110 g dried figs chopped

2 spring onions chopped

20 g coriander leaves

Salt and pepper to taste

Hang the curd till thick and creamy. Whip it up and add all the ingredients. Chill and serve with freshly cut vegetables and greens.

Carrot and Peanut Dip

200 g carrots chopped fine

50 g roasted peanuts

1 garlic clove chopped

1 green chilli chopped

125 g hung curd

15 g coriander leaves chopped

Whip up the curd and add all the ingredients. Chill and serve with freshly cut vegetables.

Sauces, dips and dressings serve to complement the meal and add variety to the play of flavours. They are like an accessory to your ensemble – adding that extra zing to your style statement. A dip, a dressing or a sauce are the cosmetic add-ons to food. A kebab does not have to be served only with a mint or coriander chutney. It can be served with a honey-chilli dip, walnut chutney, or just sour cream. I have served salads and dips as the theme for the evening, with guests actually wiping up bowls of dip as if they were main course veggies – not because they were left feeling hungry, but because they just couldn't stop. Some even took doggie bags home to use as sandwich spreads for their kids' tiffins.

Lemon Sauce

300 ml chicken stock
25 g butter
25 g flour
½ tsp grated lemon rind
2 tsp lemon juice
Salt and black pepper to taste
1 egg yolk

Blend the chicken stock, butter and flour in a blender for a few seconds, till smooth. Pour into a saucepan and bring to boil slowly, stirring constantly. Simmer till thickened. Add lemon rind and juice, salt and pepper. Cool slightly. First, mix a little sauce into the egg yolk and then stir in the entire mixture. A tablespoon of cream can be added to the sauce just before serving. This sauce works beautifully with roasted or grilled chicken and fish.

Pepper Sauce

4 tbsp peppercorns
1 tbsp cumin seeds
1 tbsp coriander seeds
4 dry red chillies
1 tbsp chana dal
½ tbsp urad dal
1 cup grated coconut
1 tbsp mustard seeds
20 g tamarind (for pulp)
½ tsp turmeric powder
Salt to taste
2 tbsp oil
Jaggery (optional)

Heat 1 tbsp oil in a frying pan; add the first seven ingredients and stir till they turn brown. Remove from fire, cool, grind to a fine paste. Heat the remaining oil, add mustard seeds. When they crackle, pour in the pulp extracted from the tamarind. Add salt, turmeric powder and ground paste, letting it boil for about 10–15 minutes. When the sauce thickens, a piece of jaggery can be added to taste. This can be used as a dipping sauce for tikkis. I use it sometimes as a salad dressing over a mango and broccoli salad.

5

Steaming Hot and Subtly Flavoured

It was that time of the night. I was getting my usual dose of *How I Met Your Mother* when Sakshi lumbered in and declared, 'I think your weighing scale is wonky. It's showing two kilos up.'

I looked her up and down, or rather, side to side, and sniggered, 'Why blame the weighing scale, babes, you need to live on soups and broth.'

Sakshi needs a simple provocation to burst into a diatribe. 'WTF, woman, soup and broth is meant for near menopausal ladies like you. Your mother-of-three paunch looks ready to burst with the fourth and don't tell me you are swollen and PMSing, you...' Her arms flailed violently. She reached over me to the snoring husband, poked him, and in her best Gujju accent, yelled, 'Ae Puppa, shifat maro.' Bunny grunted and made an attempt to shift, but his snores took over. Sakshi grumbled for the nth time, 'Why do you have this huge bed when you use only one side of it? This should have been a single bed,' and gave Bunny a heave.

She settled her head on my chest and was quiet. That worried me. I hugged her close and asked, 'Kya hua?'

'Umm, it seems like Resham is finally realizing that I'm about to leave this year. She comes in every night, when I'm studying, removes my laptop, plonks herself in my lap, and carries on with her Facebooking on my laptop!!'

I laughed, trying to figure out how Resham, with her long legs and tall frame, would look curled up on a rotund lap.

'It's not funny, Ma. I'm leaving soon. Then no one will come to entertain you. You have to admit I'm your best daughter.' She turned around and peered into my face cheekily. In the darkness of the room, the lights from the TV screen gave me away. She saw tears streaming down my cheeks. 'Mom, if Dad wakes up, he'll slap you. Stop it.'

She had been doing this for over a month now. She would walk into my office and swivel my chair around, making me groan under her weight, and launch into her daily explosions about the world, only to end it with the refrain, 'Aiyee, Mummy, sunle meri baatein, mein jaane waali hun, phir roti rehna.'

I would laugh and push her away, but not without the horrible gnawing feeling that rose up in my throat like bile. It came to me in a tumultuous rush, the thought that Sakshi was already eighteen, ready to leave home for the US, to earn her undergraduate degree in child psychology. I'd been telling Bunny, 'A phase of our life is getting over. Things will never be the same again.' I also recalled, in a flash, moments when my mom and dad must have felt the same pain when I moved to a hostel in Delhi to finish my B.A. In a second, I felt an overwhelming mixture of feelings – my little one was stepping out into the world, to learn to fend for herself. It's not easy to not protect; to let go and let them make their own mistakes, stumble and fall, get up, dust their bums, and move on. Sakshi had faced lonely, traumatic times too early in her life and kept them bottled inside her for too many years. She thought she was protecting me from taking a tumble.

I remember, too, how I'd cried the day she was born. Everyone thought I was in pain because of my stitches, but the truth was something else. 'She is going to leave us and go away. What's the point?' Bunny still teases me. 'You were such a typical Punju housewife. Thinking of your daughter getting married, the day she was born.' For him, it still is a moment of victory, to have caught me behaving like a normal mummy.

Sakshi left the room; I stared at the TV screen. I don't know how much time passed before she came back. 'Oh, so you are still at it.' My nose was stuffed, I couldn't breathe. She grabbed my nail cutter and tried to run away. Both my girls have a nail cutter and shampoo fixation – borrowing and returning doesn't figure in their way of life. What is taken is for keeps. We fought over the nail cutter and fell on poor sleeping Bunny, who protested against the weight of two ladies. He opened his eyes and said, 'Gosh, you two are heavy; you *both* need that soup diet.' And all this while I'd thought he was asleep. He looked at me and smiled. The crinkled skin around his eyes said, 'We'll make it, don't worry.'

'Mammae,' came a guttural voice in the dark, 'maammmmaaee!' Resham walked in. She must sing her 'maaammae' song every night. It is her way of being cuddled and loved. She curled all of her 5' 7" around me and patted my cheek, thankfully not noticing my puffed eyes. 'Mere ko pata hai kya khaana hai?' she asked. I let out an exasperated wail of protest. 'You've just binged on laal maas and profiteroles. You can't be hungry in an hour's time!' She gurgled, 'I am a badhta bachcha. I feel like something sour. I feel like a lemon coriander soup.' Her eyes glittered at me with sheer wickedness. 'See, I'm so reasonable. I'm asking for healthy, non-fattening soup, not like your midnight snack of Kissan mixed fruit jam, slathered on bread with bhujiya. You must savour these moments, Ma. Sakshi is leaving soon. I'll be off in two years. Then you will regret it and whine, and say to yourself, "I wish I had spent more time pampering them." She struck her Meena Kumari pose. That was it! 'Bas!' I hollered, 'You two are scheming little horrors. Out, out, out!' A couple of pillows thrown, they tumbled out of my room.

So, I guess, much soup has flowed under the bridge. Soups have been gracing our meals for the last 5,000 years. Over time, pureed vegetable soups, what I call Dickensian gruel, have been refined to a broth, the potage to a consommé, while the East has had flavoured hot and sour, tom kha, laksa and millions more. Soup is subliminal – a good friend that cools you down on a hot summer's day with its minty smoothness, or warms you up on a cold winter night, clears your stuffy nose, props up your pillows and fluffs up your quilt. A hearty soup is synonymous with home, hearth and healing. It holds you in its arms and propels you in the right direction – towards more food!

Soup, though usually served as a prelude to a full meal, can also be served as a snack or a meal on its own. For me, it's a willing choice, a perfect way to begin an evening after a full day at work and no exercise.

Clear Vegetable Soup

125 g carrots cut in thin sticks

1 onion sliced

3 sticks celery thinly sliced

125 g cabbage finely shredded

2 tomatoes chopped

1ltr vegetable stock

Salt and pepper

You can use stock cubes to make the stock. But if I were you, a vegetable stock made from onions and carrots, flavoured with a bay leaf and black pepper, is the right thing to do. Place stock to boil, add the carrots and simmer for 5 minutes. Add the onion and celery; simmer for a couple of more minutes, leaving the vegetables crisp. Add the cabbage and tomatoes, season and serve hot.

This is one of my favourite soups – 'health in a bowl' and the flavour of celery that evokes a sense of being out in the woods. It is pure, wholesome goodness. Mildly flavoured, the vegetables left crisp, it is one of those things that I would unhesitatingly add to my list of life's pleasures.

Chicken Velvet Soup

6 tbsp butter
1/3 cup flour
½ cup milk
½ cup light cream
3 cups chicken stock
1 cup chicken finely cubed
Salt, pepper to taste

Melt butter in a saucepan. Blend in flour; add milk, cream and stock. Let it come to a boil, thicken, stir in chicken and season. Garnish with fresh mint or coriander.

This is the basic chicken soup, steaming hot and mildly flavoured, which Ma always gave us when we were down with a cold. 'Feed the cold,' she'd say, popping hot buttered toasts on the side. As we grew up and she developed an angina problem, Didi simplified the soup; she pureed the chicken pieces into the stock, replaced the cream with toned milk and reduced the butter to about a tbsp, leaving out the flour completely. The soup was thinner but tastier.

Spinach Soup

250 g spinach
25 g onion chopped
3 cloves garlic chopped
1 tsp ginger paste
2 tomatoes chopped
25 g butter
½ cup fresh cream
1 tsp black pepper
2 tsp lemon juice
Salt

Wash spinach thoroughly. Sauté onion, garlic, ginger, tomatoes in butter. Add the spinach, 5–6 cups water, and pressure cook for 10 minutes. Cool the soup, blend and sieve. Add salt, pepper, lemon juice and swirl in the cream (optional).

Coconut Prawn Soup

225 g fresh prawns
1.2 ltr fish stock
4 slices galangal
4 kaffir lime leaves shredded
2 red or green chillies chopped
1 tbsp fish sauce
150 ml coconut milk
2 stalks lemon grass
Salt to taste

Thinly slice the lemon grass. Peel the prawns and discard the dark vein. Heat the stock, stir in the galangal, lime leaves, lemon grass, chillies and fish sauce. Add the prawns and simmer for 5 minutes. Stir in the coconut milk and do not let the soup come to a boil.

This is a subtly flavoured soup. The prawns melt in the mouth, the chillies and galangal add the bite, and the lemon grass remains gentle on the tongue, lending an aroma that fuses with the coconut milk. It tickles and tingles and leaves you anticipating more exotic and exciting flavours in the meal to follow. I am partial towards Thai soups and do not venture into the pureed or creamy soups. A clam chowder or a lobster bisque are preferred, but I must admit most snobbishly, 'only when I am eating at a fine dining restaurant'. To add to the snobbery, 'preferably abroad'. Though I must also admit that the first taste of a simple dal soup, which Ma used to give us as kids, is still a permanent favourite. I tried hard to make Sakshi and Resham slurp it up, when they were toddlers, but to no avail. I guess I just didn't get it right.

Hot and Sour Soup

1 tbsp oil
250 g tofu sliced
90 g mushrooms sliced
2 tbsp fresh coriander chopped
1 red chilli sliced finely

Stock:

1 tbsp tamarind pulp
2 dried red chillies chopped
2 kaffir lime leaves chopped
1" ginger chopped
2" galangal chopped
1 stalk lemon grass
1 ltr cold water

Put all the ingredients for the stock into a saucepan and bring to a boil. Simmer for 5 minutes. Remove from heat, strain, reserving the stock.

Heat oil in a wok or a large frying pan; cook the tofu over high heat for about 2 minutes, stirring constantly. Add the stock. Add the mushrooms and coriander and boil for 3 minutes. Serve hot, garnished with red chilli slices.

Growing up in a small town has its limitations. Niro's was the only restaurant in town, and the only place where we could start a meal with the typical cream of tomato soup, served in ceramic soup bowls, with a swirl of cream, fried croutons and a sprig of fresh coriander. Time passed, and a Chinese chef was added to Niros's repertory. Their hot and sour soup became a permanent fixture at every meal we ate there. Ved uncle, the man behind 'Jaipur's only restaurant', started it around the time when Ma was studying at the SMS Medical College. He would invariably sit with us for a few minutes and regale us with stories of how she would walk into Niro's, dressed in flouncy pinafores and pencil heels. It was a big deal to have women dressed in anything but a sari or salwar kameez in Jaipur in the fifties.

An extra slice of vanilla ice cream, with chocolate sauce and the proverbial pink wafer, was the regular treat for me. We all grew up on Niros's food. Going there with my cousin, Raju bhaiya, who was the best-looking boy in Jaipur in the seventies, meant a special Chinese meal – the chef at Niro's was a friend of his. When I was old enough to bunk school in the eleventh grade, mushrooms on toast and cold coffee with ice cream were tops. It was a tradition for us – my parents and my sisters – to have a celebratory meal at Niro's every Christmas, and on 26 January, to celebrate the day we had moved into our own home in Bani Park, from a rented one-room-cum-pantry where Ma and Papa had begun their careers.

Cream of Mushroom Soup

1 cup mushrooms sliced
2 tbsp onion chopped
2 tbsp butter
2 tbsp flour
2 cups vegetable stock
½ cup light cream
½ tsp nutmeg ground
Salt and white pepper to taste

Melt butter, add onion and mushrooms; blend in flour, add the stock. Add salt, pepper. Cook till thickened. Blend when cool. Swirl in cream and nutmeg just before serving.

Cream of Almond Soup

1 tbsp butter

1 onion minced

1 ltr vegetable stock

750 g almonds soaked, peeled and ground

1 cup mushrooms sliced

1 tbsp flour

½ cup light cream

Salt, white pepper to taste

Melt butter, add onion. Add the stock, almond paste and mushrooms, bring to a boil. Mix flour in a little milk, add to thicken the soup. Simmer for 10 minutes. Blend into a puree when cool. Add salt and pepper. Swirl in the cream just before serving.

Cream of Peas Soup

1 tbsp butter

1 onion sliced

1 cup peas

1½ cups water

5–6 peppercorns

1 bay leaf

1 cup milk

Salt, pepper

Melt butter, sauté onions till soft. Add peas, water, peppercorns, bay leaf and pressure cook for about 5–7 minutes. Cool, blend, sieve. Add milk, season with salt and pepper and bring to a boil. Sometimes, you may have to add a teaspoon of sugar to adjust the flavour.

Life went on, my sisters got married, but Niro's still figures on the list of to-dos, whenever they visit. Bunny took some convincing to step into Niro's after having done well in business – he suffered from what I called the 5-star hotel syndrome. I made him rediscover the joys of hot and sour soup and reshmi kebab with butter naan, topped with a cold coffee. The brain masala, and of course, the usual chilli chicken dry, became his favourites.

Sakshi, as a baby, could be found under the table whenever we went to Niro's. She would surface only to eat her ice cream and happily lick the plate, held close to her face, for all to see. Resham wanted her own bowl of lemon coriander soup and a full plate of chilli chicken, and toppled her glass of Pepsi as a rule. There are reams of memories associated with Niro's and I feel lucky to have spent time talking to Ved Uncle about how it all began. This is how his story goes:

> We were a family of landowners in Punjab's Jhelum district. I studied in Rawalpindi up to my matriculate. As a child, I used to watch my grandfather cook mutton. In those days, men used to cook non-vegetarian food, women wouldn't touch meat. What my father and grandfather cooked was something else – in desi ghee only, with lots of garlic and onion, and the masalas freshly ground! Mr Lamba and Mr Ghai, the owners of Kwality Restaurant, Delhi, were known to us. In 1943, I moved to Delhi and helped them run the restaurant on Parliament Street till 1949, as their manager, looking after the supplies, the food and the cashbook, on a salary of Rs 75 per month. I was married in 1945 and lived in a small rented place behind Regal Building. During the Second World War, British and American soldiers had their barracks just opposite Kwality and they formed our regular clientele, with a slowly growing stream of Indians, as well. We served continental food, mostly, and started serving Indian dishes only in 1947 after Partition. Once the armies left and Indians became our main clientele, I introduced the famous Pindi chana on our menu. I had never cooked before, but I developed a knack of knowing what was right or wrong with a dish just by tasting it. I taught a number of cooks to pick up flavours by instinct.
>
> I came to Jaipur to explore avenues for opening up my own restaurant. Mirza Ismail Road had a row of new buildings and the land opposite St Xavier's was all farmland. Bombay House, in 1949, was owned by two Muslim brothers who tailored the Jaipur State Army uniforms. Mirza Ismail had given them land on M.I. Road at 50 paise per yard. I walked in when the building was almost ready, met the landlord and asked, 'Hall hai? I want it for a restaurant.' In February 1949, I gave them the advance payment – two hundred rupees a month was a lot of money those days. My wife offered her jewellery to start the business with an initial investment of

Rs 18,000. I took charge of the hall in April. It was so simple then. It was just a matter of trust between the landlord and me.

Jaipur was to be the capital of Rajasthan. I loved the city and I knew it would grow. I opened Niro's in August 1949. Hanut Singhji, the first education minister of Rajasthan state, inaugurated the restaurant. We had a sizeable menu then – roast chicken, fried fish, chicken cutlet, a la Kiev, stroganoff. Sasta zamana tha – we paid ten annas per kilo of mutton. A plate of mutton cultlets cost 75 paise, roganjosh came for 80 paise per plate, and we sold tea, coffee at 25 paise per head, unlimited number of cups. Farooq Abdullah, Bhairon Singh Shekhawat have spent hours at Niro's. I remember the Suranas had a buggy, which used to be driven up to Niro's. Very few ladies came out for meals. There was only word-of-mouth publicity, and on the first day we had a sale of Rs 90. For the first two years, I used to cycle down to buy all the vegetables myself, till I bought a motorcycle. We lived at Fateh Tibba near Raja Park till 1955. I bought land for a house opposite St Xavier's at Rs 4.50 per yard.

We have many 'firsts' to our credit. We were the first in Jaipur to serve continental food. In 1950, we got a bar licence and ran a full-fledged bar till 1956. In 1962, Niro's was renovated by an architect from Bombay, and we became the only centrally air-conditioned restaurant in town. We were also the first to serve Chinese food in 1970. Satish Gujral visited Jaipur to meet his daughter, Alpana, who was studying at MGD in the seventies. The murals were made by him then and are still a part of the decor.

In those days, rajas and maharajas from the raj gharanas of Udaipur, Jaisalmer, Bikaner, Jodhpur, Jaipur, and military officers, were the ones to frequent Niro's with their families. Thakur Dushyant Singh Naila's grandfather used to come on his camel. Thakur Bissau would come to Niro's in his black Chevrolet, order three pegs of gin, drive around and come back to have his lunch. Koi log cycle par bhi aate the...

The Rambagh Palace opened a hotel in 1958 and Queen Elizabeth and Prince Phillip stayed there the next year. The Queen's visit received a lot of publicity in the international press and the number of foreign tourists visiting Jaipur got a tremendous boost, which in turn helped us.

I took my cook to Mumbai where my brother-in-law worked at the Copper Chimney restaurant as a manager. I wanted him to learn some new dishes – we came back with navratan curry, vegetable korma, malai kofta and palak paneer. What is served as Niro's Special, even today, was taken from the Volga menu, but I created my own version of it – egg white and

> cream were whipped together before being layered with the sponge. There are families who come in for a meal and the first thing they say is, 'Please reserve Niro's Special for us.' More favourites like baked cheese macaroni, mushroom on toast, brain curry have also become a part and parcel of the orders of those who eat at Niro's frequently.

Uncle passed away two months after he spent this Sunday morning reminiscing with me.

There have been many trips to Delhi, when Bunny and I have arrived with the clear intention of only eating, with our gastronomical strategy all set. On one such trip, we ate at three restaurants in a single day. It started with me staring at a black ant resting on a bed of white idli, the sambar forming a placid lake into which it looked ready to wade in for a swim. With due respect, I moved it out of the bowl, dismissing its presence as a 'human' error, that is, commonplace in government-run establishments like this one – Midway, Behror.

The theme for the dream weekend in Delhi was seafood, something that did not ever feature in Jaipur. After an 'antsy' breakfast, we deserved the divine taste of heaven unfolding on one's tongue, and that happened at Diva – the reigning diva for Italian cuisine in the capital.

The minimalist ambience, attentive staff, a mind-swirling wine list, and a go at the anti-pasti platter, set the tongue on a roll. I tucked into a classic minestrone soup, my all-time favourite, warm, tangy, hearty, and as reviving as a grandmom's caring hand through your hair. Grilled salmon in garlic-perfumed butter, with a roucale and tomato salad and a glass of Chablis came next. Open ravioli with scallops or crab meat was Bunny's choice.

In Delhi, I could pass off as a camel who stores enough food in her hump to last a few weeks in the desert. The next indulgence was grilled prawns, doused in a lemon, dill and white wine sauce, served with zucchini and carrots. The succulent whiteness of the prawns melted creamily, lemon and dill doing the teasing act, with the wine providing the kick. It is an infernal sin to leave Diva without having the chocolate melt, served with a hazelnut parfait and vanilla sauce, baked just right to allow you to break into its crust and let the chocolate fill up your senses. Another such item is the panacotta with berry sauce... so we did the needful.

'Drown further', my mind urged, and Saturday night found me at Ploof, a seafood speciality restaurant which remains a favoured haunt with aritists, designers, diplomats, politicians – as well as lesser mortals like us – who are fortunately given the same tender treatment as the likes of Shweta Nanda, Arundhati Roy and Shyam Benegal.

In my experience, each time I've ordered the same soup at the same restaurant, it tastes different. But I can never resist going back again and again to Ploof, for their roast garlic and mushroom cappuccino and their Thai prawn soup with basil. If the sea bass is Mediterranean, the salmon is a glazed teriyaki and the snapper is oriental.

I ordered a baby spinach, cherry tomato and lettuce salad in a ginger-orange dressing, and settled for a Thai soup. Viva la fusion food! Nothing like the sharpness of galangal and the tang of lemon grass to tweak a huge appetite. I ordered a lobster thermidor and crab in pepper-garlic sauce, and continued to salivate over the menu, which gave you the choice of any fish grilled with pink peppercorns and dill, or pan-seared with olive oil and herbs, or stir-fried with basil leaves, chilli, garlic and lemon grass. I had two of their German chocolate silk cakes, served with Kahlua mousse, and resigned myself to live with the title of a glutton for the rest of my life, happily. Their pine nut and chocolate marquise with a four-fruit compote was also delectable.

The epicurean journey continued at Shalom with its burnt-wood tables, sink-ins and pottery decor. Serving Spanish, Mediterranean and Lebanese food, Shalom feeds your soul. The chef vouches for the real Arabic spices and authentic recipes – that's why regulars keep coming back. The words on the wall spell out the spirit that defines the place – calm, peace, serenity, tranquillity – I would call it serendipity. Though their mojitos are famous, I preferred to swing through the evening with a Bellini. Mezze is their signature starter, but who sticks to rules while indulging?

A surreal blue flame spread like silk on the table, as the bartender quietly tipped the alcohol on burnt wood before offering my TNT with a flourish – our table was on fire! I ordered a Moroccan Harira, which is a traditional lamb soup, flavoured with cinnamon and garnished with spaghetti and lemon slices, and a Rubiyan Mashawi – prawns cooked to perfection in butter – and a pomfret stuffed with prawn mousse in orange tequila sauce. Chocolate molten cake with honey-date ice cream summed up the very joy of living. I closed my eyes and ate slowly, savouring each moment of sensuous synergy.

Smoke House Grill remains another favourite haunt. We reached there early to make sure we didn't miss out on starting with tequila shots and oysters. Bunny and I shared the six shots, so weren't knocked out before we ate anything. The atmosphere here is minimalist, all white, with earthy touches of jute and linen. Contemporary European food is what they serve, with an accent on smoked flavours in food and drink. Camembert and crushed pink peppercorn soufflé, as a starter, made sure that the tequila settled. John Dory and smoked Shimla chilly served on creamed leeks and asparagus, set off by a smoked melon mojito, came as a perfect pair. Bunny stuck to a spicy martini with his pan-seared sea bass, squid ink risotto and fresh porcini. Our combined stomach spaces could take only a shared Valrhona chocolate and kahlua mousse.

We have gone back again and again, sometimes with friends, and have always returned with drunken memories.

Tom Som Pla

175 g fish fillets skinned
¼ small cabbage
2 spring onions
2 onions
2 cloves garlic
1" ginger
2 tsp coriander root chopped
1 tsp shrimp paste
½ tsp turmeric
8 peppercorns
2 tbsp brown sugar
4 tbsp tamarind water
Salt to taste
Fresh coriander to garnish

Chop fish into small chunks. Add 2 ltrs of water to the fish in a large saucepan and bring to a boil. Simmer for 15 minutes. Strain through a fine sieve and reserve clear stock.

Shred cabbage. Slice the green of the spring onions to 1" pieces. Chop onions, ginger, garlic. Add with coriander root, shrimp paste, turmeric, peppercorns, salt, and pound to a smooth paste with a mortar and pestle.

Heat oil, add the paste and stir-fry for 5 minutes. Add fish stock, sugar and tamarind water, bring to a boil and simmer for about 30 minutes. Add cabbage, onion greens, simmer for 2–3 minutes and garnish with coriander leaves.

Spicy Mushroom and Baby Corn Soup

1 tsp garlic chopped
1 tbsp red chilli coarsely ground
1 tbsp onions sliced
1 spring onion chopped
1 tsp celery chopped
75 g baby corn sliced in long strips
50 g mushrooms sliced
1 green chilli chopped
1 ltr vegetable stock
2 tbsp paneer cubed
6–8 spinach leaves
2 tsp cornflour
1 tbsp vinegar
1 tomato cut in small slices
Salt to taste

Heat oil in a wok; add garlic, red chilli, onion, spring onion, celery and sauté. Add the baby corn, mushroom, green chilli and sauté further. Add vegetable stock, salt, paneer and let it boil. Add spinach. Stir in 2 tsp cornflour pre-dissolved in water to thicken the soup. Add the tomatoes and vinegar just before serving.

Tom Yum Goong

400 g fresh prawns or chicken	2 fresh red chillies
3 stalks lemon grass	2 tsp fish sauce
2 cloves garlic	4 kaffir lime leaves
2 tsp coriander chopped	2 tbsp lemon juice
4 peppercorns	50 ml oil
1" fresh ginger	Fresh coriander leaves for garnish

Shell and devein the prawns. Cut lemon grass in 1" lengths and pound slightly with the back of the knife. Place garlic, coriander, peppercorns in a mortar and pound into a smooth paste. Slice ginger, cut chillies in rings. Heat oil, add the prawns and stir-fry for 3–4 minutes. Add 1.5 ltrs water, bring to a boil, cover pan and simmer for 10 minutes. Strain this stock through a fine sieve and bring back to a boil. Stir in the pounded paste. Add lemon grass, ginger, lime leaves and prawns. Add fish sauce, lemon juice, red chillies. Garnish with coriander leaves.

There was a time when I yearned for a Tom Yum Goong in Jaipur, but none of the restaurants had ventured into serving Thai cuisine. About five years ago, Jai Mahal Palace took the lead. The head steward, Narendra Rathore, walked up to our table, beaming, 'Ma'am, you'll be happy with us now. We have Tom Yum on our menu.'

Rathore was a young waiter when Bunny and I first began seeing each other. In the early eighties, this small palace was being converted into a sprawling hotel. The first flush of romance, in a small town, can be torturous. 'Everyone knows you. You'll get caught. If you go for a drive beyond the airport, you have to cross the whole city, and you'll definitely risk being seen together. The families will go to war! There will be a total tamasha!'

It was almost as if Jai Mahal opened its doors just for us. Being a new hotel, hardly anyone from the city frequented the coffee shop. Table settings, placed in small alcoves, hid us from the view of anyone who walked in. We spent hours there, and Narendra always served us. He sensed our predicament and saw how much in love we were. And I taught him how to swirl and coat a glass with chocolate sauce before making a hot chocolate fudge, and how each scoop of ice cream should get a slathering of sauce and roasted cashew nuts. He got the hang of it after three or four attempts, and to pre-empt further demands, would bring a serving of chocolate sauce on the side.

Hot-and-sour soup was another such experiment. I like it to be really hot and really sour. The veggies ought to be crisp and the flavour of ginger and soya just right. The colour shouldn't be too dark. Reduce the use of cornflour, to prevent the almost gelatinous look and texture. No paneer, please, and don't be miserly with the chicken pieces. Narendra did the rounds of the kitchen and conveyed each instruction to the chef, who never showed me his face – which was quite understandable.

Bunny and I dated for a long time; we also stayed apart for two years. And then we got married. Narendra observed us slip into each role. He understood that it had eventually worked out, when he saw me in a sari. His smile remained the same.

Sakshi was born and a champagne party was thrown to celebrate the birth of Dadu's princess, again at Jai Mahal – a daughter was born in the family after fifty-two years.

Time passed. Two more kids came along and Narendra stayed faithful to Jai Mahal. He has also remained a silent witness to the linear narrative of our lives. Our conversation is limited to food. He seeks us out whenever we are there for a meal; I don't have to ask for him. The hot-and-sour soup remains the same.

It was one of those evenings when Bunny came home from work in a weird mood.

'Shall we go out for dinner?'

'Alright.'

'But we have a dance class.'

'Bunk it.' We giggled like truant teenagers.

A car was waiting in the pillared porch. 'May I?'

I smiled, it lit up his eyes.

Silence on the roads. Same old place. There aren't too many choices in this city.

Following his eyes, I walked down to the lawns, along a path lit by candles, like stars winking down on earth. Seduced by the winds, the flames tried in vain to escape. The breeze carried the fragrance of the night, lifting me up, strumming a song on my soul. Each time it rose, tiny bells chimed a tune that made a smile dance on our lips.

He looked at me. 'You still look gorgeous.'

Still? Battlelines were being drawn here, but the barman arrived.

Fruits flambéd in Cointreau and cognac, dunked into champagne, glowed a warm gold in a tall flute. The amber liquid swirled and slid down like silk. The kebabs filled the mouth with spices and kewra. The prawns made me want to drown in the sea.

He bantered about my book; I teased him by saying how I wished a young boyfriend were present to add some literary conversations to the evening. We grinned over the three devils in our life, the first time we

held hands, the way we had jalebis in the middle of the day in Defence Colony – frequently glancing back and wondering if a certain old lady had seen us, scared that she would tell my father.

'You drove to Delhi in three hours flat, straight into the driveway of my college. We haunted the shaded boulevards of Chanakyapuri in your old Fiat.'

'You are graying at the temples. Shouldn't you colour your hair?'

'No, I want my age to show. It's about growing old gracefully.'

I looked at him. 'That's quite a bulge in your middle.' I saw the picture in his eyes – a girl in a floral white skirt and a flimsy blouse, waiting for him on the steps of her house. He would arrive the moment Ma left for the hospital.

'Want to do the mobike ride again? You'd have to wear my checked shirt, though.'

'Can we drive to Delhi to meet an old friend?'

'Sure.' Mundane talk woven into meaningful silences.

I stared into the flames.

'I want to drive back,' I said.

'We'll see.' He laughed into my eyes, indulging me.

'No, don't be chauvinistic. I will drive back. I'm not high.'

I took the wheel. The world reeled.

'Your place or mine?' Our eyes met. We giggled.

'Your side of the bed or mine?'

Noodle, Mushroom and Ginger Soup

125 g thread egg noodles
2 tsp oil
3 garlic cloves crushed
1" ginger shredded finely
125 g mushrooms sliced
1 ltr vegetable stock
1 tsp light soya sauce
2 cups bean sprouts
Fresh coriander to garnish

Cook noodles for 2–3 minutes in boiling water. Drain and rinse, keep aside. Heat oil over high heat in a wok. Add garlic, ginger and mushrooms. Stir-fry over high heat for 2 minutes. Add vegetable stock, soya sauce and bring to boil. Stir in bean sprouts. Pour immediately over noodles and garnish with coriander.

Chicken Yoghurt Soup

1 ltr chicken stock

2 tbsp rice soaked

1 tbsp flour

200 ml yoghurt

2 beaten egg yolks

2 tbsp butter

1 tbsp chopped mint

400 ml water

Salt, pepper to taste

Bring the stock to boil. Add the rice and let it cook for about 15 minutes. Season it with salt and pepper. In another saucepan, mix flour, yoghurt, egg yolks and water. Let it simmer till it almost comes to a boil. Add the stock mixture and cook for another 5 minutes. Melt butter, add the mint and pour over the soup.

Hot Yoghurt Soup

200 g mince

1 onion grated

1 tsp black pepper

½ tsp cinnamon powder

1 egg

4 cups whipped yoghurt

1 tbsp flour

¼ cup rice soaked

½ cup spring onion greens chopped

¼ cup fresh coriander chopped

½ cup chick peas boiled

Salt and pepper to taste

Add salt, onion, black pepper, cinnamon powder to the mince. Make balls of the mince and keep in fridge.

Mix egg well with yoghurt, add flour, soaked rice, 4 cups water, salt, pepper. Cook on low heat for 30 minutes. Add the meat balls, spring onions, coriander, chick peas and cook for another 20 minutes.

Creamy Herbed Walnut Soup

½ cup walnuts chopped
2 cups milk
1 bay leaf
2 tsp fresh coriander
1 small sprig fresh mint
2 tbsp butter
1 onion sliced
1 large stalk celery chopped
2 tbsp wheat flour
3 cups vegetable stock

Cover walnuts with water and bring to a boil over medium heat. Boil for 3 minutes, drain, and rinse with cold water.

Pour milk over drained walnuts, add bay leaf, coriander and mint. Cover and set aside for 20 minutes.

Melt butter, add onion, celery, and cook for a minute. Stir in flour and gradually stir in the stock. Bring to a boil, simmer for 10 minutes. Remove bay leaf and add the milk mixture to the soup. Puree the soup in a blender, season with salt and pepper.

Evenings like this one always brought back memories of the time when Bunny and I were seeing each other, a fact that we managed to hide from our families for about three years. I remember being alone at home in Jaipur, trying my hand at baking a chocolate cake, in my second year of English Honours at LSR. Summers at home meant long days of lazing in bed with a good book and watching *Dynasty* on video. The cake got burnt. I looked at it and sighed. A frantic call was made to a friend. 'Divya, the cake's burnt, what do I do? Bunny is coming home in the evening!' 'I challenge you to feed him a whole slice of that cake,' she chortled back. I must confess my heart fluttered with glee at the thought of feeding a slice of rock hard, charred cake to the gullible, Farex-baby-faced twenty-one-year-old man, so desparately in love with me. The moment came. We sat in the garden and I produced the cake with a deadpan face. Bunny ate the entire slice without a wrinkle on his forehead. When he left, I let out one triumphant whoop on the phone to Divya.

Resham's eyes roll upwards each time her father narrates the incident as if it were the most exhilarating episode in our Bollywood-style romance. 'Get over it, Dad. It's not so exciting.'

'You don't value good old-fashioned romance,' he replies.

'Mum, who else did you date while you were in college?'

'No one.'

'Seriously.' Her large doe eyes look askance at me. 'You knew no one else, didn't go out with anyone else?'

'No.'

'Was Dad the only man you kissed before you got married?'

'Yes.'

She continued staring at my face, looking for a giveaway glimmer, hoping to nab me lying in an effort to portray myself as the ideal, well-behaved Indian girl and mother. I kept a straight face and gave her my favourite line: 'Yeh sab hamare "culture" ke khilaaf hai.'

A slow-paced, well-measured question followed. 'Are you trying to tell me that Dad is the only man you've slept with?'

It was my turn to stare into her face.

A couple of seconds lapsed, then I couldn't take it any more. I had to let go. There was a hoot and an explosion of laughter.

'Yes, Dad's been the only one.'

She inhaled, trying hard to gain composure. Trying hard to digest what she'd just heard.

'Boy, you've led such a boring life,' she said finally, a soft, pitying look on her face.

I have to confess, she left me speechless for once. A mother's worst fears washed over me. I looked at her for a few seconds, shook her by the shoulders and laughed – there was really nothing I could do or say.

A few days later, we were on our way to the walled city, shopping for bandhini and leheriya saris. Watching me make a call, Resham said, 'Can you get off the phone for once?'

'I'm calling Dad. He'll come home from work and won't find me home. You know how he sulks, poor man!'

'Gosh, it's been so many years; you're still attracted to each other? If you know what I mean, huh?'

There was wonder, ridicule and a note of you-guys-are-looney in her voice. The big eyes rolled once again and she sighed, 'Whatever, Mum.'

6

The Fragrance of Meat

It's decision time. One has to cook up a new story each day, and it does get monotonous for those who hold the power to plot the day's pot-boilers. Main course decisions are delicate and to be handled with kindness. Everyone should be happy, most of all, your cook.

A friend's daughter came over at five in the evening. We were working on her text for a school debate, over cold coffee and cookies, when the cook came up to ask me the question I sometimes just don't want to hear. 'What is to be made for dinner?' He added accusingly, 'You forgot to marinate the chicken,' the unspoken message being, 'You should just let me take charge completely.' Not being one to give up in the undeclared war between us, I whipped out Mummy's old register of recipes, a relic from her years as an army wife, and replied with composed calm, 'I don't need to marinate the chicken, since adrak kesari murg doesn't require it.' I quickly scribbled all the chopping instructions in Hindi for him and turned back to the debate.

The friend's daughter went back home with a story to narrate to her mother. 'Even regular, daily food gets made in Mita aunty's home after a proper recipe is consulted, why can't you cook like that?' Then followed the complaint on the phone: 'Sending kids to you for help costs me a lot. Now I am expected to cook like you every day!'

Cooking for a large family during the summers only adds to the heat. Everyone seems to have a mental block when it comes to lauki, tori and tinda. The carrots turn tastelessly English and cauliflower loses its wintry nip. Left with bhindi and aloo, there's not much one can do for dinner. Mummy is delighted, because that means it's mutton or chicken time. I sometimes strongly suspect that she thrives on her secret (well, not so secret) desire to serve only cooked flesh swimming in gravy. She runs her household on the basis of a single principle: 'How to keep her husband and two sons happy.' She prefers to plan meaty meals – it's manly and more attuned to the virile spirit of a patriarchal family.

Dinner-time democracy was infused into the menu only with time. Everyone's choices had to be met with, specially once the kids starting growing up, and both Smriti and I just went with the flow. Systems were broken – more and more veggies were made and a lot of dishes were tried, tested, rejected and accepted. Though hard to accept, the need to recognize the reality of more delicate digestions and thicker medical files stared us right in the face.

When I first stepped in and had to face mutton on the dinner menu every evening, I was revolted. It became essential to get creative with my cooking, and I vowed to myself that I would turn the family around to healthier eating habits. Balbir Singh and Jiggs Kalra became my gods; I experimented by skipping some ingredients, substituting some, reducing the fat, cream, dry fruits, and finding ways of adding texture. While making lemony cauliflower, another typical army recipe of Mummy's, I eliminated the cheese entirely, stepping up the lemon-pepper flavour. I can't explain what chemical reactions occurred, but the taste was just as cheesy. Each discovery gave me a thrill – my small kitchen victories as I called them. Triumph meant seeing the disbelieving looks around the table when they understood that there was no cheese in a dish, or that I had made two kilos of Bikaneri meat with just four tablespoons of ghee, and yet it tasted as delicious as ever.

I just had to prove my point that tasty food doesn't mean more oil, more ghee or more chillies. I'm sure my cook would love to slice me up into the 2.5" juliennes of vegetables that I make him cut painstakingly, because he thinks that food is tasty only if it has at least half an inch of oil floating on top.

When we get together at Ma's place, we sisters still go into splits over how we ate mutton every Sunday – that was a ceremony sacred to our little world. My grandmother was a staunch vegetarian and anyone who ate non-vegetarian food was only half a human being in her eyes – she treated them like rotten, pulpy onions.

Being unpredictable was Dadi's forte and she often used to drop in without a warning. 'Bahuuuu, aaj aloo pyaz bana hai kya? Bahar tak khushboo aa rahi hai,' she would call out from the gate itself, dismissing the hapless rickshaw-walla with a rupee less. Her loud voice would send us all scurrying away with our plates, precariously balancing gravy and bones. Ma would deftly remove all vestiges of the Devil's dish and cheekily place the pressure cooker with half-made aloo pyaaz on the stove. With a straight face and a welcoming smile, she would lovingly feed her mother-in-law her special Sunday lunch.

Lifebuoy-washed hands, sounds of hasty gargling, and we would come and sit with her, feigning patience till she finished her meal. I can still see Papa, running across the courtyard to receive her, faster than any of us. 'Behna, you should have called me to pick you up. Why did you come in a rickshaw?' he would ask, and her standard reply would be, 'I knew Bahu would have cooked something special for Sunday, so I just came.' The aroma of mutton curry, a bouquet of smells from badi elaichi, tej patta, kali mirch and laung lingered in the air – I have a feeling she knew, and this was her way of indulging her 'doctor bahu'. Of my grandmother's four daughters-in-law, Ma was the only working lady. Dadi gave her the kind of freedom that the others didn't get, like not having to have a bath at four in the morning, in freezing December, before entering the kitchen.

Our meat and roti lunch, at the dining table in the kitchen, was a Sunday ritual as sacred as going to the temple. My grandmother, the patriarch ever since her husband passed on, was almost like a man, with her broad face, bushy eyebrows, thin, pursed lips, puffed up cheeks – and a booming voice. I think she must have grown into that role, bringing up eight of her own, and two stepchildren, as a mostly single parent. We would wait for her to retire to the mandirwala bedroom. Her snores were like a 'next shot ready clap' for us to finish our meal and remove all traces of bones from the kitchen.

Breakfast for Papa's generation meant besan ka laddoo, mathi, milk or lassi in tall steel glasses. We moved on to eggs and toast, sandwiches, cornflakes and cold coffee. Lunch was dal, sabzi, dahi, roti, with achaar and papad. You ate what was on the table, or you went without food till the next meal. Meals were simple. One look at the dhuli moong ki dal and lauki ki sabzi, and Preeti would go, 'Yuck, Mom!' But all she got in response was a stern look and a firm, 'If you can't eat this, you can leave the table and go to your room.' Our middle sister, Preeti or Guddu, was always in trouble over food, and she was the only one of us who could not stay hungry.

A 'simple' meal in my present household means pao bhaji, rajma, rice, sukhe aloo, Bombay sandwich. This includes rajma in three versions. I have them boiled with fistfuls of cut tomatoes, fresh coriander and raw onion. The kids have them with an extra dollop of tomato puree, simmered for a longer time, the gravy remaining thin. The 'boys' have a thickened version in the office, with a stealthy dash of cream and mirchi ka tadka. There always seems to be a stock of pao bhaji in the fridge, as an emergency option, just in case Aman and Tanay don't feel like eating rajma for lunch, just as Sakshi always chooses to resort to a safer Bombay sandwich. Sakshi has a weakness for bread, and this is one of the ways I can get some veggies inside her. Resham and Rehan happily have a little of everything. They are smart, because they cash in fully on the variety of food available.

The same story is repeated for dinner. The variants this time are chicken, eggs or veggies. And it includes the option of a roti stuffed with leftover veggies, though I usually choose to stick to a soya flour roti. There are multiple choices for even a chicken salad, because there is never a single preference for a dressing with so many at the table. Boiled chicken meets with mayonnaise, 'chillified' with Tabasco for the 'aam janta'. For Dad, I like to do a curd and garlic-pepper dressing, and for Smriti and me, a simple combination of salt, red chilli flakes, fresh coriander and lemon juice, along with any fresh veggies that I can find in the fridge.

Adrak Kesari Murg

1 kg boneless chicken
1 tbsp cumin seeds
300 g onions chopped
10 green chillies chopped
25 g ginger chopped
1 pod garlic chopped
500 g tomatoes chopped
1 tsp turmeric
2 tbsp ghee
Salt to taste

To be crushed coarsely:

10 g black peppercorns
20 g coriander seeds
15 g cumin seeds
10 dry red chillies

Heat ghee in a kadhai, crackle the cumin seeds, add the chopped onions, green chillies and ginger, and fry till the onions are lightly browned. Add the garlic and sauté for 5 minutes. Add the tomatoes and let them cook. Add the turmeric and chicken, and when the chicken is half cooked, add the pounded spices. There is no need to add any water since the chicken will cook in its own juices.

This chicken is not for the faint-hearted. The pungency of the dry coriander is only heightened by the heat of the chillies. It's a dish that goes well with dosas. I have served it as a main dish in a south Indian menu and it's been loved. Though Mummy could never answer my query about why it's named 'kesari', when no saffron is used, nor is it a dish with delicate flavours. The only plausible reason could be the fiery red colour.

Dum ka Murgh

1 chicken (about 800 g)

Marinade:

50 g almonds

15 g poppy seeds

10 g chironji

5 tsp ginger paste

3 tsp garlic paste

Fresh coriander chopped

Fresh mint chopped

1½ tsp red chilli powder

1½ tsp cumin powder

2 tbsp lemon juice

Gravy:

250 ml curd whisked

250 g onions browned

8 green cardamoms

6 cloves

6 green chillies

3 sticks cinnamon

1 tsp saffron

Blanch almonds, roast along with poppy seeds and chironji till each emits its own aroma and is lightly coloured. Pulse in a blender with water, add the remaining ingredients and rub the pricked chicken with this. Leave aside for 2 hours.

Grease a baking dish with ghee, place the marinated chicken and pour the whisked curd on it. Add the browned onions, spices, chillies and saffron. Cover it with a lid and cook in the oven on low heat till tender.

This is one of those eternal Jiggs Kalra recipes that appeared in *Saturday Times*, and I still mourn the day they stopped publishing the supplement. But in my version, some 'elements' have been taken out to make life simpler! The dish may sound complicated because the prior preparation is demanding. Normally, I reduce, or eliminate, nuts from recipes, but I am partial to almonds and the way they fuse with chicken.

Murg Kesar Malai

8 chicken breasts
1 ltr chicken stock
4 green cardamoms
3 blades javitri
3 cloves
2 brown cardamoms
2 bay leaves
Salt to taste
150 g onion chopped
10 g ginger chopped
6 flakes garlic chopped
4 green chillies
Ghee to fry the onions
30 g almonds
3 tbsp milk

Gravy:

1 tbsp lemon juice
1 tsp white pepper
¼ tsp clove powder
¼ tsp mace powder
½ tsp green cardamom powder
½ tsp saunth powder
200 ml cream
2 drops kewra
Pinch of saffron soaked in hot milk

Heat the stock, add all the spices, bring to a boil. Reduce to simmer, add chicken and poach till it's done through. Keep aside, covered. Strain the stock and reserve for the gravy.

Heat ghee, add the chopped onion, garlic, ginger, green chillies and fry till the onions are translucent. Cool and blend into a paste. Blanch the almonds, blend with milk to a smooth paste.

To make the gravy, heat ghee in a kadhai, add onion paste, stir-fry till it gets a sheen. Add the almond paste, stock, and boil till it has a medium-thick consistency. Add the lemon juice, white pepper, clove, mace, green cardamom powders, saunth, chicken pieces and cream. Give it a boil. Remove from heat, add saffron and kewra.

This dish has struck the right chord with many people who have eaten at our house. The sweetness of onions still trapped within, the milky flavour of almonds combined with sensuous saffron, played up by the saunth and a hint of spices. I've laughed at people spooning the curry into their mouths, as if desperately trying to keep the taste on their tongue forever. It can never fail with rice, because the curry is rather light hearted. It's simple to prepare, and strangely, a very no-stress dish. I haven't mentioned the quantity of ghee to be used, deliberately, since you can go as minimalistic as you wish – I do. I even dilute the cream with milk to reduce the fat content. The spice levels can be heightened, or played down, so it's actually a fun dish to cook.

Somewhere along the line, I have to admit that it's easy to cook the way I do, with enough hands in the kitchen to help out. I used to watch Ma cook for parties after returning home from the hospital. The whole family got involved – there was something for everyone to do, even Papa. I can never forget peeling an endless number of boiled potatoes and laying the table. Decorating the table was exciting, and Ma let us use our imagination. But it was usually Didi and I who ran around, while Preeti simply looked on, managing to escape anything that came close to being called house work. They say that: 'The more you run away from chores that bore you, the more your destiny will take you to them.' That is precisely what happened to Preeti when she moved to Australia. Cooking and cleaning are a part of her daily life, alongside a full-fledged career in telemarketing.

My friend Shalini also belongs to the gang of procrastinators. But the real test came when we were in the same hostel in my last year at school. With large kohled eyes and thick black hair, Shalini is dusky and has a

fire that blazes from inside her, whenever she sees someone being unfair. Her room was next to mine in the hostel and Smita, her roommate, was my bumchum pal. We teased her endlessly because of her penchant for wearing irritatingly noisy silver and glass bangles.

I used to leave my coffee glass on the windowsill every night, and at the end of the week, I would be reduced to begging for a clean glass for my nightly potion of strong coffee. It was poor Shalini who was brave enough to pick up six glasses with layers of milk and fat globules that had turned a monstrous greenish yellow, to soak and wash them in boiling hot water and deposit them valiantly on the same windowsill. 'For you to start collecting grease and filth all over again!' she would say. Shalini also cleaned my room and made my bed, simply because I was studying for my twelfth standard exams. It's been almost twenty-five years since we first got to know each other. Initially enemies, then friends, we spent two years together in the school hostel, and later I stayed with her in Delhi while completing my postgraduation.

Shalini's mother is an extremely religious person and disappears into her puja room for long hours. On one such evening, the servant had left and dinner had to be made. Aunty emerged from her puja room, hoping to see the house tidy and the kitchen bustling with activity. There was only silence; the silence before the storm. None of us had moved an inch to do anything. She exploded like a tanker, shaking up the whole building with her anger. I can't remember now what she screamed at us, but everyone, including Shalini's father, retreated into his or her cubby-hole silently. No reactions, no activity. I found that strange, and feeling rather guilty that I was staying with them and adding to the general chaos, I ran into the kitchen. Aunty walked in after a few minutes to find me chopping onions with tears streaming down my eyes. It was the first time I had peeled and chopped onions. She stood there and smiled at me, while I looked at her, not knowing what to do next.

Everyone emerged stealthily, took one look at me and the onions, and began laughing. Aunty said, 'See, she is the only one who understands my pain. Now get out of my kitchen and let me cook peacefully.'

I am still teased mercilessly by Shalini and her brothers. 'Mita chopping onions!' It was a lesson learnt – if you don't have helping hands, just make sandwiches please!

Murg Malwa

2 chickens cut into 8 pieces each
2 coconuts grated
500 g onions sliced
4 tbsp oil
20 dry red chillies
20 g dry coriander seeds
2 sticks of cinnamon
1 tsp cumin seeds
1 tsp black peppercorn
5 cloves
5 green cardamoms
2 tsp ginger paste
2 tsp garlic paste
½ tsp turmeric
½ tsp nutmeg powder
Salt to taste
6 green chillies split
Chopped coriander

Grind the coconuts, soak in hot water and extract milk. Roast the red chillies, coriander seeds and other whole spices and grind to a paste. Heat oil, add onions, cook till browned. Add the ground masala paste, cook till the oil appears. Add chicken, coconut milk and salt, simmer till tender. Add the chopped coriander and split green chillies.

Murg Dahiwala

800 g boneless chicken
100 g cream cheese
½ cup cream
300 g hung curd
1 tbsp ginger paste
1 tbsp garlic paste
1 tbsp green chilli paste
4 tbsp lemon juice
1 tsp turmeric
2 tsp garam masala
Salt to taste

Mix the cheese and cream. Add all the ingredients to the hung curd, including the cream cheese mixture. Rub the chicken pieces generously with this marinade. Preferably leave it overnight in the fridge. Roast the chicken in a preheated oven at 220°C. Baste with oil, turn the pieces around and make sure they are evenly roasted to a golden brown.

This is a recipe that you can convert into a dish with gravy, or leave as it is. It allows for multiple uses. I have converted this marinated chicken into a cheesy baked chicken, or into a chicken curry by dunking it in a gravy, made hurriedly with onions sweated till blushing pink, curd and whole dry red chillies to add the bite. You could also convert it into chicken tikka and grill it in a tandoor. It works in every way.

Murg Mirch Korma

2 kg chicken cut small
2–3 tbsp oil
25–30 dry red chillies deseeded
15 brown cardamoms slightly crushed
4 x 1" cinnamon sticks
2 tsp turmeric
6 cloves
6–8 green cardamoms slightly crushed
1 garlic pod crushed

Grind the red chillies, sieve through a muslin cloth with 6 cups water. Heat oil; add the crushed garlic, chicken and other whole spices. Add chilli water to the chicken along with the turmeric and cook till tender.

This dish is Kashmiri, though it's not authentic to the region. The aromas sent out by the spices vie for your attention, as if fluttering their eyelashes seductively. And what's more, it's simple cooking, just the kind of dish which can be made even if you only have an hour before serving the meal. It's to be served freshly cooked and piping hot. If the mood demands it, I put the dekchi on the table straightaway.

Murg Irani

1 kg chicken
250 g onions chopped
10 g ginger paste
250 g curd
100 g cream
20 g garlic paste
10 g red chillies crushed
10 g green cardamom
150 g almonds blanched and sliced
1 tsp saffron soaked in milk
A few drops of kewra
Juice of 4 lemons
Salt to taste

Heat ghee, add the chopped onion, sauté till slightly brown. Add the chicken pieces and ginger. Let it cook for 10 minutes. Strain the curd and cream, add to the chicken. Add the garlic, red chillies, cardamom, almonds. Let it simmer (do not add any water) on slow fire till done. Add saffron and remove from heat when the chicken is tender; add the kewra and lemon juice and transfer to serving dish.

This is a slightly rich chicken recipe, but it's irresistible. It's unbeatable with a butter-garlic naan or plain boiled rice, and I always overeat when it's on the menu. Because of the cream and curd content, a lot of fat floats up to the top, making it look lethal – I'd ladle it out if I were you.

There is a contradiction in my cooking. I hate oily food so much that there have been times when I've walked away from the table just to embarrass my cook. But when it comes to cooking meat or chicken, I use only ghee, which in turn amuses him. The quantity, of course, is the prime issue and he watches me with an eagle eye, waiting with bated breath to catch me using that give-away extra tablespoon of fat. He's still waiting to taste victory, while I've had a series of triumphs when he's just poured oil into a cooker for the veggies and I've walked in, silently dished out at least four spoons of extra fat, and walked out with my head held high, not a word said. These days, I use another weapon. I ask Bunny to call and chide him. With Bunny's gentle, jovial demeanour, it's easy for anyone to digest anything negative. It hurts. And it works.

There is something about the months of March, April and May. Each year, these weeks are turbulent and frothing, like milk boiling over. Trouble, strife and unrest! Bunny and I have our worst fights then. He sulks; I clam up and go around as if nothing has happened. And then I have a problem with everyone and everything that happens at home. Suddenly everyone turns vicious and ugly and must be viewed with suspicion. I find the daily menu unimaginative. Why can't people think beyond the usual panch ratni dal and that oily, over-bhunnoed-onions-turned-black in a chicken curry that should appear alluringly red? I grumble and gripe to myself. 'One can't even expect anything more than an undercooked, underspiced egg curry after a whole day's work. Whatever happened to light ginger fish or pepper chicken – is it so difficult to play with the menu?'

Over the years, I've learnt to remain silent and tell myself, 'If you aren't ready to cook everyday, why do you expect others to do it? Why do you have to resent their watching those horrendously dumbed-down reality shows on TV for hours, instead of experimenting in the kitchen?' With great self-control, I calm down to the coolness of curd and remind myself, 'You are eating to survive and that's it, so just shut up and make do with what is served on the table.' Or better still, every time there is something as distasteful and tired as egg curry, I walk into the kitchen and make a laksa – sour and spicy – to retain my cool. It's a way of silent protest and driving home a point – food works as a metaphor for all sorts of emotions, not only love.

There are times when I grumble to Sakshi and Resham. Sakshi reacts with a quiet comment. 'You know, Mom, you are behaving like a man when you say things like "one can't even expect a good meal after a hard day's work, bah!" in that raised voice and commanding tone, and that is so not cool. Ggguhhgghh…' Her lips turn up scornfully.

My girls make me laugh, make each day tolerable. I look forward to what we all call 'Sakshi moments'. I used to put down Sakshi's crusade to her reading books like *Not Without My Daughter*, combined with her natural tendency to take pot shots at everyone. I couldn't make out the pain that lay latent within her. Her mask never fell away. On one of those days, she came to me while I lay in bed, reading. An angst-ridden teenager, suffering from turbulent hormonal disorder, walked in on my quiet zone.

'I know exactly what to do with men!'

I thought to myself, 'Huh? All of sixteen and already so wise?'

The whites of my room were just beginning to calm after a mad day, but alas, it wasn't meant to be. A gleeful grin made her cheeks gleam like freshly polished Chinese apples. This one has horns on her head, I thought, and braced myself for rapid-fire assault.

'Y'know, I turned my ass towards Tushar in class.'

That was meant to be insulting? I thought he'd enjoy the view. I bit back my response, giving her straight-faced attention.

'Physics ma'am asked me why I had helped Arohit with a numerical. I told her, "Gadhon ko toh help karna padta hai."'

'Since when have you become an expert in quantum Physics?' I asked.

'That Arpit rammed into my shoulder! I caught him by the collar, showed him my palm, and said, "Abe oye, tameez nahin hai kya, dekh ke chal, kheench ke dungi."'

'All these years, you didn't know the sound of your own voice, leave alone raise a hand! Am I supposed to be impressed?'

'I guess so,' she said, her voice laced with threat. 'That fucking Neerav was staring at my freshly waxed legs. I clicked my fingers at him like that, under his parrot nose. "Meri tangein kya Pamela Anderson jaise hain?"'

'Not bad, young lady, all in a day's work?' I smirked. What had happened to my little girl whose liquid brown eyes would fill up with tears if someone spoke a decibel higher? Now they glinted with evil fire.

She was off on another track. 'I don't know how you can live with the same man for so many years.'

I sighed. 'After a few years, husbands function best as "utility items". Someone who pays the bills along with you, someone you take to a party because it doesn't look nice if a woman enters alone (grrrr), someone who can pat his daughter's head in absent-minded appreciation... someone who looks the best and most lovable when he's asleep... sonorous snores being a part of the package deal.'

I recalled a bizarre conversation with a friend. 'Imagine, I'm forty and I've slept with just one man!'

I looked at my first-born now and said, 'Y'know babe, thinking about this guy makes me go all mushy. He is a friend. I can bare my insides to him. He taught me humility and crisis management.' But my subtle hint was ignored by the girl-woman.

'I think all men should be destroyed.'

'But you love kids. Where will the babies come from?'

'Hmmm, we'll put them in concentration camps; freeze their sperm before bumping them off. I'm going to be a "bhayankar feminist".'

'Well,' I said, 'more like a genocidal one. Will your father, brothers, Nanu, Dadu, also be lined up?'

A momentary frown appeared on her face. 'In that case, we can leave behind a few of the tolerable ones.'

I carried on, determined to make her see the light, 'That's being selectively unfair. If men have to go, all go or none at all! Feminism is a done-in thingie. We are in the throes of Beckettian existentialism. Nietzsche is our God, individualism is in.'

She spat, 'Not in India. It's tit for tat time here. These men need to be burnt alive for a change. Why do you keep counselling "victims" then?' Her arm was raised like Buddha imparting wisdom.

'Babe, there's someone who wakes me up with kisses on my feet every morning. Gets me a hot water bottle when my tummy hurts, massages my tired back. Sends me mysteriously flattering sms-es during a party, saying, "You stand tall in the crowd," from an unknown number. That's a lot, given I'm only five feet high.'

This too was wilfully ignored.

'Hark! So, my two aims in life are to be a marine biologist and to kill all men!' Her eyes smouldered.

I tried to explain, 'Victory lies in being yourself, being happy in what you've become, and not in putting down people, making them feel like the scum of the earth.'

'Okay, wait, I think I have the perfect solution.'

'Aha, another one to make Archimedes catch his sides and roll with laughter.'

'I think they should be relegated to being 1. domestic help (who'll dry my towel and make my bed?) 2. sex slaves (we will "queen" over them).'

I didn't give up.

'I can't help but tell you about the man who bent down to tie my shoe laces, fill my ink pen and drive me to every exam. Who walked in at odd hours to make me drink water when I was studying, because I got dehydrated easily. Who stood by me and said, "Every girl in my house gets equal opportunity." These are MAN men, if you know what I mean.'

I smiled at her. But she stormed on. 'All right, we'll leave them be. But should we stop hammering the rapists, the merchants of dowry, the pimps and...'

'No, just as we can't stop hammering the cruel mothers-in-law, sisters-in-law, women who sell women,' I said, adding, 'think about this – who raised these men anyway?'

She countered, 'Why do they see me only as a "body", whistle at me even when I'm talking about Owen's war poetry?'

'But the battle of the sexes is passé. We've beaten it out, there is no meat on the bones any more.' Her eyes mocked me. Shaking her head, she dismissed me as beyond repair.

'I'm ravenous. The thought of destroying men gives me an appetite. What's for lunch?'

'I've got your favourite methi aloo ki roti made for you.'

She whirled around. 'Me thinks all this men talk dilutes your imagination. If you think I'm eating that... how I wish there was a Panda Express here – I'd have their chicken day in and day out.'

The phone beeps. The Man sends another sms – 'You didn't pack toothpaste in my kit. I reminded you thrice.' Hrrmmph.

Sakshi walked into my office the next day, hands raised in despair. 'I need to see a psychologist...'

'Why?'

'I don't just hate men; I also think and *know* that they are retarded...'

That night I made orange chicken for madam man-hater, to cool her down, though she preferred the deep-fried, artificially coloured, cornflour-coated orange chicken served by Panda Express. I think she pretended to like orange chicken only to spite me, because I can't for the life of me imagine anyone taking to artificially coloured, batter-coated chicken, which has turned rubbery after being plunged into hot oil twice or thrice to keep it looking palatable.

Orange Chicken

800 g chicken
2 tbsp oil
2 onions chopped
4 cloves garlic crushed
4 tomatoes chopped
Juice of 2 oranges
Grated rind of 1 orange
2 green cardamoms powdered
1 cup water
Salt, pepper to taste
Fresh coriander chopped

Heat oil and sauté the chicken pieces till lightly browned. Add the onion and garlic to the chicken. Add tomatoes, orange juice, orange rind, salt, pepper, cardamom and water. Cook over slow fire, stirring occasionally. Add fresh coriander when done; throw in a few peeled orange slices before serving.

Chicken Gol Mirch

800 g chicken
Juice of 5 lemons
250 g curd whisked
Salt to taste
4 tbsp coarsely ground pepper (or to taste)
2 tbsp oil

Heat oil in a kadhai, add all the ingredients together and let the chicken cook till it is tender.

This recipe is my sister's trademark. Didi learned it from her cook when she was a new bride in Shahjahanpur. The black pepper and lemon combination is a winner and it's the quickest chicken dish to prepare. The curd and lemon juice mingle with the chicken's own juices, to soak in the sharpness of the pepper and leave your tongue tingling. But four tablespoons of black pepper can be extremely peppery for some taste buds, so it's best to add half the quantity at first, taste and add more, if required.

It's strange when you think of it, but there was a time when for a handful of peppercorns, you could have someone killed. There was a time when grown men sat around and thought of nothing but black pepper. How to get it? How to get more of it? How to control the trade in pepper from the point of origin to purchase? In *Spice: The History of a Temptation*, Jack Turner opens up the whole story of pepper, blending the exotic scents of the East deep into the history of Western culture.

Everyone knows a little bit of the story, how the desire to control the spice trade drove Western nations into the throes of the Age of Discovery; the Portuguese sponsored da Gama's push to India; the Spanish underwrote the many attempts of Columbus to get to India by another route. The West's madness for spice was just about peaking at this time, and spice would all too soon become – gasp – common. Who thinks twice about pepper any longer? It's almost an afterthought condiment for so many today, the last resort if that 'little something' is missing in a dish.

Stir-Fried Ginger Chicken

- 400 g boneless chicken cut in long strips
- 2 tbsp oil
- 3 onions chopped
- 6–8 cloves garlic crushed
- 2 tsp ginger chopped
- 4 kaffir lime leaves shredded
- 60 g almonds blanched
- 120 g French beans cut into 2" pieces
- 1 red pepper cut into strips
- 90 g water chestnuts sliced
- 3 tbsp fish sauce
- 1 tbsp brown sugar

Heat oil in a wok, fry the garlic and onions till they soften. Add the chicken and sauté till it changes colour. Add the ginger, lime leaves, almonds, beans, red pepper and chestnuts. Stir-fry, tossing them all up, leaving the veggies crisp yet done out of their rawness. Stir in the fish sauce (this adds the salt component) and sugar.

This is a mildly flavoured chicken, but each ingredient helps the others to stand out. Crisp veggies help the crunch of almonds, while the ginger and garlic add the spice.

Chicken with Chilli and Basil

400 g boneless chicken

2 tbsp oil

3 red chillies chopped

1 tbsp fresh coriander chopped

4 cloves garlic crushed

3 green chillies sliced

2 tbsp fish sauce

2 tbsp oyster sauce

Small bunch of basil leaves torn into small pieces

Pound the red chillies, coriander and garlic together in a pestle and mortar. Heat oil in a wok and sauté the chicken till golden and cooked through. Remove from the wok. Add the pounded chilli mixture and stir-fry for a few minutes. Return chicken to the wok, add the green chillies, fish sauce, oyster sauce. Cook for another 10–15 minutes on medium heat. Add the basil leaves.

Those fiery Thai red chillies were the only things I brought back from Bangkok, much to the amusement of everyone at home. Rehan and Resham watch me bite into them and enjoy the fire travelling down my throat. They can't understand my fascination with this explosion in the mouth, but Bunny assures them, 'She is only refurbishing her reserve of sharp stings. Woh kahte hain na – chhoti mirchi teekhi hoti hai...'

Gaeng Ped Gai

800 g boneless chicken
12 dry red chillies softened in water
3 onions chopped
2 tsp ginger chopped
2 tsp garlic crushed
¼ tsp nutmeg powder
¼ tsp mace powder
1 tsp coriander seeds
1 stalk lemon grass chopped
2 tsp fresh coriander chopped
½ tsp lemon peel
2 tbsp shrimp paste
1 tbsp oil
700 ml coconut milk
Salt, pepper to taste

Pound all the ingredients, except coconut milk, in a mortar till smooth. Heat oil, stir-fry the spice paste for 4–5 minutes, add the chicken, pour in the coconut milk and cook on medium heat till chicken is tender.

I got this recipe from a chef in West End, Bangalore, at their Thai restaurant Paradise Island, which no longer exists. It was nineteen years ago and I can't recall the name of the chef, though I preserved the recipe, transferring it from a paper tissue to my register.

Chicken in Red Curry

6 chicken breasts cut into bite sized pieces
600 ml coconut milk
7–8 garlic cloves
150 ml chicken stock
2 tbsp fish sauce
2 fresh red chillies sliced
Fresh coriander chopped
4–5 kaffir lime leaves
1 tbsp oil

Red Curry Paste:

10 dry red chillies chopped
1" galangal sliced
3 stalks lemon grass chopped
4 garlic cloves peeled
2 tsp shrimp paste
I kaffir lime leaf chopped
1 tsp coriander powder
¼ tsp cumin powder
1 tbsp chopped fresh coriander
Salt, pepper to taste

Blend all the ingredients for the curry paste smoothly in a food processor. Heat oil in a wok, add the garlic, stir in the curry paste, stir-fry for 10–15 seconds. Add coconut milk and chicken stock stirring constantly. Add the chicken, fish sauce and cook on medium heat till tender. Throw in the red chillies, coriander, kaffir lime leaves, and serve with rice.

The green curry paste recipe will appear in the following chapter as a vegetarian dish, but these two curry pastes can be easily switched. Freshly made, the mingling of the aromas is like a burst of sensations. I dilute the pastes and dump a bit into an incognito version of noodles that the kids demand. Sometimes I use it to flavour fish kebabs. A wee bit in a salad dressing can be an uplifting experience.

Portuguese Chicken Masala

1 kg chicken
300 g onion chopped
Salt to taste
4 tbsp oil

Masala paste:

50 dry red chillies
1 cup palm vinegar
20–25 black peppercorns
2–3 sticks cinnamon
20–25 cloves
1 heaped tsp cumin seeds
4 pods garlic
2" ginger
Tamarind lump, size of lemon
8–10 tsp sugar

Grind all the masala paste ingredients finely in a food processor. Rub the chicken pieces evenly with it and leave overnight in the fridge. Heat oil in a pan, sauté the onions till golden brown, add the marinated chicken and let it cook till tender. A little water can be added to create a gravy. Let the chicken cook through, remaining juicy.

A relative, who lives in Goa, was visiting Jaipur and we got talking about cultural influences on food. This recipe is a fusion of Indian and Portuguese flavours, and she merrily told me that she passed it off as a vindaloo by adding plenty of oil.

On the day there was laung wale aloo and lauki ki sabzi for dinner, Aman called home in the middle of his Physics extra class and moaned, 'I will die of weakness if I don't eat a Domino's pizza for dinner.' Aman is huge. He weighs around 135 kilos. 'What if I ruin my Physics exam? There is too much at stake... And I'm telling you, don't order just one. These girls always say, "We won't eat pizza," but when they see it, they grab slices of it, so just as a preventive measure...'

'How's the writing going, CM?' Aman asked later, chomping his way through his pepperoni pizza. 'Am I in it?' I grinned back and said, 'Yes, majorly.' Sakshi can't resist a jibe at Aman, and immediately chipped in, 'Why are you lying, Mom, the book is only about me!'

'Am I in it?' Resham piped up. I can't help but be wicked and said, 'Not as yet.' Bunty sprang to his fellow Cancerian's support. 'It would be wise to put her in. Your book will sell three times the number in its second, or maybe third edition, because by then Resh will be a famous stylist.'

Just to prove Aman wrong, I stuck to the aloo and lauki menu. Halfway through dinner, he realized I had had the last laugh. 'CM, you aren't eating pizza?' My soft, deadpan reply, without a crease on my face, was, 'Hmm, I really prefer gourmet pizzas, these are pretty sad, chewy, no-flavour pizzas.'

Aman gulped down a bite. He looked me straight in the eye, viciously. 'I don't want to be in your book.' General laughter rippled around the table, then he launched his attack. 'When did you last make anything "flavourful"?'

'Just yesterday, those Thai noodles and red curry you slurped down.'

'What about some good dessert, huh?' he sneered.

'Scratch your head, buddy. Dadu-Dadi's anniversary was just last week. Have you forgotten the mango mousse cake on fudge brownie base, topped with crushed cranberry roses?'

'So we are reduced to waiting for birthdays and anniversaries now, to get some decent food?'

'Considering there are eleven of us and three wedding anniversaries, there's special food on the table every few weeks. Isn't that enough, you fathead?'

'No, you last made meat on CP's birthday. That was two months back!!'

Bunny added to the smouldering revolt. 'Dekha, mera jack hai, tumhara nahin!'

Bunny's birthday is mostly, or rather, only, about food. He starts needling me a month earlier. 'My birthday is coming, what will you make?'

Even if every passing year adds to his age, I see no difference – he just doesn't seem to grow up! And there is no difference in the ritual we've established.

Each year, I get the guard to make mitti ka chulhas for me in one corner of the garden. I sit on my haunches, like a village woman, stirring the dal on a slow fire and shifting to the next chulha, to gently peer into the dekchi full of meat yielding to the teekhapan of Jodhpuri dry red chillies, salt and ghee. The whole thing is an event and there's a buzz around the house from the evening before. Finally it boils down to just dal, meat and tandoori roti, but it's the excitement of cooking in a clay dekchi over an open fire, gently coaxing the meat to smoke up its juices, while the dal thickens slowly over a few hours. I'm always told, 'All you need is a ghagra-odhni, with a ghunghat covering your face.' It's another thing that I sit on the steps with my laptop during the intervals that I don't need to watch over the meat.

Our friend Shatrunjay adamantly refuses to put proportions to jungle maas. 'It's junglee, it's made in the jungle and you have to be wild about it,' he says. 'Make it with how much ever ghee, red chilli and salt you have. It's a dish that works out best with andaaz.' We make it in a dekchi, following our instincts, while Shatrunjay instructs us, 'Pour enough ghee, ghano ghee, in the dekchi... achha, ab aath-das mirchi naak deyo. Rang kam aayo? Thodi aur naak deyo... That's how we make jungle maas. Always add a few dry red chillies in the end – woh aakhi mirch rahe toh achha rahta hai.' Grudgingly, he adds, 'Okay, you can use about 250 gram ghee for 1.5 kilos of meat, salt to taste, and about 18–24 dry red chillies.'

Ajmer-style Meat

1 kg meat
4 tbsp ghee
2 heaped tsp sabut garam masala (cardamom of both types, peppercorns, cinnamon, cloves)
2 bay leaves
250 g onions chopped
250 g onions ground
2 heaped tsp garlic paste
2 heaped tsp ginger paste
1 tsp turmeric
3 heaped tsp red chilli powder
2 heaped tsp dry coriander powder
300 g curd
100 g fresh cream
Fresh coriander chopped
Fistful of kasuri methi
Salt to taste

Heat ghee, add whole spices and let them crackle and change colour. Add the chopped onion and sauté till light golden, then add the ground onion paste and cook till it turns a warm brown. Add the ginger and garlic paste, sauté for 3–4 minutes. Add the salt, turmeric, red chilli and coriander powders dissolved in a cup of water and let the mixture cook till the fat appears on the surface. Add the meat and let it cook on high heat for the next half an hour. Add the curd and cream and let it cook for another 40 minutes. You could pressure cook the meat for about 20 minutes, but I prefer to leave it on simmer, covered, till the meat is tender. Garnish with coriander and methi.

A lot depends on the quality of meat in this dish. It is best to get the front portion of the shoulder or thigh of a kid. If the meat is from an old goat, it will remain tough and not relent to any amount of pressure or slow cooking.

Lal Maas

- 1.5 kg meat (mixed pieces)
- 4 tbsp ghee
- 250 g curd
- 24 dry red chillies, stems removed
- 1 tsp heaped cumin seeds
- 4 tsp dry coriander powder
- 1 tsp turmeric
- 60 g garlic paste
- 250 g onions sliced
- 6 green cardamoms
- 4 brown cardamoms
- Fresh coriander chopped
- Salt to taste

Clean, trim and pat dry the meat pieces. Add red chillies, cumin, coriander, turmeric and salt to the curd and whisk well. Heat ghee and sauté garlic till light golden. Add onions, green and brown cardamom and sauté till onions are golden brown. Add the meat and sear on high heat till meat changes colour. Remove the pan from fire, add the curd and return to medium heat to let it cook. When the curd has dried up and the masala looks done, add 6 cups of water. Place the lid and simmer till the meat is cooked through and tender. Garnish with fresh coriander.

You can choose to sieve the gravy; I do. You can choose to pressure cook the meat; I don't. There is nothing like trapping the flavours within the mixture of ingredients and giving them the liberty to bring the best out of each other. Don't hurry them up. Lal maas is a typical Rajput dish. If you notice, there are no tomatoes. It's made from the local ingredients that could be found easily during hunting expeditions, which was one of the favoured pastimes of the Rajputs.

This year on Bunny's birthday, it was lal maas at its reddest, hottest, fieriest best. But this time I couldn't cook on a chulha outside. It was raining all day and any thoughts of laying the table under the front porch were dispelled by the sharp winds blowing.

Lal Mirch ka Korma

1.5 kg meat (mixed pieces)	1 tsp turmeric
24 dry red chillies	1.5 ltr clear mutton stock
125 g curd	1 tsp green cardamom powder
500 g onions sliced	¼ tsp brown cardamom powder
40 g garlic paste	¼ tsp mace powder
30 g ginger paste	¼ tsp nutmeg powder
30 g almond paste	Fresh coriander chopped
250 g curd	Saffron soaked in milk
3 tsp dry coriander powder	Ghee

Clean, wash and pat the meat dry. Soak the red chillies in water and blend to a paste. Whisk curd, add the chilli paste and salt, rub the meat with this and set aside for a couple of hours.

Heat ghee, add onions, sauté over medium heat till light golden. Add the garlic and ginger pastes and sauté till onions turn darker golden brown. Add the meat, sear till moisture evaporates and let it cook till it browns, adding a bit of the stock each time it threatens to stick to the bottom of the pan.

Remove from heat, stir in the curd with the dry coriander and turmeric powders. Stir well and resume cooking till the fat leaves the sides. Add the almond paste and remaining stock. Simmer till the meat is cooked. The gravy should have a thin, sauce-like consistency. Sprinkle the cardamom, mace and nutmeg powders. Add saffron just before serving and garnish with coriander.

In Rajasthan, especially in the Jodhpur region, meat is not eaten from a bowl. I've grown up seeing Papa place his rotis overlapping each other on the plate, and the meat being served over the rotis, gravy et al. He breaks off bits from the outer edges, working his way into the middle. 'Ismein asli anand hai, mithaas hai. Hamare Jodhpur mein toh aise hi khate hai,' he'd say, each time I grimaced at his messed up plate. Bunny also learnt to have his meat like that. I can never get myself to do so, although I am convinced that it is the best way to tackle meat-roti.

Yakhni

1 kg meat (chops and marrow bones)

2 tsp dry ginger powder (saunth)

1½ tsp aniseed powder

2 cups water

3 tbsp ghee

500 g curd whisked

1 tsp garam masala powder

6 green cardamoms crushed

Salt to taste

Boil the meat in water with the dry ginger, aniseed and salt till tender and the water is absorbed. Heat ghee, add the curd, cook till creamy. Add the boiled meat and garam masala, simmer for 15–20 minutes. Sprinkle crushed cardamom and remove from heat.

The flavour lent by the dry ginger and aniseed are the main plot in this recipe. Mummy started adding 3–4 dry red chillies to the ghee before pouring the whisked curd in. It does add the right blend of spiciness, but if you are looking for authentic stuff, then it's best to stick to the original recipe. Best served with plain rice, it's a terrific dish to make on a summer evening when everyone is tired out by the heat. The meat used here is the leaner portions of the goat, so the guilt of having eaten too much red meat doesn't unleash its torture on the arteries and your mind. This is one of Resham's hot favourites, though we are all curry and rice lovers – I guess that's the Sindhi blood in us.

Nihari

600 g marrow bones

600 g chops

2 tbsp ghee

6 green cardamoms

6 cloves

3 brown cardamoms

2 cinnamon sticks

2 bay leaves

2 tbsp garlic paste

2 tbsp ginger paste

200 g fried onion paste

100 g curd

1 tsp turmeric powder

2 tsp red chilli powder

Salt to taste

1 tsp powdered rose petal and mace for garnish

Heat ghee, add all the whole spices, salt, meat and sear on high heat till meat changes colour. Add the ginger and garlic pastes. Add the curd, onion paste and let it cook on low heat till meat is tender and almost falls off the bone. Add turmeric, salt, red chilli powder and 1 litre of water and let it boil for another 15 minutes. Sprinkle rose petal and mace powder before serving.

Nihari is a breakfast dish and the best place to eat it is on the streets of Old Delhi or Lucknow. Francois Bernier talks of the bazaar of Delhi in the 1660s, with the bakers, nihari makers, kebab sellers, etc. I read this description in an essay by Holly Shaffer called 'Nawabs and Kebabs' where she quotes Bernier's book, *Travels in the Mogul Empire*. 'The rich meat broth cooked overnight, strained multiple times and flavoured by a spice bouquet. Labourers traditionally eat this in the morning to sustain them through the day. But the Nawabs equally ate it for breakfast, when they had no visitors, so that no one could bear witness to their indulgence in a common food.' Even today, on the Akbari Gate side of the old city, there are many nihariwallas, Rahim's being the most famous among them.

Mutton Korma

1 kg meat
2 cups curd
2 heaped tsp garlic paste
2 heaped tsp ginger paste
4 tbsp ghee
8 onions chopped
12 cloves
12–14 green cardamoms
3 bay leaves
3 sticks cinnamon
2 tbsp dry coriander powder
2 tsp red chilli powder
Salt to taste
½ tsp each of powered clove, cinnamon and cardamom
Few drops of kewra

Wash the meat, pat dry; marinate it with curd, ginger-garlic pastes and salt. Heat ghee and add the cloves and cardamoms. Then add the onions and sauté till golden brown. Add the meat and cook till the water dries out. Add bay leaves, cinnamon and the powdered spices, dissolved in a cup of water. Let it cook for 15 minutes. Add 2 cups of water and let it simmer till the meat is cooked through. Sprinkle the korma with powered garam masalas. Add a few drops of kewra essence just before serving.

Cooking this uncomplicated dish is real fun. I've stood on a stool with a three-feet-long ladle over a gigantic bhagona to bhunno the korma for a party of a hundred guests. There is nothing more rewarding than hearing the ladies whisper, 'Wonder where they get their meat cooked, who is this special cook that they have hidden away? Will Veena tell us?' I pass the table with a smile, laugh suppressed, and leaving them thinking, 'Oh, crap, Veena's younger daughter-in-law heard that, now she'll go and tell her.'

Andhra-style Mutton

- 1 kg mutton
- 2 tbsp + 1 tsp ghee
- 1 tsp cumin seeds
- 1 cup onion sliced
- 2 tbsp garlic paste
- 2 tbsp ginger paste
- 2 tbsp dry coriander powder
- 3 tbsp red chilli paste
- 3 tsp magaz (melon seeds) paste
- ½ tsp star anise powder
- 2 cups tomato puree
- 10–12 curry leaves
- 3–6 dry whole red chillies
- Salt to taste

Heat ghee, add cumin seeds and let them crackle. Add onions and sauté till light golden brown. Add the meat and sear on high heat till it changes colour. Add ginger-garlic pastes and sauté for about 10 minutes. Add coriander powder and sauté. Add the red chilli and magaz pastes and let the meat cook, adding a little water. Add the salt and star anise powder and simmer till cooked tender. Add the tomato puree and cook for another 15 minutes. Before serving, heat ghee in another pan, crackle the curry leaves and whole red chillies and pour over the mutton.

Kashmiri Kofta

- 500 g meat finely minced
- 30 g ginger paste
- Pinch of asafoetida dissolved in 1 tsp water
- 6–8 brown cardamoms crushed
- 2 tbsp hung curd
- 1 tsp black cumin seeds
- ½ tsp red chilli powder
- 2 green chillies pounded to a paste
- 2 tsp coriander seeds ground
- ⅓ tsp each of mace, nutmeg, cloves, cinnamon powder
- 40 g ghee
- 1 tsp red chilli powder

Add all the ingredients to the mince, except for the chilli powder, and reserving half the ghee for cooking. Mix thoroughly, and when the mixture is quite pliable, divide it into equal parts. Roll each ball into a sausage of about 2½" length, pressing the mince firmly into shape. Add ghee to a saucepan, place the koftas and cook on slow fire. Cover the pan, shake gently every now and then, taking care the koftas don't break. When they become deep brown in colour, add red chilli powder. Add 4 tbsp of hot water, little at a time, and simmer till the koftas are well done and only ghee is left.

There is only one way to describe Kashmiri koftas – melt-in-the-mouth mince balls. Mummy doesn't like raw mince, so we've tried pressure cooking the mince, grinding it and then adding the ingredients, and the taste has been appealing. I prefer using the original recipe, however.

Malai Kebab

250 g meat finely minced
1 slice white bread soaked in milk
30 g onion chopped
2 green chillies chopped
½ tsp red chilli powder
½ tsp garam masala powder
1 tsp coriander seeds ground
½ egg
1 tbsp fresh coriander
15 g ginger finely chopped
Salt to taste
Flour for coating (optional)
Ghee for shallow-frying
150 ml sour cream
¼ tsp garam masala
¼ tsp red chilli powder
1 tbsp fresh coriander
2 green chillies chopped

Add the first 10 ingredients to the mince. Knead for 5 minutes. Divide the mixture into equal parts, shape them into round, flat cakes and roll in dry flour. Shallow-fry in a little ghee till browned well. Place in a dish. Heat the cream on low heat and pour over the kebabs, sprinkle the red chilli, garam masala and coriander leaves. Cook covered on slow fire and place live charcoals on the lid. Garnish with the chopped green chilli before serving.

Korma Rampuri

1.5 kg meat
10 green cardamoms
8 cloves
3 sticks cinnamon
4 bay leaves
30 g garlic paste
25 g ginger paste
2 tsp coriander powder
1 tsp red chilli powder
1 tsp turmeric
300 g curd whisked
100 g fried onion paste
30 g cashew nut paste
1.5 ltrs chicken stock
½ tsp black pepper powder
½ tsp green cardamom powder
½ tsp nutmeg powder
½ tsp clove powder
½ tsp cumin powder
Few drops of kewra

Heat ghee, add cardamom, cloves, cinnamon and bay leaves, sauté till they change colour. Add the meat and salt, sear on high heat till the meat changes colour and then reduce heat. Add garlic and ginger paste; coriander, red chilli and turmeric (all dissolved in 3 tbsp water) and fry till the water evaporates. Remove pan from fire, add the whisked curd. Return to flame and cook till the fat leaves the sides. Add the fried onion paste, let it cook for 5 minutes; add the cashew nut paste, stir and add the stock. Bring to a boil and then let it simmer till the meat is cooked. The Rampur finishing touch, according to Jiggs Kalra, is to sprinkle black pepper, green cardamom, nutmeg, clove and cumin powders; stir, add kewra and adjust the seasoning. If you wish to add a little more finesse to the dish, before sprinkling the powders, strain the gravy through a fine mesh and return the gravy to heat with the meat.

Rampur is a small town near Lucknow, ravaged by the vagaries of time and history, but remembered by a few faithfuls committed to the delicate use of spices. These old recipes still keep the place and its memories alive. Among others, Jiggs Kalra has tried to perpetuate the taar kormas, the kaliyas and kebabs from this area.

Mutton Doh Pyaza

1 kg meat
4 tbsp ghee
600 g onion sliced
6 brown cardamom
15 black peppercorns
6 tsp ginger paste
5 tsp garlic paste
200 g curd
6 green chillies chopped
50 g fried onion paste
800 ml chicken stock
1 tsp cumin seeds roasted and pounded
Fresh coriander chopped

Heat ghee, add the cardamoms, peppercorns, onion, ginger and garlic paste; sauté for 5 minutes and add the meat. Cook till the fat leaves the sides. Remove from heat, add the curd and green chillies. Return to flame and cook till the masalas turn golden brown. Add the fried onion paste, cook for a few more minutes. Add the stock, simmer till meat is tender and cooked through. Sprinkle cumin, fresh coriander before serving.

Fish is healthy; Sakshi does not like fish. Prawns are what she understands to be seafood and the rest of the aquatic species have to be protected from human consumption. Garlic butter prawns is all she wants to order at any restaurant. For two years Sakshi nursed a dream of becoming a marine biologist and gave up eating even prawns. Her dream eased out rather smoothly when she faced the hard reality that Calculus would have to be conquered to be able to do the subject. Figures are anathema to Sakshi and she conveniently blames it on a faulty gene pool. 'Mommy, you suck at math and that's why I do too.' Now training to be a psychologist, she still reads up a lot on the marine world. I guess the vestiges of the dream remain with her.

Our yearning for seafood gets pampered only when we are out of Jaipur. In the UK or Europe, we guzzle bottles of beer while eating our way through plates of fried fish in beer batter. The family looks forward to lots of seafood whenever we travel, because they have, by now, understood the delight that comes from savouring new recipes and the way they are presented. Only Rehan and Sakshi continue to be slightly hesitant to try out seafood, though I have tricked them into eating crabs and lobsters.

Pla Lad Phrik

1 whole pomfret
Oil for shallow-frying
5 green chillies
4 garlic cloves
1 tbsp lemon juice
1 tbsp fish sauce
50 g onion
2 tbsp fresh coriander
1 tbsp sugar
1 tbsp sweet chilli sauce
1 tsp cornflour

Wash the fish and pat dry after cleaning the insides. Make 3–4 vertical cuts on either side of the fish. Shallow-fry the fish on both sides till cooked through and remove to serving dish. Heat oil in a separate pan, toss all the remaining ingredients together on high flame and pour over the fish.

Pomfret in Pepper Sauce

500 g pomfret fillet
1 tbsp light soya sauce
1 tsp ginger paste
Salt to taste

Sauce:

1 tsp white pepper
1 tbsp coarse black pepper
1 tbsp dark soya sauce
6 flakes garlic chopped
3 green chillies chopped
1 tbsp chilli oil

Prick the fish pieces with a fork and marinate with light soya sauce, ginger paste, salt. Heat oil, add the fish and stir-fry for a few minutes. Remove and keep aside. Heat chilli oil, add sauce ingredients. Add the fish and stir till well coated. This dish is best served with steamed rice.

Fish Molie

500 g fish fillets
50 g desiccated coconut
6 small onions
6 cloves garlic
20 g ginger
1 tsp turmeric
2 stalks lemon grass
3 green chillies
800 ml coconut milk
Salt to taste

Sprinkle the fish fillets with salt. Roast the desiccated coconut till golden, add to the rest of the ingredients (except coconut milk and salt) and grind to a paste. Heat oil, fry the paste till it leaves the sides of the pan, add coconut milk and stir on low heat for about 3–4 minutes. Add the fish and simmer till it is done. Season with salt and serve with rice.

This is a Malaysian version of Indian fish moilee, which normally requires the onions to be stir-fried to a golden brown and has no lemon grass.

Goan Fish Curry

4 pomfrets (200–250 g each)
2 tbsp oil
2 onions sliced
2 coconuts
1 tbsp cumin seeds
½ tsp turmeric
2 small pods garlic
30 g tamarind
3 tbsp coriander seeds
18 dry red chilli
10 g ginger
Salt to taste

Clean and cut each fish into four horizontal pieces. Apply a little salt and keep aside. Heat oil, sauté onions till golden brown and keep aside. Grind the coconut to a fine paste along with the remaining ingredients. Add the paste to 500 ml water, bring to a boil and simmer for about 10 minutes. Add the fried onions, fish and cook on slow fire till done.

Green Chutney Fish

1 whole pomfret

1 bunch fresh coriander

10–12 green chillies

10–12 garlic cloves

½ coconut

Tamarind ball size of lemon

1 tsp cumin powder

Juice of 2 lemons

Salt to taste

Blend all the chutney ingredients in a food processor. Clean the fish, make vertical cuts, rub generously with the chutney and leave for a couple of hours. Wrap the fish in aluminium foil, bake in a preheated oven at 180°C for about 20–25 minutes. Test it with a fork; if flaky white, then its ready. For variation, you can add 4 tsp sugar and ½ cup peanuts to the chutney. This chutney can also be used to accompany hot snacks or as a sandwich spread on its own.

Fish in Ginger Butter

4 whole black pomfrets 250 g each

6 tbsp fresh coriander chopped

6–8 garlic cloves crushed

3 tsp grated lemon rind

6 tbsp butter

2 tbsp ginger grated

2 tbsp light soya sauce

Salt and pepper to taste

Banana leaves for wrapping

Lemon slices and fresh coriander for garnish

Clean and pat dry the fish. Mix coriander, garlic, lemon rind, salt, pepper and spoon it into the fish. Brush the fish well with oil and wrap it in a double layer of banana leaves. Place on a tray and bake for about 25 minutes at 190°C till the fish is flaky. Melt butter on low heat in a pan, add ginger and soya sauce. To serve, unwrap the banana leaves and drizzle the ginger butter over the fish. Garnish with lemon slices and fresh coriander leaves.

Mustard Fish

1 kg fish fillets

1 tsp turmeric

2½ tbsp mustard seeds

200 g curd

8 green chillies

4 tbsp mustard oil

Salt to taste

Wash fish, pat dry. Grind mustard to a paste with a pinch of salt. Whisk curd and add turmeric, salt, mustard paste and 2 tbsp mustard oil to it. Coat the fish well with this mixture and leave for 45 minutes. Heat the rest of the mustard oil till it smokes. Reduce heat, add the fish along with the marinade. Add the green chillies. Cover and let it simmer for about 20–25 minutes. The sauce should be of medium-thick consistency. The pungency of mustard and the heat from the green chillies is a winning combination – you just can't go wrong with this.

We were at Banyan Tree, Phuket. Greeted by friendly staff with folded hands and bowed heads, I took in the lobby and sank into the first steps of sheer decadence. A golf buggy took us through vast greens, dotted by ponds and palm trees, to our villa. The private pool seemed to stretch and fall into the lagoon at the edge of the green. A waterfall on one side, an open Jacuzzi on the other; the dense foliage fused to create a pretty picture. Birds added their music to that of the lilting breeze. A lomi lomi massage, at the edge of the lagoon, was like a straight dive into our existence for the next three days.

The massage and steam made us want to skip lunch. Pink rose tea with finger sandwiches and mini almond and fruit tarts, served on a tiered platter, was a light treat. I smiled at the dried pink rose buds peeping out of the teapot spout. The hedonist in me was awakened. A swim in the pool before dinner seemed to be just the thing to do.

Dusk must be worshipped in a manner befitting the colours of the sky. We went back to our villa to welcome it with red wine – the Jacuzzi bubbled, rippling and cavorting. My goblet slipped and bounced into the water. Not a drop spilled out. The chuckling waters buoyed it up. The wine glass bobbed around gleefully, dancing on the tiny waves. I laughed and another goblet joined the dance. They met, clinked, cheered and twirled to the music merrily. We drank from the rim without holding them, so as to not interrupt their courtship.

Languorous after the wine and still drinking in the sounds and smells of twilight, we buggied our way to Saffron for dinner. I wanted to taste tom yum and tom kha in Thailand. It was more to reassure myself that we get the authentic version in India as well. Both the soups surpassed my expectations, the prawns melting on the tongue, the galangal biting and the lemon grass suffusing the over-all taste. The broth was spicy, sassy and just sour enough. I had never seen galangal sliced so fine and thread-like. The steamed snow fish with lemon and sweet chilli, and the sautéed Phuket lobster in a dry red curry sauce, accosted us with a cheeky mixture of sensations. No room for dessert. Pampered silly, we chose to fall asleep on crisp white cotton sheets.

The next morning, breakfast in bed or breakfast at the pool turned out to mean one and the same thing. Carried to our villa in a huge wicker basket, it was like Pandora's Box with an endless array of eats – omelettes, fruits, cereal, coffee and juices – laid out decorously by the staff as we sank into gluttony. A swim later, the action began with a

short walk to one of the spa pavilions. Surrounded by ebony- and gold-filigreed pillars, bird-of-paradise blooms and fish swimming in a lotus pond, the notes of divine music enveloped us. It was surreal. I could only feel hands pressing, kneading and sliding the kaffir lime scrub over my body. My limbs felt as if they were floating. Back to the villa in the buggy, driven by an ever-smiling Thai, his head bobbing as if to say, 'Now I will take you to your room in my Formula One car.' My eyes never tired of the orchids flowering carelessly all around.

Wine and fresh purple grapes were the prelude to another evening. We watched the night come in, changing from peach to orange, to a sap green, before the colours of darkness took over. We decided to dine at Lotus, one of the more famous restaurants in Phuket – a must-do, we had been told. We entered to see crabs, shrimps, lobsters and tuna swimming in tanks, to be weighed and cooked for dinner the way you wanted them. We chose to remain faithful to a grilled lobster with Penang sauce, and crab in red curry. I don't think I can ever get enough of the curry, the chilli and the lemon grass. There was lime and litchi sorbet to round off the hot, spicy meal on the beach. Thai kites dotted the skyline, their candle flames dying out in the sea breeze.

Deep, contented slumber followed till next morning, which began with a huge Thai and Japanese breakfast. Miso soup, shrimp broth, Thai omelette, wheat noodles and some fruits later, we lazily meandered into another spa pavilion for the Tranquility hydromist revitalizing treatment. Each pavilion was a delight in design. Passing through stacked graphite, lit up by red tea lights, the sense of impending luxury, of being swathed in smells and sensations, was heightened. Later, after a hot steam and gentle shower that revitalized each point of the body, we were scrubbed with a creamy ginger and honey scrub. I figured Cleopatra's life must have been kind of similar to this.

The treatment didn't stop there. More warm honey was slathered on generously. I understood what it meant to be steeped in a satiny finish, like the softest of silks gliding over your body, feathery to the touch and reaching into your very insides. Treatments like this are designed to make you ravenous. The food at the Water Court with its Mediterranean flavours of citrus salad with garlic prawns, and charred aubergine cappuccino, the intimate dinner at the Sala Terrace, left us both heavier by a few pounds. We consoled ourselves every night by saying, 'Don't worry, we'll shed it all once we get back to the grind in Jaipur.'

The two of us giggled like teenagers as the Banyan Tree staff moved noiselessly to set up the Intimate Moments evening. The entire passage through the villa was lined with purple orchids and candles right up to the open bath. Orchids floated in the water. Wine glasses and a wine bottle waited silently on the side. Bath salts, aroma sticks, et al, we slipped into the bath. A sinful chocolate mousse, bedecked with a chocolate rose, awaited us at the foot of the bed. Two decanters of 'love oil' and 'bliss oil' rested at the head. 'Love' for before and 'Bliss' for after, I was told. The 'midnight queen' aroma sticks were already sending up swirls of smoke. The satin sheets were strewn with white orchids. A jug full of ice-cold water, flavoured by half a green apple resolutely staring out of it, was placed nearby. 'Remember I have to meet the chef before we leave and take some of the fish recipes he promised me,' I said. Bunny was on the edge of losing his calm, and snapped, 'With all of this, you can only think of your recipes?' I shrugged.

Laksa Lemak

6 sprigs laksa leaves

900 ml water

300 ml thick coconut milk

20 g sugar

500 g cooked noodles (egg or rice)

150 g blanched bean sprouts

100 g steamed prawns peeled

50 g diced steamed fish

2 eggs cooked into a thin omelette and sliced

Spice paste:

8 fresh red chillies

10 small onions

1 stalk lemon grass

25 g galangal

1 tsp turmeric

Garnish:

3 sprigs laksa leaves

1 cucumber shredded

2 fresh red chillies sliced

2 spring onions chopped

6 lemon wedges

10 cherry tomatoes

Salt to taste

Chop all the spice paste ingredients and grind them with the turmeric, adding oil if necessary. Heat oil in a pan, fry the spice paste, add laksa leaves, water and bring it to a boil. Add coconut milk, sugar, salt. Reduce heat, simmer uncovered for about

10 minutes. Divide the noodles, bean sprouts, prawns, fish, omelette between the serving bowls. Add the broth to the bowls and finish with the garnish. Serve hot with lemon wedges on the side. If laksa leaves are not available, I substitute them with 5–6 kaffir lime leaves shredded. It's a hearty meal and very quick to assemble.

Pomfret Curry

12 pomfret fillets
80 g tamarind pulp dissolved in 110 ml water
2 tbsp oil
1 tsp mustard seeds
80 g chopped onion
20 g chopped ginger
25 g chopped garlic
½ tsp turmeric
12 curry leaves
6 chopped green chillies
1 tsp coriander powder
¼ tsp fennel powder
½ tsp cinnamon powder
½ tsp clove powder
220 ml coconut milk

Leave fish to marinate in the tamarind pulp for about 15–20 minutes. Heat oil in kadhai, add mustard seeds and let them crackle. Add ginger, garlic and sauté for 2 minutes. Add onions and sauté till they turn light brown. Add curry leaves, green chillies, coriander, fennel, cinnamon, clove, stirring all the while. Add coconut milk and simmer for 5 minutes. Add the fish and simmer till cooked.

Steamed Fish in Banana Leaves

750 g fish fillets 3"x3"
5 tbsp vinegar
1 tbsp oil
Salt to taste
Banana leaves to wrap the fish

Green Paste:
1½ cup fresh coriander
¾ cup fresh coconut
8 green chillies roughly chopped
8 garlic cloves
1½ tbsp coriander seeds
¾ tbsp cumin seeds
5 tbsp lemon juice
1 tbsp sugar
Salt to taste

Sprinkle salt and vinegar on the fish and leave aside for an hour. Combine all the ingredients for the paste and grind in a blender. The banana leaves should be cut to a size large enough to wrap a single fillet. Rub the fillets with the green paste till well covered. Brush banana leaves with oil and wrap each fillet separately, securing with a toothpick. Place in a steamer for about half an hour. Serve hot with lemon wedges.

When we were in Amsterdam, both the girls were thrilled by the fact that we were living in an apartment just thirty feet away from the red light district. Suddenly, discovering new flavours and new eating joints mattered a lot less to them. 'Can we also go with you for your night jaunts and see all those shows that Dad is surely going to drag you to?' they asked. Resham and Sakshi would shut Rehan's eyes, each time we walked down the street, to prevent him from glancing at the ladies posing as mannequins behind glass windows. The poor boy was pulled along, tripping, stumbling and squealing, till I yelled at them to stop.

John Travolta's opening dialogue in Tarantino's *Pulp Fiction* came to mind: 'You know the funny thing about Europe is they have the same shit as us, but it's the little differences... you can walk into a movie theatre in Amsterdam and buy a beer, not in a paper cup but a glass... you know what they put on French fries instead of ketchup – mayonnaise... and hash? It's legal to buy it, it's legal to own it, sell it in a hash bar, carry it... and you know, it's illegal for a cop to search you?' Small wonder then, that the Dutch say, 'Doe maar gewoan, dan doe je gek genoeg' – 'Be normal, that's crazy enough!'

Clusters of narrow, gabled buildings marked with dates like 1541 AD and 1603 AD, the smell of the canals mixed with tar and tulips, the soothing sound of cycle tyres: Amsterdam is fairy tale-like, making you move back and forth in time. A fishing village in the 13th century, Amsterdam grew into a 'people's capital'. My first reaction as I walked to the hyper-kinetic Dam Square was: 'This place is a 24x7 party.' The War Memorial is built on sand brought from all the provinces in Holland. The Royal Palace is used for ceremonial occasions when Queen Beatrix visits and is an architectural beauty. We walked into the Jordaan quarter: narrow streets, eclectic shop fronts, cafes; the relentless buzz was infectious. The Oude Kirk (old church), a 1306 AD mammoth structure with three naves, towers and chapels, stands conveniently in the middle of the red light district. The Sensi Seed Bank, which we visited for kicks, threw up a host of 'dopey' facts. The guy there practically adopted us, answering all my queries about the different effects of different drugs. 'More people die of smoking cigarettes,' he informed us.

Amsterdam is a voyeur's paradise. It is an in-your-face experience to pass by windows which have the 'ladies' positioned in fluorescent lingerie and black garters, throwing an occasional wink and pouting their lips at the passing gawker. I got talking to one, wanting to interview her. The rate 'per hour' was steep; I said so in Hindi to Bunny. The voluptuous lady caught on and replied, 'Nahin, bahut mehnga nahin hai.' She was an Indian, her streaked hair and heavily made-up face concealing her identity. 'In that one hour while you interview me, I'll give you a good time too,' she said, her eyes twinkling with mirth. Thanks, but no thanks, I laughed and walked away.

Amsterdam was the art, culture and business capital of Europe during the seventeenth century, after which its power waned. An on-foot tour is the best way to feel the pulse of the city. The sun was elusive and the breeze cold, but we trudged on. Our 'walking' guide, a friendly Dutch lady, made us cross the canals, which exude a romanticism that spells serenity in one way, intimacy in another. The three main canals, Prinsengracht, Keizersgracht, Hirengracht, are distinct from one another: if one is all about majestic royalty, the other is a 'gentlemanly' canal, and the third has a thriving coffee bar culture.

Wherever we were, Sakshi dragged us back to the Pancake Bakery. We had chanced upon it while randomly walking the streets – its length of sun-burnt bricks and two rows of typical café furniture gave it the feel of a school dining hall. She insisted on ordering apple and banana pancakes with Grand Marnier and Nutella, saying, 'Let's do the normal stuff first and over our second round of hot chocolate, we'll order the vooor dee pannnenekoeken specialities.' We giggled at the mouthful of Dutch in desi Indian accent. Pancakes with salami, ham, cheese and paprika followed by pannenkoek met aardbeiensuas, ijs en slagroom, pannenkoek met honing, nootjes, manderijnen en slagroom. They were ordered simply because it was a challenge to pronounce the names, and after much deliberation with the waitress, since Sakshi insisted that she must speak in Dutch (her version). We were looked after with much warmth and, of course, my elder daughter took all the credit. 'Moi, I'm special, see,' she said, with her hand moving towards her heart, just the way Supriya Pathak does in her role as Hansa in *Instant Khichdi*.

Amsterdam has its immortal stars – Anne Frank, van Gogh, Rembrandt. The Anne Frank Museum is a place of pilgrimage. I recalled a documentary, *Secret Lives,* made on Jewish kids who were hidden from the Nazis. Ed van Thijn, former mayor of Amsterdam, was eight years old when the Germans came. He hid in eighteen different places.

I could have spent hours (but for the impatience of the three children and one struggling-to-grow-up husband) at the van Gogh Museum, taking in the dark, morbid colours of the *Potato Eaters,* moving on to the brighter strokes in the artist's evolution under the Impressionist influence. Amsterdam was celebrating four hundred years of Rembrandt that year. The Rijks Museum was showing the famous *Night Watch,* with an audio-visual show that explored the psyche of that age. Paintings by Vermeer and Frans Hals prodded you to speculate on how much they might have learnt from Rembrandt.

A twenty-minute train ride got us to Zaandam, a quaint nineteenth century village. It has preserved homes, wind mills and shoe- and cheese-making establishments in an open air museum. We stepped out from bursts of wild flowers into the quietness of the Zaan river flowing past green roofs, weeping willows bending to tease the waters, and the enormous blades of a windmill moving the runner stones crushing peanuts on the pans below, to let the oil ooze out. The ancient windmill, named De Zocker, dates back to 1676 AD and has weathered many a wind of change. A warm aroma of cocoa beckoned to us from the cocoa-making factory, along with sink-into-the-mouth cream puffs at the charming local bakery. We saw different types of cheeses with their odours and overpowering tastes, and a live show on how wooden clogs are made. We tried them all, the cheese and the shoes. The cheese won, obviously.

Leidseplein, the square which rocks at night, is the place to be in Amsterdam. We were there the night France played Brazil in the World Cup. The pubs overflowed with people and beer. Low ceilings, burnt wood panels, voices and laughter. You were asked whether you'd like your beer 'black, blonde or red'. The energy was palpable, as different groups rooted for their favourite teams. We laughed our evening away at the Boom Chicago comedy show. We ate through the patisseries, with crisp chocolate croissants still warm from the oven, apple turnovers and blueberry tarts. The eateries lining this square have food to die for. Fish, prawns, lobsters were on our radar as starters, main course, teatime, snacktime, anytime. Squid, mussel, crab were no longer a no-no with the kids.

For our last night out, without the kids, much to Resham's chagrin – 'You can't treat us like kids any more, see I'm so tall already,' – Supperclub was the choice. They had a jazz band performing that night. The ambience spelt freedom and escape, sensuousness redefined. It was all white, offset by the use of colours that tended towards bizarre, as the theme changed each time there was a different performance. The combination of art, music, theatre made it a different experience. Dishes served by waiters dressed in black leather, food served on records or saddled on the backs of sexily dressed women – one of them carried oysters on a round bed of ice piled on a satchel strapped to her forehead. The wine list made me swoon before the bottle reached our table – the buzz was infectious. It was like taking a vodka shot in the arm and feeling it course through your veins. We went berserk, starting with mustard soup with eel, black pepper and creme fraiche, salad of smoked Irish salmon, champagne vinaigrette and fresh herbs; we turned decadent with fried scallops and potato salad in lobster dressing. An Amaretto parfait and white chocolate mousse, coated on the side with orange sauce, wrapped up the meal, but we continued to indulge, lingering over the music in white beds and letting a masseuse knead our shoulders, whenever she passed by. It would have been great to pass out there for the night were it not for our offspring slumbering in our rented flat.

The city is a dreamy, fast-lane destination. With 16,318,199 people, 5,50,000 bikes, 160 canals, 1,200 bridges and double the amount of tourists, it tastes of old world grandeur and new age funk, nonchalantly combining the sacred and the profane, the sublime and the ridiculous, the body and the soul. One small peeve – we missed the tulips. Another time, maybe.

7

Go Green

We hurtled up the rough, craggy hills in a four-wheel drive, swerving dangerously to avoid sharp edges. The evening breeze whipped against our faces and our racing heartbeat warned us to hold tight. There was another open jeep racing down the same hill. Why was it swaying so recklessly towards us? Shatrunjay raised his hand and said, 'Khama gani, see you at Seengh Sagar later.' The driver of the jeep was a lady. Her head was covered and the pallu of her sari was tucked under her arm. Her 90-year-old mother was seated next to her. 'She has some gumption, driving over a no-roads terrain with such ease,' I thought. Shatrunjay spoke with immense pride: 'That's my mother, she takes care of the kitchen.' What would otherwise be assumed as a normal duty for a 'head-covered' woman, had different implications here. She was on her way to oversee the cooking of the evening meal. The 'kitchen' happened to be the Deogarh Mahal's, with its huge scale of operations.

I was introduced to the lady in question over succulent soola grilled on charcoal, in a serene landscape gently illuminated by candles. The valley spread before us, the

sounds from the forest filled us with tranquillity – nature and man seemed to coexist in perfect harmony. I walked over to the chulha where another 'head-covered' lady was deftly rolling out makkai ki roti, while keeping a keen eye on the dal. A playful toddler gleefully ran up a small sand hill and rolled down, squealing happily at the clouds of dust he raised. Throwing green chillies, ginger, garlic into an earthenware pot and smiling at the protesting sizzle, the lady said, 'Dal ko chamka lagayo.' 'Chamka' as in tadka, or tempering. It made the meal dance for me. In many ways, cooking is like performing a dance – the rhythm, beat, timing, expression...

I smiled and went back to the Rani of Deogarh, Bhoo Ratna Kumari, who has led an action-packed life with her husband, the ruling Rawat of Deogarh, Nahar Singhji. She immediately launched into food talk.

> I had no idea about cooking at all. When I was growing up, my mother used to tell me, 'Start learning! What are you going to do?' After I was engaged,

I stayed with my family at Shahpura, where my uncle and aunts taught me a few dishes. I learnt to make jajariya (a type of halwa) with wheat or corn, and some meat and rice dishes. I learnt to rustle up palak ka halwa. Kaka was a very good cook, he taught me how to make mutton – doh pyaza, rogan josh, biryani.

When I came to this house, it was quite a change for me, because here the day-to-day cooking was done by the ladies, and they were so interested in it. It was quite unnerving for me. I didn't know dal kaise banti hai, roti kaise sekte hain, saada chawal kaise banta hai. I slowly picked up by observing how things were done.

We moved to Ajmer when my husband took up teaching at Mayo College. One day the jeep overturned and our cook was hurt. The task of daily cooking fell upon my two younger sisters-in-law and me. We went through the usual mishaps – a very big deal then! We had no idea how to do the atta – my sister-in-law kept adding water to the flour, but it never turned into dough. Finally, the roti looked more like a naan.

We were friendly with Mr Gibson, one of the towering educationists in Rajasthan and the principal of Mayo College. Eating a meal with Mr Gibson meant that you would have meat cooked in one of two ways – a roast or a curry. He'd always say, 'You ruin the taste of the meat by adding so many spices,' but in the end, his meat remained very tough because he didn't let it cook for enough time, while ours would be ready to fall off the bone, nicely done...

One evening, my kaka commented on how tasty the clear soup Mr Gibson had served us was. Mr Gibson, known for his glibness, answered, 'All you have to do is take the bones from today's dinner and put them into tomorrow's soup.' I was horrified and couldn't bring myself to have the soup, even though he reassured me, saying, 'But it's all boiled now.'

Rani Sahiba's Bible was a book by Balbir Singh, and that was a connection we made across the generations. My mother-in-law had introduced me to this treasured cookbook when I was newly married in 1989. 'Her chutneys and murabbas, her rogan josh...' We both lapsed into our personal 'oohs and aahs' over Balbir Singh.

'I learnt to cook partridge from my nani,' Rani Sahiba reminisced. 'She used to add hara chana to the dish, now we add the same chana to chicken, which came into our menu much later.' The topography and climate of Rajasthan has pre-determined the nature of its cuisine. In the Mewar

region, corn or makkai is used for making a variety of sweet and savoury snacks, as well as main courses. Corn was first imported from South America and its versatility made it a universal ingredient. Rajasthanis make corn pakoras, meat soyeta, chicken soyeta, roti, dhokla, jajariya (made from tender, milky corn), corn pulao, and batter-fried tender corn cob. 'Makkai ka raab' in buttermilk is a type of Mewari broth. Raab is also made with green, milky wheat in the same way. Raabodi is makkai atta cooked in milk, dried in the sun, like a papad, and then cooked with spring onions or in gravy. Corn can also be dried, roasted and added to meat or kadhi, or simply turned into a dish by itself, with a masala base. In Marwar, bajra or millet is used with the same degree of flexibility.

Rani Sahiba and I could have rambled on forever about food in Rajasthan, had we not been interrupted by Bunny with his usual refrain, 'I'm hungry, let's eat'. My request for that night was lal maas with moong ki dal and gatte ki sabzi. Bunny chuckled at my preference for moong ki dal over mutton, but it has always been comfort food for me. 'You are being a typical woman, you know,' he said, trying to get a rise out of me. I was too pleased with the food to be bothered and ignored him with a shrug. 'Auntie,' he said, 'Mita is behaving herself because of you, otherwise such statements would have led to me being chopped and served on the table like raw salad.' We laughed him off and soon I was engrossed in foodie talk once again.

> Deogarh Mahal is a part of the village and we wanted to keep the food served here as authentic and local as we could. Mewari cuisine is what we make at home. What the Italians call polenta, we call makkai ka daliya. We serve this daliya and bajra ka meetha kheech for breakfast, and it's a big hit with our guests. We make it a point to be there at meal times to explain the history and origins of the food, so that people really savour it.
>
> Jungle maas was created by Rajput warriors while they roamed the forests, hunting or fighting wars. Onion and garlic is not available in the jungle, only ghee, salt and red chillies are carried with the supplies. Khada masala meat was also the result of such wanderings. Even if there were ingredients, there would be no tools to grind and chop, so they all went in whole with the meat, and the result was one of the tastiest meat dishes.
>
> Most gravies in Rajasthani cuisine are without tomatoes. When I got married and came to Deogarh, tomato and ginger weren't available at all,

they weren't even grown locally. I had to buy lemon and coriander from Ajmer, whenever we went there. Till 1964, vegetables were not available in Bikaner.

Originally, soola was made with deer meat marinated and grilled on charcoal. Rabbit meat was eaten in summer because it's supposed to keep you cool and protect you from the 'loo' or warm winds. Rabbit, which was fed on greens, was not considered tasty; the same was true of wild boars. Rabbit meat is traditionally served with baati, buttermilk and whole onion. Baati is also the result of not having anything to roll out chapattis with in the jungle – it was much easier to bake a ball of dough! Jungle mein roti kaise banaoge?

Women in Rajasthan have remained predominantly vegetarian. Gatta sabzi and panchkutta are dishes typical of Marwar. Rajasthani food is quite rich, because traditionally curd, buttermilk, ghee and fresh butter were used instead of water. We believe that biloya hua makkhan does not have bad cholesterol and is healthy. I keep telling my sons, we must serve more of our food, pickles, chutneys...'

The Rajasthani kitchen was able to create much from little, and it also had to cater to different communities, each with its own ritual observances. The Rajput warrior, for example, was not averse to going on shikar, to put game meat in his pot at night. The Vaishnavs, followers of Vishnu, were vegetarian, as were the Bishnois, a community known for its passionate conservation of both animal and plant life. However, even among the Rajputs, there were many royal kitchens where only vegetarian meals were cooked. The Marwaris were vegetarian too, but their cuisine, though not very different from that of the Rajputs, was richer.

Our conversation was interrupted once again by a dish of jajariya and Bunny's protests. In spite of being so fond of typical Rajasthani dishes, I've never tried making gatte ki sabzi or jajariya, although I grew up in a household where they were made very often. I guess there are some things you just don't end up doing in life!

All of eight years old, Sakshi watched me while I ate my way through a simple lunch of moong ki dal and cabbage. Her round face was framed by a mop of dark hair, and her expressive eyes spoke before she voiced her young but condescending views. 'You are very old fashioned.'

'Why do you say that?'

'You eat old fashioned food like dal and cabbage.' Keeping my laughter at bay, I replied, 'So, what is the latest fashion in food?'

'Oh, y'know, pizza and noodles, cakes and burgers. Who eats dal-sabzi these days?'

We have all been part of such conversations and more: 'Ghaas phoos kaun khata hai,' or 'I'm a *pure* non-vegetarian.' The baingan ka bharta made at our home is famous in all of Jaipur. But if someone has the temerity to place it on the table in front of Bunty, he is sure to get a tongue lashing. 'Remove it immediately, I can't look at it, why are you bent on making me retch?'

Poor Bunny, on the other hand, has always politely listened to Dad, who would pass him the arbi, doused with chat masala and lemon juice, saying, 'You must eat this, it's just like chaat. Arbi acchi hoti hai, khao.' I would giggle each time, and now I say the line before Dad can say it, whenever arbi is served. The day there is only chicken curry on the table, Bunty strums a different tune. 'Why don't we have any veggies on the table, why are we such voracious carnivores? Such gluttony, tsk tsk.'

I wonder how anyone can resist aloo gobi ki sabzi, made just ten minutes before serving, the florets a sunny yellow, fragrant with the flavours of freshly chopped coriander, green chillies and ginger? Or a medley of carrots, peas, cauliflower and potatoes made the same way? Or tender green peas in a tadka of loads of chopped ginger, green chillies, fresh coriander and cumin seeds? The colours of winter vegetables are spritely and uplifting. I survive on bowls of lauki, tinda and tori all summer, made piquant with sweating onions, tomatoes and the usual dash of coriander, green chillies and mint. They taste refreshing, fill up the stomach, and are basically guilt-free veggies – eat two full bowls and you feel like you've had a complete meal. Cheat the calories of all the satisfaction they get from sitting smugly on the paunch and the bottom.

Resham loves the rassa that tomatoes leave when cooked with tinda. She has stuck to eating veggies since she was a baby, unlike Sakshi, who can survive on plain bread or roti, jam-bread, funny egg, or only chicken – no impurities allowed here.

But there must be something about the dal-sabzi combination. Why do most of us yearn for dal, rice and sukhe aloo on our return from a two-week vacation abroad, even if we have just feasted on the finest of world cuisine?

Potato and Cauliflower with Methi

1 kg cauliflower cut in medium florets
600 g large potatoes with skin, cubed
200 g methi (fenugreek) leaves chopped
2 tbsp oil
1 tsp cumin seeds
15 g ginger chopped
3–4 green chillies chopped
2 tbsp fresh coriander
1 tsp turmeric
1 tsp red chilli powder
Salt to taste
Fresh coriander and ½ tsp kasuri methi for garnish

Blanch the potatoes in salted boiling water till done, drain and keep aside. Sprinkle salt over the fenugreek and wash well after 10 minutes.

Heat oil, add cumin seeds and let them crackle. Add the ginger, green chillies, coriander and stir-fry till they exude an aroma. Add fenugreek, cauliflower, salt, turmeric and red chilli powder, cover and let it cook in its own steam. Add potatoes, cover and cook till well mixed. Garnish with fresh coriander and kasuri methi. This dish would serve a hungry army of 10 people.

Vegetables with a Mediterranean Touch

250 g baby potatoes parboiled
250 g cauliflower florets
150 g brinjal sliced
100 g peas shelled
200 g tomatoes cubed
2 tbsp olive oil
4 dry red chilli broken, deseeded
4 flakes garlic chopped
2 onions chopped
1 cup white wine
Salt and pepper to taste

Heat olive oil, add dry red chillies, garlic and sauté. Add onion and cook till soft. Add the brinjal, sauté for a minute. Add white wine and let it simmer for 5 minutes. Add the cauliflower, potatoes, cover and simmer till all vegetables are tender. Add the peas shortly before other vegetables are done. Add tomatoes and cook them only enough to leave them crisp. Add the seasoning.

Spinach and Peanuts in Moong Dal

- 3/4 cups raw peanuts soaked for 30 minutes
- 2 bunches spinach, washed
- 3/4 cup moong dal washed
- 4–5 green chillies slit, deseeded
- 1 tsp turmeric
- 1½" piece ginger grated
- 2 tsp ghee
- 1 tsp cumin seeds
- 3–4 green cardamom
- 3–4 cloves
- 4 tomatoes chopped
- Salt and lemon juice to taste
- Fresh coriander for garnish

Pressure cook moong dal with the green chilli, salt, turmeric and ginger for one whistle, and then let out the steam to make sure the dal remains khilwa or grainy. Pressure cook the peanuts separately for 3 whistles. Heat ghee, add cumin seeds, cardamom, cloves, tomatoes and sauté till tomatoes are done. Add the spinach, peanuts and salt to the dal and stir. Garnish with lemon juice and fresh coriander.

Jackfruit the Mutton Way

- 2 kg jackfruit
- 4 tbsp oil
- 2–3 bay leaves
- 2–3 sticks cinnamon
- 6 green cardamoms
- 4–5 cloves
- 500 g onion sliced, not lengthwise but across
- 2 tsp garlic paste
- 2 tsp ginger paste
- 2 tsp red chilli powder
- 1 tsp turmeric powder
- 2 tsp dry coriander powder
- 500 g tomato skinned and chopped
- 2 tbsp gram flour roasted on low heat
- Salt to taste
- Fresh coriander for garnish

Slit open the jackfruit, remove the thick peel and cut into 1½"cubes. Shallow-fry in 2 tbsp oil till lightly browned, keep aside. Heat 2 tbsp oil, add the whole spices and let them crackle. Add onions and sauté till light golden. Add the ginger and garlic paste, sauté for 2 minutes. Add red chilli, turmeric, coriander and a little hot water, let it cook till the oil floats on top. Add tomatoes and let it cook some more. Add the fried jackfruit and gram flour, mix well. Add 2 cups water and pressure cook for 20 minutes. Adjust seasoning. Sprinkle fresh coriander.

The kids call this vegetarian meat. It's the texture added by the roasted gram flour, combined with the hunt for the seeds that spill out of the flesh, which makes it a fun dish. Cutting the onions 'the other way round', according to CB, is what is extra special about it. But I have realized that onions cut across soften sooner!

Ghutwa Gobi

1 cauliflower cut into small florets
1 potato cubed
1 tsp ghee
Pinch of asafoetida
1 tsp cumin seeds
150 g curd
200 g onion
2 tbsp oil
1 tsp red chilli powder
½ tsp turmeric powder
½ tsp garam masala powder
2–3 green chillies chopped
Fresh coriander
Salt to taste

Heat ghee in pressure cooker and do a tadka of asafoetida and cumin seeds. Add cauliflower, potato and pressure cook for 10 minutes (with ¼ cup water). Mash the cooked vegetable, add curd and cook for 5 minutes in the open cooker. In a separate pan, sauté onions in oil till golden. Add red chilli, turmeric, garam masala and green chillies. Add this to the cauliflower mixture and stir well. Garnish with fresh coriander.

Lemony Cauliflower

1 large cauliflower cut into medium florets
3 tbsp butter
3 tbsp flour
2 cups milk
Juice of 2 lemons
Rind of 2 lemons
60 g cheese (optional)
3–4 dried red chilli deseeded and broken
2 green chillies sliced diagonally
Fresh coriander chopped
Salt and pepper to taste

Blanch cauliflower till done but crisp. Drain and keep aside. Melt butter, stir in the flour and sauté for 2–3 minutes. Add milk and bring to a boil, stirring constantly, till the sauce is only slightly thick. Add lemon juice, rind, salt, pepper, cheese. Add the cauliflower to the sauce. Add red and green chillies and let it cook for 2 minutes. Garnish with fresh coriander.

This is a recipe that I would call 'old fashioned'. It belongs to Mummy's army years. She used to make it with double the amount of butter and cheese, and no green or red chillies, giving it a very 'propah' feel. The citrusy tang to a white sauce is what caught my fancy and I simply upped the tang and added some chillies to make it more 'homey' and appealing to the Indian palate. White sauce can put off many, since baked dishes are not trendy any more. But it looks appealing if it's left rather thin and the red chillies leave a swirl of orange in the whiteness. It's a nice change eaten with crisp garlic toast.

I came back from Delhi, satiated after yet another meal at the House of Ming. Rehan, now eight years old, was with me. I told him stories of how Tina, Anamika and I used to come to Ming clutching a few crushed hundred-rupee notes. We could afford to order just one dish – either the chilli garlic noodles or the chicken home style. It was quite a triumph to be able to do that.

The Maitre d' had fussed over Rehan and he lapped up the attention. The spicy prawn and lemon broth went down well with both of us; I immediately lapsed into old memories, only slightly distracted by a girl from Jaipur, now married into a rich Punjabi family of Delhi. She squealed her 'helloooo' at me and waved a long distance hug. We watched her settle down with her coiffured friends. 'Oh, no, no, I turned vegetarian twenty-four years ago,' said one of them. 'Oh, you did?' said another lady, fluttering her diamond-studded fingers. 'But we *must* order some "chikkan"!' Out went her imported accent and I muttered to myself in my roadside Hindi, 'Aa gayi na apni asli aukaat par'.

Tofu with Vegetables

500 g tofu cubed
2 tsp oil
4 garlic cloves crushed
1 onion sliced
1 carrot cut into juliennes
1 red pepper sliced
250 g snow peas
1 stick celery sliced
125 g broccoli cut into florets
125 g French beans halved
2 tbsp oyster sauce
1 tbsp tamarind pulp
1 tbsp fish sauce
1 tbsp tomato puree
1 tbsp chilli sauce
1 tbsp light soya sauce
2 tbsp sugar
1 tbsp white vinegar
Pinch of ground star anise
300 ml water
1 tsp cornflour

Heat oil, add garlic and sauté. Add the tofu, stir-fry over gentle heat, remove with a slotted spoon and keep warm. Add onions, carrot, red pepper, snow peas, celery, broccoli, beans and stir-fry for 2–3 minutes till tender-crisp. Add all the remaining ingredients, except the cornflour and water, mixing well to blend. Mix the cornflour with the water and add to the pan along with the tofu. Stir gently till the sauce boils and thickens slightly.

Stir-fried Greens

4 spring onions sliced finely
230 g water chestnuts sliced
500 g spinach
2 tbsp oil
2 garlic cloves crushed
1 tbsp vinegar
1 tbsp light soy sauce
Pepper to taste

Heat oil on high flame. Add garlic, sauté till golden and remove. Add the spring onions, water chestnuts, stir-fry for 2 minutes. Add the spinach. Add vinegar, soy sauce, pepper and cook for a minute. Add the fried garlic. Use a slotted spoon to drain off any excess liquid and serve immediately. This dish should be cooked just 5 minutes before serving.

The Perennial Stir-fry

6 fresh red chillies sliced fine diagonally
6 tbsp white vinegar
6 cloves garlic crushed
1 onion sliced
90 g cauliflower
90 g broccoli
1 red pepper sliced
120 g baby corn
2 carrots
90 g mushroom
4 spring onions diagonally sliced
2 tsp brown sugar
2 tbsp light soy sauce

Combine chillies with vinegar to serve as a dipping sauce. Heat oil, add all the vegetables at once. Stir-fry for 4 minutes, till vegetables are done but crisp. Stir in the sugar, soy sauce and toss well. Serve with dipping sauce. Bean sprouts and Chinese cabbage can also be added to this recipe, or can be made as a separate dish based on the same style.

I tried to draw Rehan's attention away from the loud women by saying, 'I've come here very often with both your sisters. Sakshi didi loves the prawns here.'

'You remember when we went to eat Gujju food and she was so horrified that it was pure vegetarian?' Rehan said, his memory of eating Gujarati food at a small eatery in Jaipur coming back to him. 'Yes, I love their meethi dal.' I screwed up my nose and said, 'No, it is not even authentic Gujju food. We took you to this other place in Mount Abu, when you were just four. *That* was a total feast.'

'Chalo, Kapur friends, chalo,' invited Kailash, the cheerful owner of Arbuda, a multi-speciality food joint in Mt Abu. One look at the crowd buzzing inside made you want to take a step backward, but the smiling face of the host-cum-owner kept you rooted to the spot. A cacophony of sounds and smells hit you: the mingling and merging of loud human voices, the clanging of steel dishes, the waiters deftly weaving their way between tables, the aroma of fried, bulbous bhaturas vying for attention with crisp, neatly folded dosas. The master of ceremonies, Kailash, was the loudest, as he manoeuvred the guests to their tables. 'Aao, Amisha Patel, aao.' I twirled around expecting to see the Gujju diva but found a visibly flattered Amisha ben from Ahmedabad being seated at her table!

Arbuda has been around on the food scene since 1957, and Kailash appears to draw his life force from the customers who return repeatedly to eat at the restaurant. On weekends, it normally has a two-hour waiting period and fifty per cent of the clients are permanent visitors, mostly from Bhavnagar, Ahmedabad and Palanpur. Kailash and his food savvy wife, who supervises the kitchen, make a winning meal plan.

The Gujju thali was sumptuous, with the typical dhokla served with a hot and sweet chutney, the celebrated khatti-meethi dal, lauki ki subzi, gobi, aloo rasse wala, aam ras, puri and a unique mix of bundi and bhujiya. The food was simple but tasty, and sat heavy on the stomach only because you tended to ate like it was your first meal in days. It was certainly very light on the wallet – the entire spread came for just Rs 50. Fast was the keyword here: in the blink of an eye, your order appeared, and before you knew it, the waiter was grinning at you, ready to serve another helping from the traditional 'chaar khane waala' serving dishes. Whenever I crossed the restaurant during my three-day stay, I found Kailash at the entrance and people waiting to be seated!

Mount Abu, for most people, is synonymous with the stunning, intricately carved Dilwara temples, and entwined with the mythological tale of how the serpent Arbuda descended to rescue Nandi, Lord Shiva's bull, from a deep chasm. Like any other hill station, it has a lake, a market teeming with Softy corners, a Sunset Point and a Honeymoon Point to complete the picture.

One romances with the rocks here. The Aravallis are dressed to kill – the unique rock formations have a magnetic pull, making it mandatory to trek along the mountain trails. The magic of the gigantic rocks, towering over the 1,220 m granite table, is spellbinding. The rocks are igneous and due to the weathering effect of wind and water, large cavities have been formed, giving them fascinating shapes.

An early morning trek along the rocks, a sudden burst of wild flowers amidst thorny cacti, an occasional scrape against prickly bushes, an uphill climb, the noisy chirping of birds, it's the most exhilarating experience. You can look down on creation from atop a majestic rock and feel as if you've conquered the world. Inversely, stand beneath their looming shoulders and look up awestruck at their grandeur taking in the immense power of nature's playfulness.

It's like a virtual reality scene from the *Panchatantra* where you come upon a hermit, swathed in saffron, living in a cave. Yes, it still happens. It's amusing, though, to see a gas stove sitting on the cavern floor, with

gleaming steel utensils arranged in a row on a natural shelf and an ancient rain-fed well nearby.

The aam ras and puri at Arbuda remind me of the Jodhpuri tradition of serving mithai before a meal. It is common to serve meethi bundi mixed with bhujiya right in the beginning, before the main dishes are set out on the table. All over Rajasthan, there are quirky customs that fascinate and apall one simultaneously. The time Preeti and I accompanied Papa to Kota, a local family invited us to a meal, and I was witness to the most ghastly sight while crossing the kitchen. The lady of the house was deftly swiping each roti from the tawa, dunking it whole in a bucket full of ghee, and sending it out with a flourish. I was stunned into speechlessness and Papa couldn't figure out why and how my stomach ache could have taken on such a sudden and painful intensity. To add to the revulsion I felt, the host passed around a sinister-sized serving dish of ghee and insisted that we add at least a ladle full to the dal, vegetables and rice as well. Papa enjoyed himself thoroughly, his Jodhpuri upbringing bursting to take on a fresh identity. That trip came to an unfortunate end with us rushing back to Jaipur upon Didi's frantic call that Ma had been hospitalized with her first heart attack. From a ghee-laden evening, we entered a phase of clear soups, salads and tossed vegetables.

Baingan ka Bharta

2 large brinjals

1 tbsp oil

½ tsp cumin seeds

300 g onion chopped

250 g tomato

3/4 tsp red chilli powder

5–6 green chillies chopped

Fresh coriander chopped

Salt to taste

Roast each brinjal on the gas till the skin starts peeling off and gives out, what I call, a purple haze, heady when inhaled. Mash the roasted brinjals into a pulp. Heat oil, add cumin seeds. Add onions and sweat them till tender but white. Add tomatoes, salt and sauté till the tomatoes blend with the onions. Add red chilli powder and green chillies.

Put in the mashed brinjal and cook for another 10 minutes. Sprinkle fresh coriander before serving.

This is one of the most underrated dishes in Indian vegetarian cuisine, but one of my favourites – I have always sided with the underdog. It's important to capture the aroma of the roasted brinjals. Eating bharta with plain rice is a great way to enjoy the dish. Aman loves it, which is rather unlike him, since 'liking' veggies is not 'cool'. 'Its 'coz it gets disguised under all the onions and tomatoes, catch me eating baingan any other way,' he says.

For a quick breakfast, CB stirs up loads of crushed garlic, sliced brinjal, potatoes and onions, quartered tomatoes, whole slit green chillies, and a generous helping of red chillies – it's one of the tastiest dishes, spicy, hot and crunchy. Had with bread and washed down with tea in a steel glass, it is one of Resham's favourite breakfasts. It helps her escape the egg and toast, which she has never liked. As a toddler, she used to sit on the floor mats in the kitchen with all the helpers and maids and have her breakfast with them. Mummy says Bunny did the same as a child.

Khatti Arbi

20 medium arbi
2–3 tbsp lemon juice
2 tbsp oil
1 tbsp urad dal
12 flakes garlic chopped
1 tsp mustard seeds
1 tsp cumin seeds
6–8 dry red chillies
15–20 curry leaves
220 g onion chopped
200 ml tomato puree
6–8 tbsp tamarind pulp
2 tsp coriander powder
1 tsp turmeric
2 tsp red chilli powder
2 tbsp jaggery
Salt to taste

Boil arbi; add lemon juice while boiling. Peel, quarter lengthwise and leave them submerged in water. Soak jaggery in 4 tablespoons of water. Heat oil, add urad dal, garlic, mustard seeds, cumin, whole dry red chillies, curry leaves and stir. Add onions and sauté till golden. Add tomato puree, tamarind pulp, red chilli, turmeric, coriander and stir-fry till the oil separates. Add salt and 3 cups water, boil. Reduce heat, add arbi and jaggery and boil again. The gravy should reach a sauce-like consistency.

The usual lazy Sunday morning turned into a day of tumult, like a good suspense film slowly unfolding into colour and chaos before ascending to a climax. It started with my being accused of near sacrilege: 'Oh, you haven't been to Pushkar all your life? And you were born and brought up in Jaipur?' So we drove off there to be greeted by Madhu jija, an elegant Rajput lady dressed in jeans, playing charming hostess at the Rajasthan Tours campsite ('Come have some poha and jam-toast before you dive into Pushkar'). A camel cart carried our luggage to our tent. There was a Krishna statuette under a tree next to the hot-water boiler. 'You start your day by praying here and all will be well,' a friendly staff member advised.

We walked into the mela ground to see rows of Rajasthani dancers ready to perform. I asked a foreigner if I could sneak a look at the day's programme. She looked me straight in the eye and said, 'Five rupees please.' We burst into loud laughter. Camel carts, decorated like young brides in riotously multi-hued finery, stood lined up on the edge of the ground. The camels flaunted nets and pom poms of vibrant red, fluorescent green, oranges and royal blue, confident that they had our attention. A wrinkled old palmist told me, 'Tata to Tata free calling... you can call me anytime.' The main street was like a microcosm of India, and all that is right and wrong with it – colourful, chaotic, bustling, yet beautiful. The filth and the squalor didn't seem to detract from the merry confusion, there was a rhythmic flow to the entire panorama… it seemed the only way to be.

The road, at one sweeping glance, was a long, serpentine channel teeming with human traffic, cows, camels, dogs, and jeeps with blaring horns belting out 'sri ram, jai ram, jai jai ram' to compete with the loudspeakers. It was a bazaar that never seemed to end, but kept turning the corner into narrower lanes. The entire prism of earthly existence refracted angles of life, such colours that I had never imagined, ever since I moved on from reading E. M. Forster's passages on India.

And that's not all that Pushkar is, for it has a side to it that's far more modern than Jaipur. I took in German bakeries, Israeli cafès, Italian-style coffee, smartly cut pants and jackets, being sold along with bandhini skirts, camel decorations, silver bracelets and carved silver cholis. Pink Floyd was eternalized in a cyber café named Wish You Were Here, nestled in a corner with a halwai selling dal kachori. A palmist sat on the roadside with an array of semi-precious stones, chunky beads and Hanumanji's picture, garlanded and enthroned on a battered old trunk. He was hunchbacked, and had hennaed hair and a forehead smeared with gold acrylic paint, which set off sparks each time he turned his head to face the afternoon sun. 'Pushkar's Nostradamus', he called himself. 'I've learnt to speak English,' he claimed, which explained a Frenchman listening to him intently. 'Take this tabeez, your work will get sorted out,' he said. Will that gold paint be lucky, I wondered.

Amidst this torrential stream of humanity, the saffron garb became increasingly prominent as we neared the world's only Brahma temple. Lost in frenzied worship as they were, the flies, rotting flowers and fruits, the feet landing in puddles of mud and water, the jostling elbows, none of it mattered. My mouth gaped open on seeing a skeletal sadhu hanging on a swing with half his body dangling over. 'This is a regular sight; he's vowed to stand for a year, so this is the way he sleeps,' somebody explained. Strange vows – the feverish will to submit to the almighty power above, while ignoring the reality of daily life, shook me up. It was so real that it translated into the surreal. Religion was blatantly a business here. There was no bhakti; it was the politicking pundits who stood out. Our family pundit took us to the ghats, where you could choose to do a puja worth Rs 501, 1,001, 2,001 or more – there was no limit.

The supposedly holy water was green and murky, and yet people plunged into the lake with the fervent belief that it 'cleansed' them. The chanting of pundits and devotees at the ghats rose and fell like a symphony. Our pundit dipped a saucer into the lake and made us sip the water while the mantras were being chanted. We prayed... yes, the pulse of the place just makes you slip into the spirit. The pundit asked me to wash my husband's feet. 'He's your keeper,' he said. A loud, obviously male, cackle followed.

Legend goes that Brahma's children were killed by the demon Vajra Nabha. Brahma, in turn, struck him with his weapon, a lotus flower. Vajra Nabha died at the impact, and the petals of the lotus fell in three different places. One of them was Pushkar, where a lake sprang into being. Brahma is supposed to have performed sacrifices at this lake on Kartik Purnima (the full moon day of the Kartik month), thus purifying the place. Thousands of people flock to Pushkar to observe the ritual on this day, or on any of the four days preceding it.

We walked into a narrow alley, Pushkar's food street, to devour hot puri-aloo and malpua. The 'best' place for a meal was a dirty dhaba with an old glass cabinet near its entrance, stacked with mounds of malpua and thick jalebi. On the other side sat the proverbial halwai in a stained white, nearly grey-brown dhoti hitched up to his upper thighs, frying hot dal kachoris. He broke them roughly as he placed them in the daunas, poured kadhi and imli chutney over them, and deftly passed on three servings at a time to a waiting boy. The moment we were seated, steel glasses of water appeared. No orders were taken. The plates appeared, and spoons too, but only if you asked for them. The boy-waiter came with a chaar khaane waali dish, welded together to a single steel handle, to serve us rasse ke aloo. Hot puris were placed in mounds on the table and you could ask for chilli pickle and curd. You only became aware of these extras once you saw them on someone else's table. There was a thick layer of oil floating on the aloo but the rassa was arresting – I couldn't stop at two puris. It reminded me of the pundits who came home to eat sharaadh ka khaana and wouldn't stop eating. I burped as loudly as they used to after drinking endless bowls of kheer.

Sakshi couldn't keep her hands off the malpua, though she made sure she wiped the bench and the table with a dozen tissues, repeating, 'If I get a stomach infection, I will never eat veggies in all my life, and that's the price you will pay for making me eat here.' I had already warned her to refrain from any more 'eewuus' with my usual lecture on 'more than half of India lives on this kind of food' and 'you need to remain connected to your roots'.

To digest all the oil that came as a package deal with an aloo-puri-malpua meal, we took a spin over the dunes on a desert mobile. The cattle fair grounds were dotted with more horses than camels, though I was told the numbers had reduced greatly. The tents at the Rajasthan Tours campsite were cosy. A relaxing massage later, I got into a deep discussion about what was wrong with Indian tourism with a Canadian who had been coming to India every year since 1999. Talking about the Incredible India campaign, she said, 'They've got the bone structure, but they need to add the meat to it.' And Rehan piped up, 'Mum, didn't you say Pushkar is a vegetarian place?'

Kala Chana

500 g kabuli chana
3 tea bags
4 brown cardamoms
3 sticks cinnamon
1.5 ltr water
Salt to taste
2 tsp black salt
1 tsp pepper
2 tsp red chilli powder
2 tsp coriander powder
3 tsp chaat masala
2 tsp amchur powder
3 tbsp oil
1 tsp cumin seeds
400 g onion sliced

Garnish:

15 g ginger julienned
3–4 green chillies sliced
1 lemon sliced
1 onion chopped

Soak the chana overnight with 1 tsp cooking soda. Pressure cook chana along with the tea bags, brown cardamoms, cinnamon, salt and water for about 35 minutes. When done, strain the water and reserve. Add black salt, pepper, red chilli powder, coriander, chaat masala, amchur to the chana and leave aside for 15–20 minutes. Heat oil, add cumin seeds, onions and cook till well browned. Add chanas and cook for about 10–15 minutes. Add ginger and green chillies, adjust seasoning. Serve with lemon slices and chopped onion.

Mangodi

250 g yellow moong dal soaked overnight
1 tsp cooking soda
3 ltr buttermilk
Oil for deep-frying

Tadka:

1 tsp ghee
6 dry red chillies
2 tsp cumin seeds
2 sprigs curry leaves
Pinch of asafoetida
½ tsp turmeric
1 tbsp coriander powder
1 tsp red chilli powder
½ tsp garam masala powder
Salt and to taste

Finish:

1 tsp ghee
1 tsp red chilli powder

Drain soaked dal and grind in a mixer with 1 tbsp water. Blend 2 heaped tbsp of the ground dal with the buttermilk and keep aside. Beat the rest of the ground dal mixture for about 10 minutes with a beater until light and fluffy. Add soda to the dal mixture and stir well. Heat oil in a deep kadhai. Shape small balls of the mixture with your hand and deep-fry in oil.

In another large pan, heat ghee and add red chillies, cumin seeds, curry leaves and asafoetida. Make a paste of turmeric, coriander, chilli powder in a little water and add to the pan. Sauté for a minute. Add the buttermilk mixture to the pan and boil on high heat, stirring constantly. A little water can be added to keep the consistency of the gravy thin. Bring it to a boil and add the fried balls. Add a little boiling water on top of the balls. Keep pressing the balls down to keep them submerged in the gravy. Simmer for about 40 minutes. Sprinkle garam masala only when it's ready to be served. Finish it with lal mirch singed in ghee.

Food such as this evokes memories of an age that are locked away in the recesses of my mind. Bunny's grandmother belonged to a landowning family of Bareilly. Her grandfather was a Rai Bahadur when the 1857 uprising broke out. He gave the Britishers refuge in his home, for which he was rewarded with a hundred villages. Over the years, this land was sub-divided among the sons and eventually some of it went to Bunny's grandmother, Savitri. She used to tell us stories of the opulent household she grew up in and how gold and silver coins were stored in gunny bags in the basement of their home during her grandfather's time. They were never counted, only weighed by the 'mann'. The basement had a double door and was guarded by lathdaar, or men with staffs, at all times.

Badi Mummy, as we all called Bunny's grandmother, had two sisters and no brother. She grew up in a strictly vegetarian household and was a cook of some authority. She planned each meal with a fervour that bordered on religiosity. When she cooked, it seemed as if she devoted her soul to the making of that one dish. It was as if it consumed her being, right from the point when she collected all the ingredients, to the peeling, chopping and cooking, till it was served on the table where she sat quietly watching everyone's expressions to judge how tasty the dish had finally turned out to be. While cooking, she didn't leave the kitchen for a second, not trusting the servants to even swirl a ladle through the gravy.

If mangodi was being made, it became an occasion in the house. The dal was ground on a sil batta and not in a mixer. It was spread in a parat and 'phaintoed' by hand till it became light and fluffy. Badi Mummy never added soda to make the balls airy and melt-in-the-mouth. It was simply pre-ordained: they were subjected to precision at every step, left with no option but to be soft and spongy.

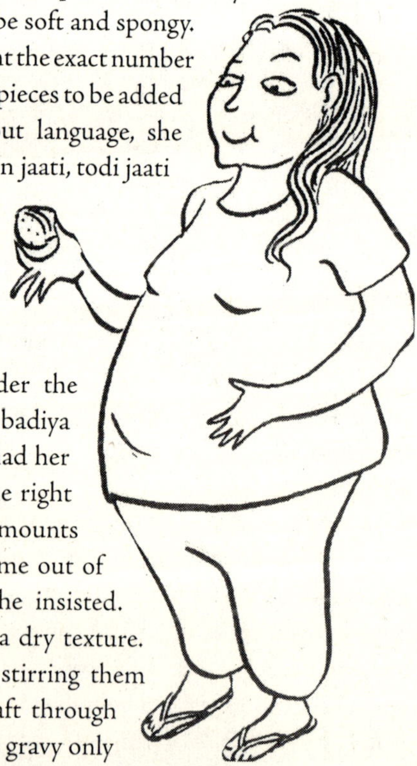

I have seen Badi Mummy count the exact number of cauliflower florets and potato pieces to be added to badiya. Very particular about language, she used to say, 'Badiya banaayi nahin jaati, todi jaati hain.' Never one to buy badiya from the market, she used to make them herself with moong dal, and the paste was piped in little rosettes on chatais, then left to dry on the terrace under the hot sun. Insistent on cooking badiya only in a 'peetal ka pateela', she had her 'fundas' very clear. To cook it the right way, there had to be generous amounts of ghee. 'Your fingers should come out of the bowl covered with ghee,' she insisted. The logic was that badiya have a dry texture. She'd fry them in 'khula' ghee, stirring them deftly and letting the aroma waft through the walls. Curd was added to the gravy only after it was removed from the fire and all the steam had escaped. Garam masala was added right before serving, the lid shut firmly the second it was sprinkled, to capture the flavour 'properly'. Her cooking had all the drama and intensity of a well-rehearsed stage play.

Badiya with Potatoes, Cauliflower and Peas

- 100 g moong dal badiya
- ¼ cup oil
- 2 medium potatoes cut in cubes
- 10 cauliflower florets
- 100 g peas
- 10–15 sengri
- 1 cup beaten curd
- 2 tbsp coriander powder
- 1 tsp red chilli powder
- ½ tsp turmeric
- 1 tsp cumin seeds
- Pinch of asafoetida
- Salt to taste
- Garam masala and coriander for garnish

Shallow-fry badiya till light brown in hot oil, stirring constantly to prevent them from turning dark and losing their flavour. Remove from oil and keep aside. Shallow-fry potatoes and cauliflower separately. Heat oil in another saucepan, add asafoetida, cumin seeds. Make a paste of coriander, turmeric, salt, red chilli with a little water, and add it to the pan. Cook till the oil separates. Add the sautéed vegetables, peas, sengri and cook for a couple of minutes. Add enough hot water to make a curry. Cover and cook till the vegetables are cooked through. Add the badiya. Remove from fire, stir in the curd and simmer for 3–4 minutes. Sprinkle garam masala and fresh coriander just before serving.

When I was expecting Sakshi, Badi Mummy kept up my supply of besan laddoos throughout. The morning sickness rarely left me in those nine months, and it would go only when I ate something sweet. At the end of it, I was twenty-five kilos heavier. I was made to walk and a walnut rolled alongside to prove the similarity in our wobbling passage across the hall. This was also filmed to be preserved for posterity. An epoch ended in our family when Badi Mummy passed away in 1992. The mangodi and badiyan are no longer made with the same devotion and delicacy. Everything is mechanical and matter of fact – like life itself, in patches.

8

The Taste of Home

There have been evenings when Bunny dragged me to a party saying, 'It doesn't look nice if you don't go,' or 'Our host is an important bureaucrat,' or simply, 'I hate going alone, I miss you.' These are no-win situations, which can be very frustrating. Coming back from many such reluctantly attended parties, from which I have run away without eating dinner, I often find myself shuffling around the fridge looking for leftover rajma chawal. And then there are the rare evenings when Bunny turns benevolent and surrenders with, 'Okay, you look tired, stay home and I'll go for the party.' This is *the* actual party for me. There's nothing like being alone in my room with a bowl of hot food and silence – to have the whole bed to myself and the luxury of sharing it only with my laptop.

I was thinking of doing just that, one such evening, when Sakshi walked in, biting into a slice of bread from which I could see jam oozing. It was a cue for me to launch into, 'If you think you can keep eating so much white bread and get away with it, you're mistaken. I'll beat you up next time...' while I grumbled to myself, 'There goes my quiet-time-with-my-dal-chawal-bowl.'

'There are some things I want to tell you…'

'Shoot. But let me heat up my dal chawal first, and then we can talk, okay?'

We both trooped down to the kitchen. She was quiet, which was rather strange. She gulped and her eyes filled up. I parked myself on the kitchen island, alert, alarmed.

'Out with it.'

'Remember I told you I can't sustain a relationship? I have trust issues, Mom.'

'As in?'

'I find it difficult to trust people, especially boys.'

I measured her thoughts and said, 'It's your strength, in a way. You'll be living alone in the US, it's best to be sharp and question everyone's motives… you'd be wiser to not trust people easily.'

That was me going off again, being a typical Indian mother, fretting over the usual 'my daughter's going to be living alone in a strange country…'

'You don't get it. I don't want to be in a relationship… I don't want to be attractive to men… I don't want to get intimate with anyone.'

'Why is it so difficult? You see so many couples around you who are happy and content being together.'

'Yes, but I don't want to. There's something I need to tell you. I hid it from you all these years… you remember, I told you how Prem Bahadur felt me all over when we were in our old house. I didn't tell you the whole truth.'

I didn't want to hear it. I numbed out. I couldn't feel a thing.

She sat there, looking at me, gauging my expression; it was a struggle, but I managed to keep calm.

'What happened – tell me,' I finally said.

'He didn't just feel me all over,' she gulped. 'He touched me… inside.'

I remained outwardly calm, trying very hard to keep my voice steady. 'How often, when, how? I was always at home, why didn't you tell me?'

She kept looking at me. Her tears stood stiff on her eyelids, as she willed them not to fall. I willed mine to evaporate.

'It was the year you were expecting Rehan. It happened three or four times, I can't remember clearly now – in the afternoon, when you weren't home for some reason. He told me not to tell anyone or they would hate me. I believed him.'

'We speak about everything under the sky, why didn't you tell me? Haven't I always been frank with you? Haven't I always discussed everything with you? Don't you remember the year you turned ten and I explained all the facts to you? Did you think I'd brush you aside and not believe you? How much did it hurt? And you've been bearing it all these years – nine years? Why didn't you trust me to help you?' The questions came pouring out.

'I didn't think you'd be able to handle it. You were a very strict mother. Remember how you slapped me whenever I didn't study? I was terrified of you. You weren't the mum you are now.'

It sliced me up. Yes, it was true. I wasn't a patient mother. Short-tempered and easily given to flashes of anger, I tolerated no nonsense. It took me years to accept motherhood – it took me years to grow into a mother who looked upon her daughter as her best pal. I've often told Sakshi that if I live with one regret, and one intense wish, it is that I'd like to have her as a baby again, and this time be the mother I should have been from the very first day.

A noose seemed to grip my heart, now tightening, now letting go, and the pain seared through my being.

'It's a very vague memory now, Mum. I can't even recall it clearly. But yes, I didn't want you to face it.'

She sat there, looking tiny, vulnerable and yet, mature.

'You need to realize that you shouldn't carry it within you as a burden. Yes, you've suffered the trauma, but it doesn't make you a lesser person. You are not tainted in any way. We need to look at the positive side – you will have the strength and conviction to handle so many tough situations in life. You'll come out stronger and you know we are always with you, by your side, at every step. I wish I could take the hurt and the pain and your loneliness away… I wish…' I choked up.

'It's not that I didn't trust you to believe me, I just felt you wouldn't be able to handle it… I think that's why I don't bother about losing weight. I don't want to. I am happy being me, very comfortable, and I don't want to be in a relationship. I don't want to appear attractive to men, I don't need men in my life. I am happy being on my own.'

Questions knocked around in my head. How could I let this happen to my own child? I had fought for the rights of so many women who had been victimized, raped, sexually harassed. I wrote about them... and I failed to protect my own.

She laid her head on my shoulder. 'I can't make it disappear, even though I wish I could,' I said. 'But Papa and I are with you... you've always been special and I'll say it again: I wish I could rewind your childhood and make up for all that's lost.'

'Mum, you've more than made up in these past few years; you came back with a bang...'

'Saksh, I don't like small kids. I never wanted to have any kids. I didn't want to have any of you. I saw kids as a threat to my freedom. I don't have the patience to deal with younger kids. The older they get, the easier it is...' Those were the first few years of my married life, when I just did what I was expected to do – I had both the girls and carried on living, bringing them up, taking care of the house. Something was constantly smouldering inside me. I just wanted each day of feeding, sterilizing bottles, ironing baby clothes and making pureed food to be over. It's not that I wasn't happy. I was. But I was in a limbo for many years.

'I guess that's what made me such an awful mother,' I tried to explain. 'I found both of you when you were about eleven, twelve... It was then that I grew to be your friend, and now I can't imagine it any other way.'

She looked at me. 'I'm not surprised. Most women don't ever wake up from the limbo... they walk through life in a sedated state.'

We sat in the kitchen, arms around each other, struggling to be brave for each other. I felt splintered, helpless, angry, and a complete failure.

She spoke again. 'Mom, it's over.'

I shook my head. 'I'll never be able to get over this.'

'You have to. It's all so vague in my mind now.'

'You still want to eat?'

She nodded and we reheated the dal chawal. The whir of the microwave was familiar comfort.

I said, 'Don't confuse being strongly aware of your feminist beliefs with feminism. There's nothing wrong with looking good or being attractive. We don't have to apologize for female vanity. You are a strong girl and nothing can take away your personhood, you know. You need to lose weight for yourself, to feel well, to be healthy. I'm not asking you to lose weight just because you are a girl.'

'I am happy and super-confident the way I am,' came her reply.

I left the argument for the moment and wished that Bunny wasn't away. That night was a long night. I kept trying to get into my little one's mind and heart, wanting to live her pain and erase it from inside her. That night I faced all my failures.

Sakshi remained calm and strong. She spoke about the many, many moments of fear and self-doubt she held inside herself while growing up. 'But now I can hold these boys by their collars and holler them down. No one dares to act smart with me in school.'

I saw the familiar spark in her eyes. The fire. I knew it was true. Aman had told me how she had punched a couple of boys and that no one in school dared to misbehave with her.

The next day, Sakshi and I instinctively veered towards 'nani house'. 'Ma, please make arhar dal ki tahiri. Sakshi and I are coming for lunch,' I told my mother.

Basic living. Simple meals. An uncomplicated life. The smell of ghee snaking up from freshly cooked rice, spiced with salt, turmeric and red chillies. The arhar ki dal sits daintily on the yellowed rice grains, like a sunny side up. Ma can't recall who she learnt this dish from, but it's frequently made in the kitchens of Uttar Pradesh. It's one of those things you can hastily throw into a pressure cooker for a quick, last minute meal. It's a lazy day dish, most apt for the day after a party, which has left you out of sorts and in a not-wanting-to-cook-for-a-month mood.

Arhar Dal Tahiri

2 cups rice soaked for 10 minutes

1¼ cup arhar dal soaked for 40 minutes

3 heaped tbsp ghee

A pinch of asafoetida

1½ tsp cumin seeds

1½ tsp turmeric

2 tsp red chilli powder

Salt to taste

Heat ghee, add asafoetida, cumin and let it crackle. Add turmeric, salt and red chilli with a little hot water and let it cook till the fat separates. Drain the rice and dal and add to the masala. Add 5½ cups water. Ideally let it cook in a wide-bottomed, deep pan, till the rice and dal are cooked through. The tahiri should be 'khilwa', each grain of rice visible. Serve it with plain curd, mango pickle and papad.

Any recipe using arhar ki dal has to have an extra dollop of ghee. Its dryness has to be countered, like a sharp-tongued lady has to be mollified with smooth talking. I have grown up listening to my father saying, 'A katori of dal should have an equally thick layer of ghee on top.' Horrifying thought, but I can never forget Dadi spooning ghee into dal that had just been taken off the fire. No early morning cooking for her. Everything had to be fresh and made-just-then. There was an ideology at work here. The timing was as crucial as the peetal ki dekchi in which the dal *had* to be cooked. Ma still makes rice just fifteen minutes before she sets out lunch. Otherwise, it doesn't smell or taste as good. She has a fetish for freshness. I could never fathom, even as a child, why she had to get up at 5 a.m. to fill fresh water for cooking and drinking. She still does it at the age of seventy-six. 'Stored water is stale,' she says, screwing up her nose. Nothing can convince her that the water travelling through rusted pipelines from the Ramgarh Lake, where it stagnates, cannot be called fresh or 'pure'.

That day, Ma sensed something was the matter, since we didn't normally land up at lunchtime. She asked, 'Kya hua aaj, din mein kaise man kar gaya aane ka, kaam chod ke?' Sakshi took charge. 'Arre Nani, Mum is getting old and sentimental. She is just too stressed out, so I pulled her out of her blessed red office chair and dragged her here.'

Ma knew I would open up if I wanted to. But I decided I didn't want to make her suffer as well. A lot was left unspoken. She bustled around, getting the salad ready to eat with the tahiri. 'Sakshi, fridge se tamatar lekar ao.'

'Eeuww, Nani, I will not touch tomatoes, and you still haven't learnt to pronounce it right, have you? It's not T for tabla, it's T for table.'

Ma grinned and Papa piped up, laughing, 'She still says bhatura with a soft T.'

Ma defended herself, saying, 'I can't change what I learnt as a child. The Spanish influence in the Philippines is too strong to throw away so easily. You can't imagine the times I have seen when I was a child. We grew up in the middle of the war and went through weeks when we didn't know if we'd live to see the next day...'

Sakshi never tires of listening to Ma's childhood stories. She sat her down. 'Tell me again... just the way you always have, like a storyteller.'

Ma was sensitive to the underlying mood, realizing that both of us wanted to turn away from something. She began:

> My father Dayaram Vaswani moved from Hyderabad in Sindh, to Philippines, in the early 1920s, with his wife Kishni and eldest son, Tikam. Three daughters and two sons followed in quick succession while he worked hard to set up his general merchandise shop and an ice cream parlour in Davao City. I was the second daughter, and childhood for me meant school with birthday parties where cakes and ice creams were served and also, a frail mother who fell ill frequently. I was eight years old when the Japanese attacked our city in 1941 and razed it to the ground in just one day of continuous bombardment.
>
> Tikam went out to survey the damage, dressed in the khaki uniform of boy scouts. He came back with stories of the destruction he saw all around him on the streets, not realizing that Japanese soldiers were following him back to our house. They barged in, caught him by the neck, and declared he was a spy. They were about to behead him before our eyes, when one of Dada's influential Japanese friends almost banged the door down and saved him. Tikam was only thirteen then.
>
> That didn't stop Dada and his friends from taking rounds of the city during curfew hours. One night, they were caught and kept in jail. His connections helped him to get out once again. We were never worried when members of the family didn't return for a night or two. No one was afraid,

no one cried. War makes you live life in a different spirit. Everyone was alert. Our influential Japanese friends sent us a supply of rice, sugar, potatoes and onions. We lived on cheeni and roti for a few months.

The Japanese ruled over Philippines for the next five years and every aspect of our life changed, to suit their way of living. It was compulsory for all schools to teach Japanese. Our hair had to be cut with a fringe. Gymnastics was made compulsory. We even had a new currency, the Filipino Yen, which was used till the ceasefire in August 1946.

The US attacked the Philippines in 1945. We had received news of the impending bombardment. We had been trained to protect ourselves during a bombing, we were taught how to wear our headgear, to lie down flat on our tummies and crawl. We slept in our shop for two months, while the bombing continued relentlessly. One day, the shop was engulfed by a fire. We had to run out... we kept running till my father realized he hadn't brought any money with him, and he ran back to get it. We continued walking late into the evening till we couldn't see where we were going in the dark.

Davao city had fires raging everywhere... all the buildings were burnt, save for churches and schools. We found some abandoned Filipino huts, where we took shelter. Machine gun fire kept coming at us sporadically. We were told later that our house had escaped being burnt down. My father was the chairman of the Indian National League in the Philippines and was in constant touch with Subhash Chandra Bose. Because of his position, he was given a supply of rice and flour, which he generously shared with the rest of the Indians, who looked up to him as the senior-most in the community.

In 1945, when the news came that the Americans were about to attack, the Japanese gave us a truck to escape in. We were not scared because of our connections with the Indian National League and Bose. My father made us pack three or four trunks of essential clothes and utensils to load on to the truck and we moved to our farm outside the city.

We went back to farming and raising poultry for survival. Some of the other Indians who were with us took to selling food, like pakodas, in the nearby market, on a barter system, since money had no value. There was no school and we all did our chores – I had to fetch water from the spring, Tikam worked with my father in the fields, Gurdas managed the poultry.

We worked barefoot since, by now, all our shoes had worn out and there was no way we could buy any. Even at the farm, we had air raid shelters where we rushed to hide whenever we heard the warning buzz of an approaching airplane.

After about a year, Japanese soldiers arrived while we were having lunch and warned us about an American attack. We were asked to evacuate the farm by evening. We buried most of our belongings and my mother made us wear as many layers of clothes as we could. Gurdas tied as many chickens as he could by their feet to a long pole. Tikam tied bundles of rice and flour to two ends of a long pole and slung it across his shoulders. We walked away from the farm, barefoot, into the interior, to escape from being bombed.

We settled down in some abandoned huts with a group of Indians. One day, we heard a plane, and my father shouted at the men who were cooking rice for lunch to douse the fire. But they didn't heed his warning. Seeing the smoke rising out of our huts, the Americans dropped their bombs and the huts were destroyed. My father was angry and decided to break away from the rest of the Indians.

Since Sundays were off-days for bombing, food was cooked that day. In a couple of days, it would start smelling and we used to clamp our noses and push it down our throats to fill our stomachs. My father took to eating only once a week to make the food last longer for the rest of us. There were times when bullets whizzed past Baby's neck, head or shoulders while she was cooking. We had to forage for sacks of rice around the burnt down huts. Stumbling upon dead bodies of soldiers was not uncommon. A couple of times, a Japanese soldier put a bayonet to my chest and asked me, 'Hindu or Filipino?' I said 'Hindu' and was left free.

My father became very weak and skeletal. He had an infected thumb and the infection spread to his blood. The American soldiers came after the ceasefire and took him to the hospital in the city. We could see only American soldiers milling all around the place. We all went back to Davao City and Tikam was supposed to get my father back home on the same day. Amma had cooked chicken to celebrate the fact that life was coming back to normal once more. But Tikam came home alone from the hospital. It was 14 August 1945.

Tikam took my mother in a jeep for my father's funeral. Only one child was allowed to accompany them, so I went, and the others stayed back. We had to bury my father since we didn't have the money to pay for his cremation.

Tikam was very popular in Davao and had many friends. He arranged for us to go back to school and no fee was charged from us. We stayed in Davao for a year till my uncle called us to Manila in August 1946. Uncle Hemant Das had a huge house and most of his businesses had survived the war. He had a number of Filipinos working for him. I loved the soupy one-pot meals they used to make for themselves, fish in fish broth with rice or noodles, vegetables in vegetable stock with rice or noodles. Soup and rice, with bamboo shoots and pichai or fish sauce, formed the major part of their diet. Most of their food was light and flavourful and was boiled or steamed to retain the basic flavours. We kids used to exchange our Indian food with them.

I took your mum to Philippines when she was four years old and she insisted on eating only chicken noodle soup and whole fried fish with the head and tail intact, every night, for all the months we were there!

Ma moved to Jodhpur, to her maternal uncle's home, after Partition, where she remembers attending school set up by a philanthropic Sindhi. 'Our classes took place on the steps of a mandir since he had no other place to teach us. Jodhpur winters were bitterly cold and Amma always had a hot bowl of sai bhaji and freshly steamed rice waiting for us when we came home.'

I always grumble that Ma has completely forgotten how to cook Sindhi food, and she defends herself by saying, 'I was asked never to cook Sindhi food at home. Ours was a love marriage and I had to take certain steps to be accepted by Behna.'

Sakshi, as usual, spluttered with anger. 'How could you give in, Nani?'

Ma smiled, 'In those days, we all did. And see, it paid off. Behna loved me the most. In the end, I was the most respected daughter-in-law.'

We polished off heaped plates of tahiri with curd and pickle. From habit, I lay down on my favourite couch in the living room for a snooze, listening to Ma and Sakshi talking softly in the next room.

Hyderabadi Biryani

4½ cups rice
1 kg mutton
1 tsp raw papaya skin paste
1 pod garlic ground
Ginger twice the quantity of garlic, ground
300 g curd
1 tsp red chilli powder
500 g onions sliced
10 cloves
12 cardamoms
4 sticks cinnamon
1 tsp shahi jeera
4–6 blades javitri
8 green chillies sliced
I bunch mint chopped
1 bunch coriander chopped
Juice of 4 lemons
Salt to taste
Generous pinch of saffron

Apply ginger, garlic and papaya skin paste to the meat. Add salt, red chilli powder to the curd, whisk well. Shallow-fry the onions till well browned, reserve half a cup, and add the rest to the curd, along with the whole garam masala pounded (reserving the javitri and 6 cardamoms). Add half of the green chillies, mint and coriander to this mixture and marinate the meat. Leave this overnight in the fridge or for at least 4–6 hours.

Soak saffron in hot milk. Wash and soak rice for half an hour. Bring sufficient water to a boil, add salt, pounded green cardamom and javitri. Drain the rice and add to boiling water. Remove from heat after 2 minutes and drain.

Heat ghee in a dekchi, add the marinated meat, cover and let it cook on slow fire till tender. Take a deep dish and arrange a layer of rice in it. Top it with a few pieces of the cooked meat. Spoon in some thickened gravy as well. Sprinkle some green chillies, chopped mint and coriander and sprinkle some of the soaked saffron. Add another layer of rice and repeat the process, sealing the meat under a final layer of rice topped with all the garnishes. Seal the dish with aluminium foil, cover with the lid tightly, or use chapatti dough to seal the rim, and place it in a preheated oven for about 20 minutes. Serve with mint and garlic raita or kachumbar salad.

Tanay and Sakshi have loved biryani ever since they were toddlers. Aman picks out all the meat pieces and lines them up on the periphery of his plate. He eats the rice first and then systematically chews on each piece of meat, relishing it – 'I'm making it last longer,' he says. Resham, not being too much of a meat eater, likes to dig into the saffron rice, like Rehan. Rehan's food tastes are refined beyond his age. He was never subjected to baby food beyond the Cerelac period of 6–12 months. I never had the patience to make him pureed foods, khichdi and mashed banana. He was handed a chapatti or a whole banana, which he peeled like a monkey and squished his way through. He was eating mathi and mirchi ka achaar by the time he was three. Chilli chicken, bhujia sandwich, Nani's spicy meat pulao are still his favourites. And vegetable fried rice was one way I tricked him into eating a good amount of veggies as a toddler.

Nothing can be more delightful than carrying a pressure cooker full of vegetable pulao and eating it seated on a beach towel on Bondi Beach in Sydney (with my sister Preeti and her family). The Indian flavours taste heavenly and reassuring after a few days of angrezi khana – especially when you bite into a firm, fiery green chilli with each spoonful, and top it up with green coriander chutney. On that trip, Sakshi was too small to fret over 'how desi' we were – she was only nine or ten and yet to develop her strong views and biting vocabulary. Both the girls ate up the pulao, a sign that they were missing home food. It was quite evident that Preeti had evolved into a fairly decent cook: each grain of rice was cooked just right and it wasn't a moist mish mash. I had carried a copy of Balbir Singh's *Indian Cookery* as a gift for her – 'Just take this as a broad hint that you need to learn a few things about cooking tasty food.' I said. 'And I'm also making sure we eat palatable food while we are here with you.' She almost threw me out of her house.

There are reams of anecdotes surrounding the creation and evolution of biryani and pulao. Asaf Khan, a respected Mughal noble, is known to have invited Shah Jahan to his palace in Lahore. Food was served ceremoniously in silver and gold dishes by women, and the meal, with its vast repertoire of dishes, including varieties of pulao, lasted for four hours.

The pulao is essentially a Central Asian dish. Its existence has been traced back to the early nineteenth century and is mentioned in the chronicles and travelogues of European scholars as a recipe that combines melted fat, chunks of meat, vegetables, spices and rice. There is also a mention of rice being cooked on a slow fire, after being set in alternate layers with the meat, with red-hot coals placed on the lid. Humayun brought Persian cooks to India. The caliphs of Persia were known for their Epicurean tendencies and used to spend large sums of money on lavish spreads of food prepared with minute attention.

Pulao was considered to be a royal dish in the court cuisine of Persia. With cooks travelling to Baghdad from Turkey, Arabia and Egypt, their typical food traditions were absorbed into the culture, adding to the richness of the cuisine that evolved rapidly. Strangely, rice was imported from India. The Persians were known to be very finicky about the quality of rice – it had to be white as snow and fluffed up, without turning sticky. The pulao was judged by the aromas that wafted from the delicate balance of spices. From Persia, pulao spread to other parts of the world, and became paella in Spain, pilav in Turkey, risotto in Italy, and biryani in India. Culinary osmosis is itself a divine boon, its results fascinating and long lasting. Synthesis and regeneration led to the biryani becoming a classic delicacy in India. Marinating meat before adding it to rice is a Persian practice. Abul Fazl's *Ain-i-Akbari* has recipes that use a mixture of Indian and Persian spices, fragrances and dry fruits, along with saffron, added to curd, which was used for marinating the meat for biryani. Rice as a preparation percolated down to the diet of a rural peasant by the seventeenth century. Khichdi made from millet, or a mixture of rice and dal, became common in ordinary households.

Yakhni Pulao

400 g mutton
1¼ tsp salt
500 ml water
20 g onion chopped
2 bay leaves
12 black peppercorns

Pulao:

300 g rice
120 g onion
40 g ginger
8 cloves garlic chopped
6 green cardamoms crushed
2 blades mace
1 tsp poppy seed
2 sticks cinnamon
12 black peppercorns
5 cloves
1 tsp cumin seed
120 g curd
1 tsp red chilli powder
¾ tsp garam masala
20 almonds
Fresh coriander and mint leaves
3 green chillies chopped
1 tsp salt
4 tbsp ghee

Clean and wash mutton, add salt, water, onion, bay leaves and peppercorns. Pressure cook for 15 minutes or cook on slow fire for an hour till the meat is three-quarters cooked. Separate the meat from the stock or yakhni.

Heat ghee, brown the boiled mutton and keep aside. Add onion, ginger, garlic and green cardamoms. Add ground mace, poppy seeds, cinnamon, peppercorns, cloves, and rice and fry for 5 minutes. Add meat, cumin, curd, chilli powder, garam masala and the stock. Pressure cook for 15 minutes or cook on medium heat in a dekchi till half the water dries up, reduce to low heat and cook till done all through. Garnish with almonds, green chilli, coriander, mint. Serve the pulao with a simple raita.

In the good old days of heavy duty eating, mothers used to fry almonds and a fistful of onions to sprinkle over dishes. I suggest roasting the almonds, after giving them a swift rub with olive oil. I have changed the proportions from the original yakhni pulao recipe, increasing the quantities of spices, since everyone at home prefers stronger flavours. It has taken them a while to appreciate subtle flavours. The sensuous suggestiveness of food, the sense of mystery and revelation, run much deeper than we can fathom.

Korma Pulao

Stock:

300 g mutton bones

1 tsp salt

400 or 550 ml water

Pressure cook mutton bones with salt and water for half an hour or cook on slow fire with 550 ml water for 1½ hours. Strain and keep aside.

Korma:

400 g mutton
8 cloves garlic chopped
60 g onion sliced
½ tsp red chilli powder
20 g ginger grated
2 tbsp ghee

Marinade for mutton:

1 tbsp coriander seeds
12 almonds
2 blades mace
1 stick cinnamon
5 cloves
2 brown cardamom
1 tsp poppy seeds
120 g curd
65 g onion chopped
12 cloves garlic chopped
½ tsp black cumin seeds
1 tsp red chilli powder
1½ tsp salt

Wash and clean mutton, pat dry. To prepare the marinade, grind coriander seeds, almonds, mace, cinnamon, cloves, brown cardamoms and poppy seeds. Mix with curd, salt, onions, garlic, cumin seeds, red chilli powder. Add mutton and leave for 2 hours.

Heat ghee, add onions, garlic and cook till golden brown. Remove from heat, add the marinated mutton and ginger. Cook for about 40 minutes or till it is cooked through. Alternatively, it can be pressure cooked for about 15–20 minutes, but korma cooked on slow fire is the best.

Rice:

250 g basmati rice
1 tbsp ghee
½ tsp black cumin seeds
1 stick cinnamon
12 black peppercorns
3 bay leaves
8 cloves
6 green cardamoms
400 or 550 ml stock

Soak rice in 400 ml water for half an hour and discard the water. Heat ghee, add cumin seeds, whole garam masalas and rice, and sauté for about 5 minutes. Add 400 ml stock and pressure cook. Alternatively, add 550 ml stock and let it cook on slow fire till done.

Korma Pulao:

Fragrant cooked rice
Cooked korma
½ tsp saffron
1 tsp kewra essence

Mix the cooked rice and the korma, sprinkle saffron, kewra over it. Remove the pan from fire, keep it on hot ashes and place live charcoal on the lid for 15 minutes. Alternatively, place in an oven, covered tightly in foil for 30 minutes at 180°C. Before serving, garnish with almonds, fresh coriander and sliced green chillies. Serve with a mildly flavoured raita.

Food from various regions of India tend to creep into our kitchens and take root. In Bengal, rice is the staple in a poor man's home, while in Rajasthan, it is jowar or bajra roti with an onion and a green chilli. Potatoes and dal get included in the meal if the harvest has been good. Ayurveda has also influenced food habits from times immemorial.

Rice can be made into a cooling dish, or a hot spicy dish, according to the climate and the time of year.

Shahjehani Pulao

Stock:

Bones from the mutton used in pulao
60 g onion chopped
8 cloves
16 black peppercorns
1 stick cinnamon
1 blade mace
Small piece of nutmeg
1½ tsp salt
750 ml water

Wash bones and add onion, cloves, peppercorns, cinnamon, nutmeg, mace, salt and water. Pressure cook for 25–30 minutes.

Pulao:

750 g deboned mutton
400 g rice
Prepared stock
200 ml curd whisked
200 ml cream whisked
½ tsp salt
1 tsp red chilli powder
Half a nutmeg grated
2 blades mace
150 g onion chopped
20 g ginger paste
20 g garlic paste
2+1 tbsp ghee

For sprinkling over:

1 tsp red chilli powder
1 tsp garam masala
1 tsp black cumin seeds

Garnish:

Green chillies, fresh coriander, almonds, raisins

Heat ghee, add onions and cook till they are golden brown. Remove and keep aside. Add mutton pieces and sear till juices dry up. Mix the browned onions, salt, red chilli powder, nutmeg, mace and cook for another 10 minutes, adding a little water at intervals. Add ginger and garlic paste and continue cooking the same way till the ghee surfaces. Add 150 ml water and pressure cook for 15 minutes.

Soak rice in 600 ml water for half an hour, strain and discard the water. In a heavy-bottomed dekchi, fry the rice in 1 tbsp ghee for 2–3 minutes, add 750 ml stock. Bring to a boil, then leave it covered on slow fire till the rice cooks through.

For finishing, alternate layers of rice, cream, meat and curd respectively. Sprinkle each layer with red chilli powder, garam masala, black cumin seeds before covering it with the next one. Finish with a layer of rice. Cover the dish, place live charcoal pieces and place it on hot ashes for 15 minutes. Alternatively, place in an oven, covered tightly in foil, for 30 minutes at 180°C. Garnish with chilli, almonds, raisins, fresh coriander.

Balbir Singh suggests unmoulding the dish before serving. But I feel nervous about this and simply place the dish straight on the table, even if it's a large brass vessel. Balbir Singh's recipes have withstood the test of time and experimentation, and have yielded gracefully to slight changes in proportions. This pulao has been one of Tanay's favourite rice dishes for as long as I can remember. On his first visit back from his freshman year at Indiana, the first meal he requested was this pulao.

A few days after 'that' night, Sakshi trooped into my office. Her tread was defiant and I knew something was brewing in her mind. 'Why should I lose weight? I am happy this way,' she said. I sensed she was fighting against reality and was resisting being convinced, so I took a different route.

'Y'know how sad and frustrated I get when I shop for you kids – I can pick up pretty stuff for Resham, but I can't do that for you. I keep searching for something that will fit you and hate even looking at the synthetic rubbish in the plus size stores. It is one of the joys of being the mother of two girls. Why do I have to be deprived of that little thrill of dressing you up?'

Her eyes glimmered with disbelief as I continued the emotional onslaught.

'I have two damn good-looking girls. Resham is conventionally pretty, tall, slim, large eyes and long hair. Do you realize that your eyes, hair, mouth speak their own language... You have a personality that reflects depth and intensity, you carry yourself with a dignity that is very uncommon for a girl of your age. You feel strongly about so many things, you stand up for what you believe in. But the world is not going to make an effort to scratch the surface. They just look at you as "that fat kid" and overlook the rest of you. I don't see them recognizing your beauty, and that makes me feel cheated as a mom. Why should I not be able to flaunt you? I am so proud of you... it's human nature to want to be appreciated.

Why shouldn't you be told you are beautiful? The world is full of clichés and conventions. We can't change that, but we can change ourselves.'

I heard a soft, 'You really think so?'

I knew it was working.

'Yes, looking good is not a crime, Saksh. It doesn't dilute your principles. Tell me, who doesn't like being told, "Hey, you look great today." I am forty-four, with tons of white hair and crow's feet around my eyes. But when I walk into a party in a pretty sari, I know I look good. I can see heads turn, I can feel eyes following my back, and I enjoy every moment. I always tell Bunny when I sense it, and we both laugh about it. So don't tell me that you don't like being told that you are pretty.'

'But I don't want to look good for men, eeuww,' she sneered.

'Babe, we don't look good for men. We look good for ourselves. You think I dress up to go out for other people's sake? Duh!! I do it purely for myself.'

'You are actually making me want to lose weight, Mum.'

'Saksh, all this is peripheral. It's your basic well-being that worries me. You are starting out to live alone in another country – it's miserable being ill all alone and having no one to take care of you. And your self-esteem... I'm not saying it will do a somersault just by your losing weight, but once you start feeling happy about the way you look, it all adds up.'

'I love me,' she said stubbornly.

'Then it's time for some more self-adoration. And you know I am not psyching you into this because you are a girl, I'd do the same for Rehan.'

Her eyes widened. I had struck home.

'Okay, let's do it... give me a diet and I'll show you how much will power I have.' We laughed – out of relief. We had both been grappling for solutions within ourselves.

The diet began and I was back to my usual wicked mother role. 'It's a feast to see you in motion,' I said, watching her run on the treadmill that occupies half my office. 'You can't imagine what it does to my heart – the glee of making you eat all the veggies that you so steadfastly ran away from...'

I fed her every two hours with fruit/bhindi-roti/broccoli with burnt garlic/stir fried veggies/spinach-lettuce salad/egg white/grilled chicken.

'You'd better realize that I am giving you room service and be grateful' became my refrain while entering her room. My grumbling became ritualistic – 'why are your clothes always on the floor?' I asked her every day. Sakshi's reply was as repititive: 'This is my space, shut your eyes if you don't like it.'

And then came the day when Rehan, as if echoing Sakshi's feelings, stuck a blotchily scrawled poster on his room door – 'This is my room, take it or leave it.'

Thai Fried Rice

1 egg beaten

1 tbsp thin coconut milk

120 g chicken breast cubed

2 red or green chillies chopped

1 tbsp green curry paste

2 tbsp fish sauce

600 g cooked rice

120 g French beans cut into 1" length

6–8 spring onions sliced

Heat wok, brush it with a little oil, beat the egg with the coconut milk and swirl in the wok to make a thin omelette. Flip it over, cook it on the other side as well. Allow omelette to cool slightly, roll it up and cut it into thin strips. Heat a little more oil in the wok, add the chicken and cook on a high flame for it to become tender quickly, stirring frequently. Add the chillies, curry paste, fish sauce. Add the beans and cook till they are tender but crisp. Stir in rice and spring onions. Pile into a serving dish, garnish with shredded egg.

When a Thai meal is ready, they say, 'kin khao', which literally translates to 'eat rice'. Every meal revolves around jasmine rice and the Thais are rather particular about the taste, fragrance and whiteness of it. The Asian version of a rice cooker is a highly sophisticated piece of machinery, though I've never used it. A Thai chef is careful not to stir the rice too much while it cooks since that would release the starch from the grains and make them stick together.

Green Rice

500 g rice soaked for an hour
2 tbsp oil
750 ml coconut milk
1 tsp salt
1 bay leaf
2 tbsp fresh coriander chopped
2 tbsp fresh mint chopped
2 green chillies chopped

Heat oil, add rice and stir-fry till it becomes translucent. Add coconut milk, salt, bay leaf. Bring to boil and cook till the liquid is absorbed. Lower heat, cover tightly with a lid and cook for 10 minutes. Remove the bay leaf, stir in coriander, mint, green chillies. Fork through the rice to fluff it up gently and serve hot.

Meal in a Rice Bowl

4 spring onions chopped
4 garlic cloves crushed
1" ginger piece chopped
2 red chillies chopped
½ capsicum sliced
150 g baby aubergines quartered
90 g snow peas, trimmed, blanched
90 g bean sprouts
90 g baby corn sliced lengthwise, blanched
500 g cooked jasmine rice (or normal rice)
2 tbsp light soy sauce
2 tbsp tomato ketchup
2 tbsp oil
Fistful of fresh coriander chopped

Heat the oil, add spring onion, garlic, ginger, chillies. Stir till slightly softened. Add all the vegetables and bean sprouts, stir for about 4–5 minutes. Add rice, lift and stir with two forks, adding soy sauce and tomato ketchup. Serve immediately, garnished with fresh coriander.

Massaman Curried Rice

Curry Paste:

1 tsp coriander seeds
1 tsp cumin seeds
1" cinnamon
1 tsp cloves
1 whole star anise
1 tsp green cardamom
1 tsp white pepper
1 tbsp roasted peanuts
6 spring onions chopped
6 garlic cloves chopped
2" piece lemon grass sliced
4 fresh red chillies chopped
1 tsp oil
Grated rind of 1 lemon
Salt

Grind the spices and peanuts in a spice grinder or a pestle and mortar. Heat oil in a wok, add the spring onion, garlic, chillies and lemon grass and sauté. Grind together with the dry spices. Stir in the lemon rind and salt.

Curry:

250 g tofu cut in 1" cubes

125 g green beans cut into 1" length

250 g cooked rice

6 spring onions chopped

2 tbsp roasted peanuts

1 tbsp lemon juice

1 tbsp oil

Heat oil, sauté the tofu on high heat for 2 minutes. Add the curry paste, salt and beans. Add rice, using two forks to lift and stir over high heat for about 3 minutes. Sprinkle with spring onions, lemon juice, peanuts before serving.

This rice dish literally tickles the tongue with its piquant flavours. It can be made with very little oil and it turns out to be a meal in itself. For a greater variety of vegetables, you can also add celery, red bell pepper, snow peas and shredded cabbage.

Fried Rice in Pineapple Boats

1 large pineapple
4 garlic cloves crushed
2 onions diced
1 celery stick sliced
1 tsp coriander seeds ground
1 tsp cumin powder
175 g mushrooms sliced
250 g cooked rice
3 tbsp light soy sauce
½ tsp sugar
30 g cashew nuts
Salt
Spring onion and coriander for garnish

Halve the pineapple lengthways and cut out the flesh to make 2 boat shaped shells. Cut the flesh into cubes and use 125 g with this recipe. Heat oil in wok, cook garlic, onions, celery, over high heat for 2 minutes, stir in coriander, cumin and mushrooms. Add pineapple cubes and cooked rice. Stir in soy sauce, sugar, salt and cashew nuts. Using two forks, lift and stir the rice for about 4 minutes. Spoon it into the pineapple boats, garnish with spring onion, fresh coriander.

One day, Sakshi tried hard to put on an 'I am a gourmet' tone and said, 'I hated the scrambled egg you made for my dinner.'

'But I made it the same way, with mushrooms, capsicum, onions, carrots and broccoli.'

'I don't know when you'll stop trying your gourmet recipes on me. Can I have simple ande ki bhurji, minus the tomatoes?'

'It is a simple scrambled egg, Sakshi.'

'I am your best critic, Mom – you'll have to give that to me.'

'Huh, no, Aman is.'

That was enough. Her hands sliced through the air and she began spluttering, 'That, that... but he is a boy... yuck, Mom, how can you stoop so low?'

'He understands flavours. Last night, he loved what I did to the plain boiled rice for dinner.'

'Huh, *what* did you do that elevated a simple dish like rice to such a status?'

'I burnt garlic in olive oil and tossed the rice in it.'

'So that makes you a fine cook and him your best critic? Get a life, Mom!'

The argument would never end. We bumbled our way through senseless conversation, which was a way to unwind for both of us.

Each time Sakshi and Resham have gone for summer courses over the past few years, I have had to deal with their absence by living in 'brave denial' as they claim. At these times, I also hold Rehan close, since he misses them even more. Loneliness and comfort food make a good pair – all warm and squishy, heaped on a plate, which somehow conveys that the girls will be back soon and things will be merry again. I get this kind of reassurance from eating dal chawal, or a bowl of piping hot moong dal khichdi with coriander chutney and a squirt of lemon. Rice has a quality that comes from the warm steam rising from its flaky grains, it makes me feel cured, or well, less stressed. Every other day, I reach for a bowl of freshly boiled rice just half an hour before lunch and sprinkle a generous amount of bhujiya on it. The softness of the grain against the crisp, spicy crunch of bhujiya is as satisfying as sticking your neck out of the window in a speeding car.

Tamarind Rice

400 g cooked rice	Pinch of asafoetida
200 ml water	1 tsp mustard seeds
50 g tamarind	12 black peppercorns
20 g dry red chilli deseeded	1 tsp turmeric
50 g chana dal	1 green chilli
50 g urad dal	1" piece of ginger, julienned
150 ml oil	2 sprigs curry leaves

Soak tamarind in 200 ml water, extract the pulp. Roast chana dal, urad dal, red chillies, separately and grind to a coarse powder. Heat oil, add asafoetida, mustard seeds, peppercorns, turmeric, green chilli, ginger, curry leaves, and sauté for 1 minute. Add tamarind extract, powdered dals, salt. Cook till the water dries up. Add to the rice, mix well and serve.

Since it was the year that Sakshi was leaving for college, she wanted to go to Deogarh with all our friends and their kids. So, thirteen of us piled into a bus and made our way to Deogarh. I had crossed the same wind-eroded rock faces and boulders along the winding road thrice before, yet each time

I visit Deogarh, the place reinvents itself. Each time the plot unfolds, there is a new story being told. It's always like driving into the unknown.

The bus farted, roared, revved, spluttered and then sank into a slow trundling motion. The drive from Beawar turned green and gradually the bullock cart pace ceased to matter. We emerged with cramped, staccato steps to be greeted by Shatrunjay beating on the nagada to welcome us. The tone of the visit was set – it was a dramatic entry to say the least.

We traversed narrow village lanes to reach Deogarh Mahal. In the quaint bazaar, sacks of dried coconuts and red chillies were stacked next to a shop with tailors stitching sequined fabric, which in turn was nestled alongside a silver antique shop run by two girls with kohl-lined, almond-shaped eyes. These young girls had charmed me into buying silver bracelets at double the price on my first visit. Bright red, heavily embroidered zari saris fluttered from the next shop, reflecting the rising aspirations of the village in their glitter. Antique locks and ghungrus in all sizes hung casually on a faded red velvet hard board, which spoke of years gone by. The chiming of temple bells blended with the whiff of spices that wafted across. To add to this colourful chaos was a traffic jam, which, for once, left me amused.

A robust lunch and a deep snooze later, we climbed back into Bhacheedo, the official Deogarh four-wheel truck, to drive through the rising and plunging rocky terrain. Our first stop was to admire the vintage car collection, which the family holds in much affection. 'They are like wives, they take time to start and are expensive... this Jaguar was actually modelled on the female anatomy,' Shatrunjay said, pointing towards the car.

He drove us into the valley and then careened up the hill. Everyone gasped for breath. What was Shatrunjay doing? Was he crazy driving the one-tonne truck up the hill? He stopped just as we reached the peak – we were literally on the edge. Everyone stepped out gingerly, relieved that they were alive, while I laughed with sheer glee at their faces. 'How are we going *down* the hill?' was the question on everyone's lips, as they took in the vastness of the valley at their feet. 'The same way we came up,' was Shatrunjay's casual answer. The drive to Kotra, a small village near Deogarh, was steadily uphill. The road left off somewhere and we were ducking under tree branches and sidling past mud boundary walls of rain-washed fields. The thrill factor was going up in degrees with the ascent over sheets of rock, with sharp turns and dangerous inclines. The village kids made friends with Resham and Sakshi. Resham clicked their pictures and called out to them, 'Bahut achhi picture aayi hai.' One of them replied, 'Oh my God!' Resham couldn't believe she had heard them exclaim in English, and her response, 'Oh, shit!' was cheerfully echoed by them. We had a bevy of half naked children hanging on to the bumper of the open truck and the retinue followed us to the hilltop effortlessly.

Shatrunjay, a natural storyteller, held forth. Miles of pastoral land, with the far off Aravalli mountains, floated under the setting sun in a haze of translucent clouds. 'Though it is undocumented, there is enough evidence that Gorakhnath and Machchendranath spent some part of their life around this village,' he said. Gorakhnath is supposed to be the founder of hathayoga and legend has it that he invented the Devanagari script. He is believed to be the founder of the Nath Sampradaya, which was created to spread the message of yoga and meditation in the world. The cult of the Nath Pant is known to have existed in this area and they were called 'kan parhas' – its practitioners had their ears pierced and they wore large earrings. There is a sense of mystery around each legend that Shatrunjay narrates, and there are many such mysteries that I discover each time I go to Deogarh... it is inexplicable, but I feel a force here that is almost surreal.

We were driven to a lakeside for pakora and chai. The countryside whipped up an appetite, which was satiated at dinner with laal maas, chicken soyeta and bharwan baingan, topped with makkai jajariya for dessert, steeped in the grainy sweetness of broken corn and the tanginess of jaggery and raisins.

Our group of varying ages hit common ground on a straight forward walk to the Seengh Sagar Fort, instead of an arduous trek to the Saand Mata temple, which had also been deliberated. The early morning sounds blended with the teasing smell of rain, while peacocks strutted around, livening up the grey cloud cover against the ancient mountains. We detoured off the road into the rocky terrain. I lay down on a steep cliff, face to the sky, and felt an invisible hand guiding the orchestra as the wind played its tune, with the birds picking up the cue. Silence stepped in quietly to lull me into a wakeful sleep.

Sakshi took me by surprise by asking for last night's lal maas with rice for breakfast. 'Are you feeling all right?' I asked, aghast. 'Why would anyone want to have rice first thing in the morning?'

'Will you come and cook for me there? Will I have the luxury of having freshly boiled rice with meat ka rassa produced before me on demand like this?' she shot back. I figured this was her way of dealing with a lot of baggage she wanted to leave behind. I left my matar ki puri and aloo bhaji breakfast and waited patiently for the rice to boil. The chef at Deogarh would never have entertained such a strange request before.

Our lunch had been planned at the lakeside in Kalaseriya. A parachute had been stretched across and pegged over poles to create a shaded area. The mudhas and manjis, covered with colourful checked cloth, flanking a well-equipped bar, were a welcome sight. We were served the most succulent maas ka soola in daunas, arranged in a thal. I walked to the lake to watch a black coot and a sloppy duck frolicking. The tall grass swayed in the breeze as the waters lapped gently at the rocks. A blue winged teal flew past.

Fires of wood and charcoal had been lit close to each other. The cook threw cloves, cumin, pounded garlic, green chillies into smoking oil, added green tomatoes, turmeric and dry coriander powder, and let the tart sourness of tomatoes seep out. Kair sangri lay soaked and laal maas gravy bubbled in a dekchi with the hum of garlic and red chillies. Chilke wali urad dal, bajra churma laddoos decked with raisins and sweetened with jaggery, and roasted baatis dunked in ghee, came up in delightful continuity. Shatrunjay had yet another joke to crack – 'a roanni baati is one from which ghee drips like tears… a haasni baati is one that breaks open into a toothy smile.' The scene was typical of a rustic lunch, with vegetables roughly chopped in copper parats, makkai and bajra dough being kneaded by women in floral lehngas, heads covered. Laal maas with baati proved to be an equally lethal combination, but the kids preferred their meat with rice, not minding the repetition at all. The dal was not the usual one served with baati and the churma. It showed the influence of both the Jaipur and Jodhpur versions.

I spent the rest of the morning with the cook. His laal maas proportions were '750 ml oil for 4 kg meat, all the "akhiya" garam masalas,

500 g chopped onions, freshly ground red chillies with the seeds intact, turmeric, dry coriander and salt.' You had to add these along with the mutton to the well browned onions, bhunno this for at least 15 minutes, then add 100 g dry coconut paste and let it bhunno some more. Finally, you had to add 500 g curd, cook, add 250 g crushed garlic and water and let it simmer ('agni kam karna') till well done. It was the use of crushed garlic and red chilli paste that did the trick.

For the baati, unlike in Jaipur, the cook had used split urad dal instead of plain urad and arhar dal. You had to heat water, add the dal and 'machne do' – let it cook. For the 'chamka', heat 100 ml oil, add crushed garlic, red chillies, dry coriander, turmeric, salt, mixed in water, and let it cook. Add the cooked dal to this. Rehan found the lal maas made by the locals rather spicy. He safely had his fill of dal with rice. His mind was obviously on the churma.

The churma laddoo was the first of its kind I had eaten anywhere in Rajasthan. The cook's eyes lit up as he spoke about it. I sensed his bond with the food of his land; the connections ran much deeper than just his cooking it. For making churma, you have to grind the bajra separately; it's got to be more coarse. Put the bajra and oil in a parat and 'masalo' it with your hands. Pour water in a steady stream, constantly moving your fingers through the dough. Add crushed green cardamom powder and make rough balls out of it. Light up a cow dung 'thaapdi', add broken wood, and place the balls of churma on it to roast. When firm, remove the balls, brush away all the ash, and replace them, covering with the ashes – 'ugaadi nahin dikhni chahiye' – they shouldn't appear naked – and bake for half an hour. Remove to a big pan, crumble the balls, using your hands to rub the mixture. Add 'mote taar ki chashni', sieve it twice through a metal sieve. Pound this mixture in a 'hamam dasta', add jaggery (1 kg for 2 kg churma) and use your fingers to mix it well with strong 'muscular' motions. Add 500 g ghee for 2 kg churma and make small laddoos. Wow!

The cook, with his curled moustache, got a big smile of gratitude from me. My friends heaved a sigh of relief, knowing that I would not have budged till I had extracted the last bit of information from him. We left Deogarh feeling uplifted, although so much food was unlikely to defy gravity – it showed up on the weighing scales the next morning...

9

Desserts and Departures

India time – 15.20 p.m. Dinnertime in Sydney. A telephonic war has been declared. The 'target' is already weak, has always been. Preeti is in pain – her calves are swollen and she can barely walk a step without wincing. The doctors there haven't been able to diagnose the problem. 'So are you coming to India to get treated? With or without your legs?' I ask.

'You are all heart, aren't you?'

'Yeah.'

I continue in the same breath, coming straight to the point, 'You remember the apple pie we both baked soon after Didi got married, and I had appealed to your virtually non-existent sisterly-bordering-on-maternal feelings?'

Her tone becomes guarded immediately. 'Hmm, that was more than thirty years ago, I can't remember it at all.'

'Well, you couldn't have forgotten how we kneaded the pastry dough, which seemed pretty okay at first.'

'Go on...'

'The picture showed the pie edges standing firm and

since we didn't have a pie dish, you decided it would be wisest to turn the cake tin upside down and place the rolled out pie dough on the upturned base. You arranged the thickly sliced apples and sprinkled cinnamon and sugar before sliding it into that hideous black Racold oven.'

The protests are bordering on shrieks, like the whistling of a Hawkins cooker. 'That's so idiotic, that wasn't me. You must have made it with one of your friends. Shalini, maybe?' The long distance combat continues. 'I'm going to call Ma and Papa and give them my side of the story... you won't get away with this so easily,' Preeti screeches into the phone. I continue firing my shots. 'Then the sugar started caramelizing. It melted and trickled down in brown rivulets and sizzled at the bottom of the oven.'

'That certainly wasn't me. I know I've made kadhi without adding haldi and waited for it to turn yellow, and I've made halwa without adding sugar, *aand* in those days, hubby darling was gentler and all he would say was, "It'd be nice if the halwa had some sugar, the way it's

supposed to." But *this* is not me,' she belted out her defence in rising decibels. 'If I had been in my right mind, I wouldn't have entered the kitchen,' she ended weakly.

'You are fibbing. I remember it very clearly. We even called Raju bhaiya home to give his expert comments, but that was only after the damn sugar started melting down.'

'Nonsense.'

'You watch it, everything you say is being recorded.'

Trying hard to sound the elder sister, Preeti said, 'Aiyeee, that's illegal, you can't record me without prior warning. I'll take you to court.'

'Bhaiya was horrified, looking at the sorry apple pie and shook his head in disgust, saying, "I'm ashamed to call you my sisters."'

'Total lies. Nobody remembers such an apple pie being baked at home. I called Ma and Papa and they can't recall anything. All Ma could recall was that you tried to teach a new servant how to knead dough and it soon became a huge puddle of atta with ten times the amount of water required. See, I got dirt on you as well, miss pretending-to-be-perfect-cook,' she finished, almost as if she was wiping her hands off the whole matter. The threats continued to come in over the phone...

Baking a chocolate cake with Didi is one of the earliest memories I have. She'd measure each ingredient precisely and then start beating the cake with a spatula – we didn't have electric beaters back then, so the preparation of cake batter needed some amount of physical strength. One had to keep beating till the batter formed a regular pattern, dropped with the right consistency, and acquired the ready-to-go-into-the-oven sheen. I'd sit by the oven patiently, watching the cake rise; sometimes a bump would pop up and subside. As it changed colour and the crust formed, the anticipation grew. It was the news of the day – how well the cake had risen or sunk – and the celebration used to rise or fall in proportion to that.

We had one of those really old, circular aluminium ovens, which always reminded me of a round-faced, podgy grandmom with a warm smile. There is nothing to beat the smell of a freshly baked butter cake. And I could never wait for the mandatory ten minutes cool-off time to unmould it. Best eaten while still very hot, each morsel is sure to melt in your mouth.

When Didi got married and went away, such moments were turned into memories, because Preeti was never the baking type and the historic apple pie was the first and last episode. After she got married, Preeti continued her tradition of culinary mishaps with unbeatable consistency. There are a few cooking disasters tucked away in everyone's closet and I'd never told Preeti mine – luckily, she moved to Sydney the year Sakshi was born and was a comfortable distance away.

There are times when the disaster can't be salvaged. It was one of those evenings when Smriti and I decided to try our hand at gulab jamuns. I love homemade jammus. That day, Mummy was at the neighbour's. We chose to play safe and opened a packet of Gits, following the instructions to the T. I rolled the balls, each ½" diameter, as stated. Smriti laughed. 'Why are you being so kanjoos, make them bigger, at least the size of table-tennis balls.' Slipping the balls into the kadhai to fry them, I saw them swell in slow motion to a size larger than that of a cricket ball. I was stunned. 'Yeh kya ho gaya?' We were a sight in the kitchen, laughing hysterically, holding our tummies and looking helplessly at the huge balls bobbing around merrily in a hot kadhai.

Mummy came and spluttered louder than the fat in the kadhai with a full on Hindi film dialogue, 'Mujhe sharam aati hai tum dono ko apni bahu kahlate hue,' before she collapsed with laughter. She insisted on serving it as a special dessert for dinner that day and made a speech about the cricket balls – 'Never in the history of the Kapur khandaan have such jammus been made.'

As a household, we are not into making mithai and pakwaan during festivals. It was different before I got married. Makhane ki kheer, barfi, gujiya, kutubkhani, ram dane ke laddoo, besan and atta laddoo, khus khus ka halwa, gaund ki barfi, suji and badam ka halwa, shakarkandi ki kheer, sewiyon ki kheer... the list was endless. Makhane ki kheer was made for Janmashthami and shakarkandi ki kheer was made the night we began making the hatri, a week or so before Diwali. Papa measured out the soft wood for making a square hut with a conical roof. The hatri was meant to house the gods – Ram, Sita and Lakshman. The doli and tesu were smaller, one triangular like a Red Indian's hut and the other slightly squarish. All three structures were constructed by tying the sutli firmly at the corners and edges. Coloured paper was stuck with lai, made from shakarkandi, and frills of silver and gold paper were stuck on by us three sisters, with Papa guiding us to add more layers to make it look all sparkling and beautiful. 'Jitna lagaoge, utni Lakshmi aayegi.' We used to sit together after dinner to complete the trio and install them for the Diwali puja. Preeti, as usual, escaped doing most of the work, but landed up at the crucial moment when Ma served freshly made hot kheer.

Ma makes gur and atta ka halwa on navratri sthapna – the piquant sweetness of gur mingles with the rich texture of wheat, to make a halwa that coats the tongue with a teasing, velvety luxuriousness. To have it with puri is ultimate bliss. Ma arranges two puris and a ladle full of halwa on them in a thali, for each one of us, and keeps it ready in the kitchen for devi ki puja. After the puja, we all attack the prasad with the same fervour. It's just one of those things that never changes, no matter how old one gets.

Taste is more about the sentiments it nurtures. There are nights, in the dead of winter, when I get this sudden urge to eat steaming hot meethi roti. I call up Ma and tell her I am coming over. I hop into the car in my night suit, bundle the kids in as well, and leave Bunny cautioning us,

'You girls shouldn't be driving alone at night.' Sakshi retorts, 'Keep quiet, Puppa. It's alright, you go to sleep.'

The smell of roti sizzling under a spoon full of ghee, being pressed down on a tava, and the granules of sugar slowly changing colour, letting the caramel seep out and coat the speckled brown surface of the roti… the deep aroma rising out of the kitchen to spread its warmth and cosiness – it's like curling up under your duvet with a favourite book.

For Papa, homemade sweets mean besan ka laddoo. He never tires of telling us how his mother used to make them in kilos – 'kanastar ke kanastar laddoo banaati thi – that used to be our breakfast with mathri and our dessert after dinner.'

There is a general belief that I am very 'Western' in my tastes; that Indian food, and especially mithai, just don't gel with my 'image'. At a friend's place for dinner, there were about thirteen couples and the host decided to make us play a game. The husband had to write down correct answers to his mother-in-law's birthday, his wife's bra size, her favourite colour, favourite cuisine, favourite actor and movie, favourite dessert, which of her habits got on his nerves, what he liked best about her as his wife, and so on. The wives also had to write down their answers to these questions. I could see all the women scribble very truthful (read boring) answers to the queries. The couple that had the most number of matching answers won the game.

Bra size – 38 C, favourite actor – Brad Pitt (I knew he'd write Naseeruddin Shah, which is the other half of the truth), favourite dessert – malpua. Life throws up unexpected truths! There was the sweet silence of victory when the friend announced 'malpua' while reading from my sheet of answers, and an obvious open mouth at the 38 C – did I read a how-I-wish on his face? Bunny's expression was worth a million dollars and the hooting that followed was the icing on the cake. He gasped, 'Agli baar Mom ne malpua banaya aur tune na khaye, chhe ek saath, toh itna marunga, saali.'

Mummy's malpuas are the best. I can't say more. Resham and Rehan can't stop binging on them and I could actually run the Lays advertisement tagline for them – 'No one can eat just one!'

Malpua

1 cup flour

400 ml milk

2 to 2½ tsp rice soaked in very little water

Saffron soaked in milk

3 cups sugar

1 cup water

Ghee for frying

Mix flour and milk to a thick, but pouring consistency. Grind the soaked rice along with 2 tsp of the flour-milk mixture. Add this to the rest of the mixture. The rice paste is what makes the malpuas crisp. The trick is to be exact on this paste – too much of it will make the malpuas stick to the pan.

Make sugar syrup of a thread's consistency, add saffron to it and leave aside. Heat ghee in a kadhai and spoon in the mixture with a medium sized ladle. The ghee should be hot, but not boiling. Turn the fire to simmer when you add the mixture, watch it bubble up and turn a rich brown on the edges. Flip it over and let the other side cook. It will turn deep honey-brown towards the middle. Turn the heat on high to make it crisp. Lift it out and slide it into the sugar-saffron syrup. Let it soak well, lift it out with a jhar (a perforated spatula) and serve piping hot.

Malpuas are not meant to be like pancakes. They are uneven and have holes in them. Resham calls them doors and windows. The contrasting textures of soft and crisp mix in the mouth, while the saffrony sweetness engulfs your senses. I have seen people with a stiff resistance to sweets dissolve into simpering helplessness and ask for more.

Besan ka sheera

1 tbsp gram flour

¾ tbsp ghee

1 tsp dry ground almonds

Sugar to taste, about a tsp will do

About 150 ml water

Heat ghee in a kadhai, add the gram flour when hot, cook, stirring it continuously till it lets out the most heavenly aroma and turns golden brown. Add almonds, water, sugar and let it boil. The consistency of the sheera is a personal choice – so the quantity of water used depends on that. I like to add broken bits of almonds for that added crunch. This makes a small glass full and works wonders for a bad cough. The perfect way to pass into deep slumber, cuddled in a warm comforter, on winter nights.

Gur Wheat Halwa

1 cup wheat flour

¾ cup ghee

1 cup gur dissolved in 2½ cups of water

Heat ghee in a kadhai, add the wheat flour, cook, stirring continuously till it turns dark chocolaty brown. Add the gur and water mixture and mix well. More water can be added, if a thinner consistency is preferred. Serve hot with puri.

Mothers cook with this inherent quality called 'andaaz'. Mummy and Ma had no problems deciphering how many cups/tablespoons of gram flour, wheat flour or maida they needed to dish out the most perfect halwa, kheer or laddoo. They grew up watching their mothers cook with their style of 'andaaz' – 'Ek muthi suji, cheeni, andaaz ka ghee, khushboo aaye, rang badle, toh paani dal doh. Thodi elaichi peesi hui – bas halwa ban gaya.' They sensed things – knew exactly when the dal would be ready, without bothering with the number of 'seetis' from the pressure cooker. Rice was done to perfection, relying on 'Hmm, ab time ho gaya.' It's a reflection on their lifestyles that had an intuitive cultural connect. Cooking wasn't taught to them, they picked up stuff simply by hanging around in the kitchen – it was a part of the process called 'growing up.'

Ma has never opened a recipe book, but still makes the best chana, mutton curry, pulao, brain fry, gatte ki sabzi, kadhi. Her methi ki paranthi is light, flaky, and doesn't leave a stain of ghee on the fingers. Her laung wale aloo with sainda namak has got Resham and Rehan to declare her the best cook ever. Rehan was aghast when I told him, 'Nani doesn't know how to bake a cake – she's never baked one in her entire life.' Things haven't changed all that much with us – I mean those born in the sixties. We are still 'naturally' comfortable with making dal, sabzi, pulao and basic Indian food, as we are experimenting with set recipes. Kids these days look upon boiling an egg as an occasion. When I was ill, Sakshi preferred to chomp her way through cucumber and a bowl of curd, instead of boiling an egg for her dinner. I am the one who feels the culture shock now.

Rehan can't understand how his grandmothers cook 'just like that' – it is an alien thought to him, since he has grown up in a milieu that has a smattering of all kinds of cuisines and he sees me carry recipe books to the kitchen. At eight years of age, he has tasted black, and white, sesame seed ice cream, wasabi sorbet and vodka chilli cheesecake – I can't blame him for such thoughts. He has observed that if we need Indian mithai, we get it from the sweet shop, and if we need a dessert, we make it at home. Yet, bonds with native dishes don't break. Kheer, halwa, malpua, gulab jamun are still reigning favourites thrice a year – on Holi, Rakhi and Diwali we all go overboard, eating double the amount we should. Mummy very conveniently quotes Badi Mummy while tucking into a bowl of ice cream: 'She used to say that a dessert is like a Viceroy, there's always a place for him.'

Khubani ka Meetha

250 g dried apricots
3 tbsp sugar
1 tsp lemon juice
1 tsp vanilla essence
½ cup cream

Custard:
1 ltr milk
3–4 tbsp sugar
1½ tbsp custard powder

Wash and soak apricots in enough water overnight till they are soft and swollen. Simmer them in the same water till they are tender and about to break. Mash them with the back of the spoon, lift out the seeds. Crack them open to remove nuts. Skin the nuts by dropping them in boiling water for a couple of minutes. Add sugar to warm mashed apricots, cook till thick, stirring constantly. Cool. Add essence, lemon juice, nuts, reserving a few for decoration. Pour the cooled mixture into a glass bowl. Make custard. Cool and stir in the cream. Add this to the apricot mixture when completely cold. Serve with a swirl of cream and nuts.

Khajoor ki roti

1 cup maida
¼ cup atta
½ cup milk
1 tbsp cream
250 g seedless dates finely chopped
1 tbsp castor sugar
1 tbsp green cardamom powder
Ghee

Knead the dough with milk, cream and both the flours, adding a little water only if required. Roll out a thin chapatti. Spread dates mixed with sugar and cardamom powder on it. Cover with another thinly rolled out chapatti. Roast on a tawa, adding a little ghee, cooking till it turns a warm brown on both sides, like the way one makes a paranthi. Cut into four quarters before serving.

Simple homespun sweets can be more exciting than perfectly scooped out green tea sorbets with fruity foams and curled chocolate ribbons. Each dish needs an ambience. I can't imagine eating a khajoor ki roti in a restaurant – it takes on another avatar, minus the cardamom, as date pancakes in a Chinese eatery. Ingredients travel their own paths, journeying into lands and taking on local flavours, morphing into symbols of the culture of which they become a part.

Corn ka Jajariya

500 g corn kernels grated
250 g ghee
3 cups full cream milk
2½ cups sugar
½ cup almonds blanched and sliced
A fistful of raisins
1 tsp green cardamom powder

Grate the kernels off the cob, taking care not to include the husk. Heat the ghee in a non-stick pan and fry the grated corn kernels till you get a nice roasted aroma. Add the milk stirring occasionally. It should be soft to the touch, like halwa, when pressed between the fingers. Add the sugar and allow it to dissolve. Add the almonds and raisins, and sprinkle over with the crushed cardamom. Enjoy this during the rainy season.

There are two types of people in this world – those who love chocolate and those who love chocolate. Chocolate is a synonym for dessert/pudding/anything sweet. For every birthday at home, the question is asked, 'Which cake do you want this time?' I really don't have to bother with the answer. 'Anything gooey, chocolaty, sinful.' Since the kids have grown up, there is an additional comment: 'Make it with a dash of Tia Maria.' 'What about a swig of Bailey's or Grand Marnier in it?' The latest is a concoction of Tequila and orange mousse cake with a fudge brownie base – that's right, chocolate is a permanent fixture.

Each time a new cake had to be made, the kids surrounded me and demanded shapes that they knew would challenge me. Aman wanted Jughead's bust. His crown and his nose just wouldn't stay put. It did get made, but it was one of the many disasters that I've tucked away into the mind's recesses. Sakshi wanted a 'sexy backside of a hot chick in denims studded with crystal.' That was simple, to shade the cream in denim blue and mark out a curvaceous butt with two pockets outlined with glinting crystal studs – which had to be picked out with tweezers before the cake was finally served. Kites, cricket fields, space rockets, bumblebees have all been made for some birthday or the other. For the 'elders', I have normally stuck to the usual round cakes, irrespective of the flavour and type. It's not a very happy feeling when you discover a half-eaten black forest cake sitting helplessly in the fridge, when you have made it for a birthday the next day. Bunny and Sakshi (she must have been four years old) had a go at the cake the night before Bunny's birthday, after I had placed it in the fridge to set. It had to be made again. There were chortles and chuckles echoing through the house the entire day, while I grumbled my way through soaking the fresh cake in cherry liqueur and curling the chocolate.

Mummy taught me how to bake the perfect butter cake. She gave me tips like, 'Either add an extra egg yolk for a creamy texture, or add 10–15 g extra homemade butter, for the same effect.' She stood with me patiently while I went through the drill; she saw me through hardened cakes, sunken cakes, half-cooked-in-the-centre cakes, till I finally had the confidence to bake the cake for Aman's first birthday, for a party of hundred people. The cake was in the shape of his name – A M A N. Seven sponges, of eight eggs each, were baked – chocolate and plain – to be turned into pineapple cake and black forest cake. It was the high point for a young, enthusiastic mother, and it gave me the confidence to keep experimenting and learning.

Birthday cakes became more of an occasion than the birthday itself. I went through the drill of creating Mother Hubbard's shoe, complete with a latticed window, creepers with purple rosettes; a pair of funny faced smiling kites intertwined, Humpty Dumpty, a racing car, a white cake with pink marzipan hearts for Sakshi, a fruit basket for Smriti, and a balloon cake for Rehan's first birthday.

Learning and experimenting on my own, I figured out a light, frothy melon mousse, profiteroles, shortcakes, walnut pies, white chocolate parfait, and lots of other desserts by 'trial and error'.

Butter Cake

4 eggs

Flour

Castor sugar

Homemade or white butter

1 tsp vanilla essence

1 tsp baking powder

Weigh the eggs and measure out the same quantity of flour, sugar and butter. Sieve the flour with the baking powder. Beat eggs with sugar and vanilla essence till pale yellow and creamy, shining proudly. Add butter and whisk till well blended. Add flour and beat for another 5 minutes till the batter starts to form a regular pattern. Total beating time should be between 8–10 minutes. Bake in a preheated oven at 180°C for about 40 minutes. Test with a toothpick – it should come out clean. Some cinnamon powder can be sprinkled over the butter cake, before it goes into the oven.

Topping – chopped almonds, cashew nuts, walnuts and raisins mixed with a couple of tablespoons of granular sugar. You can pour hot custard over a slice before serving it.

Chocolate Cake

The same measurements above have to be used. The proportion of flour has to be reduced to make place for 50 g cocoa. Sift the cocoa and flour together. An extra 10–15 g butter counters the drying effect that cocoa has. Since folks at home are chocoholics, I use 60 g cocoa to satisfy their taste for a richer chocolate experience.

Caramel Cake

Caramelize 4 tbsp sugar. Add very little water when it turns brown. Just before pouring the cake batter into the cake tin swirl in the caramel lightly. If the caramel is thin, it's wise not to use the entire quantity. Just follow your instincts.

Apple Almond Cake

125 g homemade or white butter
2/3 cup castor sugar
2 eggs
1 cup flour
1/3 cup milk
1 apple grated
¼ cup slivered almonds

Grease a cake tin well. Cream the butter and sugar with an electric blender till light and fluffy, beat in the eggs one at a time. Stir in the flour, in two batches, beating with a little milk to smoothen out. Spread the batter in the cake tin. Sprinkle the apple and almonds and bake in a moderate oven for about 45 minutes.

Mud Cake

250 g homemade or white butter
150 g dark chocolate chopped
2 cups castor sugar
1 cup hot water
1 tbsp instant coffee
1/3 cup whisky
1¾ cup flour sifted
¼ cup cocoa
2 eggs lightly beaten
½ tsp baking powder

Grease cake tin. Combine butter, chocolate, sugar, water, whisky, coffee in a double boiler, stir over hot water until the chocolate melts and the mixture is smooth. Cool till lukewarm. Transfer mixture to a large bowl, stir in flour, baking powder, cocoa and then eggs. Pour into cake tin, bake in a moderate oven for 75 minutes. This is a dense, moist cake. Serve with whipped cream or vanilla ice cream.

Raisin Walnut Orange Syrup Cake

125 g butter
2 tsp grated orange rind
1 cup castor sugar
2 eggs
1 cup raisins chopped
½ cup walnuts chopped
1¼ cup flour
2/3 cup milk

Syrup:

½ cup orange juice
1/3 cup castor sugar
1 tsp grated orange rind

Grease cake tin. Cream butter, rind, sugar till light and fluffy, add eggs one at a time. Beat till well combined. Transfer mixture to a large bowl, stir in raisins, walnuts. Fold in flour and milk in two lots. Pour mixture into the cake tin and bake in a moderate oven for about an hour.

To make the syrup, combine all ingredients in a saucepan, stir constantly over low heat, without boiling, until sugar dissolves. Bring to a boil once and remove from heat. Pour hot syrup over the hot cake before serving.

Banana Walnut Cake

125 g butter
1 tsp vanilla essence
¾ cup castor sugar
2 eggs
1 cup banana mashed
1½ cup flour
½ tsp soda bi-carbonate
½ cup chopped walnuts

Grease cake tin. Cream butter, sugar, essence till light and fluffy, add eggs one at a time. Beat well. Stir in half the banana with half the dry ingredients and half the walnuts, then stir in the remaining banana, dry ingredients and walnuts, stir until combined. Pour mixture into cake tin, bake in a moderate oven for 45 minutes.

Date Nut Cake

500 g dates

1 cup water

½ tsp soda bi-carbonate

½ tsp baking powder

185 g butter

2/3 cup castor sugar

3 eggs

1 ¾ cup flour sifted

¼ cup walnuts chopped

Remove seeds from dates. Chop, add water and soda, leave overnight. Grease cake tin. Cream butter and sugar till light and fluffy. Beat in eggs one at a time, till well combined. Transfer mixture to a large bowl, add the sifted flour, walnuts and date mixture. Stir till well mixed. Bake in a moderate oven for about an hour. Serve hot with whipped cream or hot custard – it has a nice homely feel to it.

For converting this into a chocolate date cake, sift ¾ cup cocoa with 1 cup flour.

Strawberry Shortcake

2 cups flour sifted

2 tbsp sugar

3 tsp baking powder

½ tsp salt

½ cup butter

1 egg beaten

2/3 cup milk

3–4 cups strawberries sliced and sugared

1 cup cream whipped

Mix flour, salt, sugar, baking powder, cut in chilled butter till mixture resembles coarse breadcrumbs. Mix the beaten egg and milk, add all at once to the dry mixture and stir enough to mix well. Pour it into a cake tin and bake for about 20–25 minutes. Remove from tin, cool on a rack for five minutes. Split in two layers, spoon strawberries and cream on the bottom layer. Cover with the top layer and spoon more berries and cream over that. Serve immediately.

Chocolate Mousse Cake

3 eggs separated

½ tsp baking powder

½ tsp vanilla essence

90 g castor sugar

30 g cocoa sifted

60 g flour sifted

4 tbsp milk

½ tsp instant coffee

Beat egg whites and vanilla essence till soft peaks are formed. Beat in egg yolks one at a time. Add sugar in two lots and keep beating till the mixture is light and fluffy. Sift flour, cocoa and add in two lots. Pour into a greased cake tin and bake for about 30 minutes in a moderate oven.

Mousse:

300 g cream

200 g dark chocolate

2 tbsp honey

3 egg yolks

1 tbsp brandy or any liqueur

1 tsp vanilla essence

4 egg whites

Heat the cream but don't let it come to a boil. Place chopped chocolate, honey, egg yolks, brandy, vanilla essence in a blender. Pour in the hot cream while blending at high speed for about a minute or two. Pour into a large pan and fold in stiffly beaten egg whites.

Slice off the top layer of the chocolate sponge cake. Settle the sponge in a loose-bottomed cake tin. Soak the sponge with 4 tbsp of milk and ½ tsp coffee dissolved in it. Pour the mousse over it and leave to set in the fridge for a few hours.

Place the set cake on a flat plate. Decorate as you wish. It is best served with whipped cream or vanilla ice cream. For a variation you can add 2 tbsp grated orange rind to the chocolate mixture.

Lemon Cheesecake

2 packets Philadelphia cream cheese
1½ cup cream
Juice of 4 lemons
120 g castor sugar
4 tsp gelatine
3 egg whites
20–22 digestive biscuits
45 g butter melted
4 tsp granular sugar

Beat cream cheese, cream, sugar, lemon juice till well blended. Soak and dissolve gelatine over a pan of simmering water. Add gelatine to the mixture. Beat egg whites till stiff and fold into the mixture.

For the base, heat butter in a pan, add crushed biscuits, granular sugar and let it roast for a short while, constantly stirring. Settle the biscuit base and chill in the fridge till hardened. Now pour the cheesecake mixture on top and again leave it in the fridge.

This is a basic cheesecake recipe to which variations can be easily done. For a mango cheesecake, I add 1½ cup mango puree and adjust the sugar content according to taste. Strawberries and lime juice can also be an option, just for a change.

This recipe for cheesecake is a winner. I prefer changing the toppings and serving sauces with it. Summer fruits – plums, peaches, apricots, lichi, mangoes, pineapple, cherries can be simply tossed in a layer of sugar to give them a glaze and piled on the cheesecake, giving out a bountiful feeling. There is a more lethal version of cheesecake which I chanced upon in Mumbai – a vodka chilli cheesecake.

Vodka Chilli Cheesecake

2 packets Philadelphia cream cheese
1½ cup cream
Juice of 2 lemons
120 g castor sugar
4–6 tbsp vodka
2 tsp strained green chilli paste
3 egg whites
20–22 digestive biscuits
45 g butter melted
4 tsp granular sugar
4 tsp gelatine

Beat cream cheese, cream, sugar, lemon juice till well blended. Add the vodka and chilli paste and blend well, using an electric beater. Soak and dissolve gelatine over a pan of simmering water. Add gelatine to the mixture. Beat egg whites till stiff and fold into the mixture. For the base, heat butter in a pan, add crushed biscuits, granular sugar and let it roast for a short while, constantly stirring. Settle the biscuit base into a loose bottomed cake tin and put it to chill in the fridge till hardened. Now pour the cheesecake mixture on top and leave it to chill in the fridge.

The quantity of vodka and green chilli can vary according to taste. It is wise to taste the mixture and decide for yourself.

'Have you ever walked down Juhu Beach and looked at people?' a friend once asked me. I'd never walked down any of the beaches in Mumbai. Visits to that city in the past have been rather antiseptic and mechanical. On one of those trips, I had trudged with the kids to the Gateway of India, the Aquarium, Chowpatty – where we had done the chaat and ice cream thing – and shopped at Breach Candy and Kemps Corner like typical tourists. The next couple of visits were spread out over a few years, to attend weddings in a great hurry.

In Mumbai, it's the relationship you forge with the city that counts. You need to feel its pull, its power, its failures. You breathe in its air, heavy with water-laden smog; you battle the humidified sunshine and wonder how much sweat will balance on your forehead before it trickles off, because it will never evaporate. And then in the middle of it all, you strike out idealistically to find the 'real' city that is Mumbai. For this city has a different feel; it grows, morphs, contorts, mutates, and meets again, to simply carry on. It mustn't stop. It can't.

'Mumbai is surreal,' said another friend. Yes, it is.

Driving past the Gothic structures of the VT Station and the *Times of India* building, head sticking out of the car window to take in the gabled windows of the High Court and University, the sense of history is palpable. 'We could well be in a European city, if only we could retain the top half of the picture,' I murmured. But it's the 'bottom' half that makes this city what it is.

The blaring, rushing traffic, the cantankerous autorickshaws, the old Fiat taxis, BEST buses, so many faceless pedestrians, the ubiquitous vada pao and bhelpuriwallas, Katrina Kaif and John Abraham billboards, all work as scaffolding to hoist up the city. Many kinds of water rush past, carrying the remains, the slush and sewage, dreams and failures of millions. The motion is constant, like a film in fast forward mode; you see it and then you don't, because it blurs but refocuses. Bizarre – that is what is real about Mumbai.

There is a 'waiting' everywhere. We had to wait outside each and every eatery we visited. Sunday morning began with a fifteen-minute wait outside Madras Café. The hot June morning did not deter people from milling around the eating joints. There is a living, throbbing food culture that survives here. There is a sense of diehard loyalty to food traditions and to signature eateries. I glanced around the café, with the feeling that its tables, fans and fittings had remained the same for some decades now. Years' worth of smells and colours of food must have climbed up the walls. Mumbai feeds on this unchangedness. It demands it.

No normal person, even for a heavy Sunday breakfast, would land up ordering a rasam vada, idli sambhar, udundu dosa, pesserattu dosa, raagi dosa, upma sheera, and coffee to finish. Aah! Sheer bliss and a rotund paunch at the end of it. The upma sheera, a typical breakfast dish, was totally new to me. The sheera was sunny, light and 'khila hua', its sweetness just touching the tongue. It wasn't cloying with the heaviness that follows when ghee meets sugar in a kadhai to sweeten semolina. A sip of water seemed like sacrilege. I didn't want to dilute any of the flavours.

Puran Poli

Atta, as kneaded to make chapattis

190 g chana dal

200 g sugar

Saffron soaked in 3 tsp milk

1 tsp cardamom powder

½ tsp nutmeg powder (optional)

The dough should be pliant and soft. Soak the chana dal for at least 2 hours before putting it to boil in a pressure cooker. Let it cook till one whistle blows, and leave it on low heat for 10 minutes. Strain the dal, let it cool. Add sugar and blend together in a mixer. Roast this mixture in a kadhai, stirring constantly till it becomes a thick paste. Add the saffron. To test whether the mixture is ready, sweep the mixture to one side of the kadhai – if the spatula with which you stir the mixture stands straight, the mixture is ready to be stuffed. Add the cardamom and nutmeg powder.

Be careful to cool the mixture down completely. Roll out a small chapatti.Take dal, double the size of your atta ball, and place it in the centre of the chapatti. Enclose the dal mixture inside the chapatti, like we do for a kachori, making sure its packed in well and sealed. Roll it out again but very gently and mostly from the edges outwords. Avoid putting pressure, especially in the centre. Let it roast on a tawa like you roast a chapatti. A little ghee can be applied on a hot puran poli before serving it, with a bowl of warm, very lightly sweetened milk.

At 6.30, on a Sunday evening, we waited outside Aswad in Dadar. The road was jam-packed and the pavement couldn't be seen. I felt like I was walking on a non-stop conveyor belt. We were called in to share a table with a mother and son. They watched us place our order and shared the waiter's amusement. Misal, pohe, kothimbir vadi, thalipeeth, sabudana vada, puran poli, piyush and kharvas. This was my first taste of Maharashtrian snack food. Watching me invade plates of the stuff, one of my friends remarked, 'You realize you are repeating yourself? Are you really enjoying it so much, or are you doing it only to please us?' I looked at him, aghast, and said, 'You are insane, I love every bit of it.'

Finally, when the puran poli with hot milk arrived, he was ready to disappear under the table as I went into loud raptures. I'd had the fried version of puran poli, but this was thin, light, delicately sweetened and baked like a chapatti. 'What is the funda behind the Marathi balance of spices and flavours?' I swooned. I was dismissed with a curt, 'There is no funda, only the French have fundas about food. We Indians like good taste.'

The next morning I was put in my place again as I gushed over how subtle flavours were 'so very much my kinda thing.' Mihir retorted, 'When you talk about food simply – this is salty, this is theekha – you are at one level. When you start talking about aromas and subtle flavours, it's time to see you zipping around in a Mercedes.' I protested, 'Every Indian kitchen has aromatic spices like javitri and jaiphal.' Mihir's eyes twinkled mischievously as he said, 'Yeah, inse miliye, yeh hai meri behen, javitri, married to jaiphal.'

A step into Britannia & Co restaurant in Ballard Estate takes you back to the pre-World War era. The faded green checked table covers match the dirty green walls and patches of chipped plaster on the ceiling. White boards on the walls, with chipped tiles, announce the specials for the day. Old wall fans whir and rustle up the air, as if careful not to disturb the decor which is obviously much more than a 'decor' – it is the very grain of the place.

The restaurant's famous berry pulao was placed on the table. Boman Kohinoor, the owner's wife, had worked in Tehran for seven years, where she learnt to cook the zireshk, or berry, pulao, and had improvized by adding kebabs and masalas. The barberries, after which the pulao is named, are specially imported from Iran. Boman, a charming Parsi gentleman, still appeared to be a resident of colonial India, with his accent, mannerisms and English diction. His father, Rashid, opened this typical Parsi eatery in 1923, the year Boman was born. 'I wanted to become a doctor. My father died leaving me with eight brothers and sisters to take care of, so I was compelled to join the restaurant,' Boman said, continuing to count ten-rupee notes to return as change against a bill that had just been paid... 'Ek, do, teen, char, paanch, there you are...' He motioned to the waiter in his black bow tie on a white shirt.

The berry pulao lived up to its reputation. The barberries genuinely add the extra zing to the rice. The sali chicken and dhansak came as a must-do, but the caramel custard was to die for. There are certain desserts that are classic and you can't get bored with them. There were rumours of Britannia being sold. The old man explained, 'My two rascals wanted to sell this place even before I kicked the bucket!' The deal fell through and all of Mumbai must have heaved a collective sigh of relief. Boman's words were slow and measured. 'Bush and Dick Cheney have eaten here. You know Abhishek Bachchan? He comes here for lunch.'

That evening, walking around VT station, we decided to stop for our evening fix – vada pao. The notice on the wall said, 'Aaram vada pao.

Eating House Grade II. 8.30 am to 9 pm. Sunday closed. Please take care of your luggage.' Mihir put his arm around me and said, 'She's my luggage.' The vada pao came with pohe, dahi misal, sheera and kharvas. Kharvas, a lightly sweetened, cardamom-flavoured milky cheese, set in a perfect square, is supposed to be made from the first milk given by a cow after she has delivered a calf. I wondered how many calves would need to be delivered in any dairy farm, to produce such large quantities of first milk. If served at any fine dining restaurant, kharvas could easily be passed off as a fancy rare-milk cheese, garnished with roasted almond slivers, wild berry reduction or passion fruit foam carelessly dribbled on the side, and sold for Rs 550 per serving!

'Shall we go to Samovar? It's peaceful and I want a break from the noise,' said Mihir. I was taken aback. 'No, I love the noise. I simply *love* the fact that everyone shares tables here, you don't know who it is you are sitting next to and having your meal with. It could be just about anyone – a BEST bus driver, a dabbawalla, a supermodel!'

'Oh, so she actually *shared* a table, our madame! You are slumming it here, aren't you?' The guy took my case full on. 'Shucks, you are so touristy – but, of course, you come from the land of DBC takeaways and LMB.'

'DBC?'

'Dal, baati, churma, woman!'

I explained to him, with utmost seriousness, the travails faced by warriors who could only roast balls of atta in rugged jungles, but was interrupted. 'Oh, so it was more a case of grenade practice, right? Lobbing those balls of dough into a pit of live charcoals? Too bad they never exploded!' The vada pao with its spicy potato filling went down rather quickly.

'What next?' The answer was an obvious 'Alphonso mango ice cream and custard apple ice cream at Bachelors.'

The next stop was Theobroma, where we sat with a lemon mountain cake, vodka chilli cheesecake, blueberry cheesecake and chocolate nutty pudding lined up on the table. We chatted about graphic novels and animation movies and spooned our way through the desserts, looking longingly at the banoffee high, tiered temptation, orange mousse and rum-soaked cake with truffle sauce. But there are abdominal limitations... no place to even wash down the sweetness with coffee... I needed to breathe.

'For the last lunch, we will eat at this typical Malwani place tomorrow,' Mihir announced. Highway Gomantak, in Bandra East, can be seen from the highway, tucked away in a corner of the decrepit buildings of Pranav Coop Housing Society. The menu card is painted on a series of continuous white enamelled boards, which run the entire length of the dining room. Tables are arranged like in any other dhaba, edge to edge, and you can hear the conversation between folks sitting at the next table, which makes it a total eating experience. Sharing imparts layers, and can't be labelled or categorized, and that's what this city gives you on a platter.

We launched into plates of bombil fry, coated in crisp batter – the fish broke in the hand, soft, pliant, melting in the mouth. My eyes took in the menu – pomfret kaliputi, mori masala – Rs 65. The rhythm of reading the menu – bangde tikhale, kurliya masala, tisriya masala – was interrupted by the clang of utensils. Waiters in maroon shirts and shorts bustled about, waiting at tables, carrying dishes, scurrying back to the kitchen with empty plates and chewed up bones. It was like another facet of the living food culture.

Our second course was pomfret fry followed by mussels, hot crab curry with red chilli and oyster masala in coconut. Fried prawns, surmayi and chicken liver came next. Keema masala and suka were extra special – not too spicy, but flavourful. We ended with another round of bombil fry. No place for dessert once again.

Back home to a watermelon and tori-ghiya-tinda diet, it took me a while to stop missing Mumbai, the food, and most of all, my friends. Back to the treadmill and swimming routine, back to monitoring Sakshi's diet.

Everyone at home gets into a flap everytime it is announced casually, 'Oh, a very important client is in town and will have lunch with us – of course, it has to be the best.' Mummy can splutter with anger at the short notice as much as she likes, but we have to swing into action– from thawing the chicken and fish, to quickly getting all the vegetables chopped, and assembling dressings for salads. Dessert has to be the tops. I manage a quick job by layering fresh mango pulp alternately with whipped cream, crushed digestive biscuits and pulsed frozen cranberries dusted with sugar – it tastes luscious and juicy, with the cranberries adding a zesty crunch. I set it in shot glasses and espresso coffee cups and there is total silence at the table when it is served. 'I have messed up!' I think, dreading the aftermath. But the silence, I discover, is because they are struck by the stylized simplicity of the dish.

Profiteroles

50 g butter
150 ml water
65 g flour
¼ tsp baking powder
2 eggs beaten

Filling:

1 tsp vanilla essence
50 g castor sugar
150 g cream
1–2 tbsp Grand Marnier (optional)

Chocolate Sauce:

1 tbsp butter
3 tbsp cocoa heaped
1 tsp instant coffee
180 granular sugar
1 tbsp honey
185 ml water

Grease a cookie sheet. Sift flour and baking powder. Place water and butter in a pan and heat gently until the butter melts. Bring to a boil, remove from heat and immediately add all the flour, beating with a wooden spoon until smooth. Gradually add the egg, beating vigorously after each addition, until the paste looks glossy and leaves the sides of the pan clean. Allow to cool. Preheat oven to 220°C.

Place the choux paste in a piping bag fitted with a 2 cm plain tube. Pipe out 24 balls of paste, each about the size of a walnut, keeping them well apart. Bake for about 15 minutes, till well risen and golden. If the profiteroles have still not risen enough, reduce temperature to 180°C and continue baking for another 5 minutes. Slit each puff while hot and leave to cool on a rack.

To make the chocolate sauce, melt butter, add cocoa, coffee, sugar, honey, and stir till well mixed over a pan of simmering water. Add water, stirring continuously till smooth. Let the sauce cook for at least 15 minutes, till it starts to thicken. Remove from heat, cover and leave it aside to cool.

For the filling, whip cream, sugar, vanilla essence and liqueur, if being used. Pile a heaped teaspoon on the base of each profiterole and cover it gently with the top. Normally, they aren't slit all the way through but I prefer to do it because it somehow tastes better and looks more alluring with cream oozing out lustily. Make a pyramid of the filled profiteroles on a flat platter, dousing each layer with thick chocolate sauce. Once piled up, they are a perfect visual treat. I like to scoop out the extra dough from inside each profiterole before filling it with cream. This leaves a feathery touch on the tongue.

Bunny calls profiteroles temptresses. Baking them, in batches, for over forty dinner guests, can be a back bender. But observing them pop a profiterole into their mouths and closing their eyes, as if transported into another world, is enough to make the backache go away. The sight always reminds me of the children's delight as they watch Roald Dahl's *Charlie and the Chocolate Factory* for the nth time.

The chocolate sauce is a universal recipe – it can be had with ice creams, or as an accompanying sauce for any dessert that demands to be uplifted. I've caught Bunty, Bunny and all the five kids tipping the decanter straight into their mouths to sample it neat.

Creating desserts by combining basic recipes is not so demanding. A simple run of honey, cream, milk, gelatine and egg whites gives rise to a honey mousse; a chocolate sponge serves as the base. Profiteroles doused in thick chocolate sauce can alternate layers of honey mousse; toasted, slivered almonds or crushed caramel can cover the sides. Thick strands of chocolate sauce running randomly across can serve as a garnish.

Mocha Granita

100 g dark chocolate broken in pieces
3 tbsp instant coffee
50 g castor sugar
600 ml boiling water
150 ml whipped cream
1 tbsp icing sugar

Put chocolate in a bowl. Dissolve coffee and sugar in water and pour over the chocolate. Leave it to stand for 5 minutes, by which time the chocolate should soften; if not, stand the bowl over hot water for a short while. Stir until the mixture is smooth and leave it to cool. Pour it into a shallow container and freeze till the edges are firm. Transfer to a bowl and beat again till smooth. Return to the container and refreeze. Whip cream with icing sugar. Serve small portions of granita scooped into stemmed glasses and top it with the cream. For a special occasion, drizzle 1 tbsp Tia Maria or Kahlua.

Chocolate Soufflé

15 g gelatine
3 tbsp water
1 tbsp instant coffee
60 g cocoa
400 ml milk
115 g castor sugar
2 tbsp thick cream
3 eggs separated
1 tsp vanilla essence

Soak gelatine in water and let it swell. Mix cocoa, coffee with milk and stir over low heat till blended well. Bring the mixture to a boil and simmer for a minute. Let it cool. Beat egg yolks with sugar till blended well. Gradually stir in hot milk mixture. Strain mixture back into the pan and stir over gentle heat until it lightly coats the back of a wooden spoon. It mustn't be allowed to boil or the mixture will curdle. This can be done in a double saucepan. Leave it aside to cool. Dissolve gelatine over gentle heat and stir into the mixture. Whip cream lightly and add to the cooled mixture. Whip egg whites till stiff. Stand the pan of soufflé mixture on a bed of ice cubes, stirring constantly. As soon as the mixture begins to thicken and set, fold in stiffly beaten egg whites. Pour into a soufflé dish and chill until firm.

The cooling down of the basic custard is most crucial since stark temperature differences result in the soufflé breaking up into layers. Whenever I am in a mood of hurried impatience, I've had to face this as a punishment, and then there's double the amount of labour, because it has to be made all over again!

Caramel soufflé

5 eggs separated
500 g sugar
750 ml milk
1 tsp vanilla essence
60 g gelatine
25 g almonds roughly chopped
25 g cashew nuts roughly chopped
15 g butter
2 cups cream

Cream egg yolks and 6 tbsp of sugar together. Bring the milk to boiling point and add gradually to the mixture. Heat over boiling water for a few seconds, remove from fire and cool. Add melted gelatine and vanilla essence. Strain and place on ice, bring it nearly to setting point. Fold in egg whites (stiffly beaten). Caramelize the rest of the sugar with the butter and add the nuts to it. Crush and sprinkle it over the soufflé.

Walnut Pie

Short crust pastry:
300 g flour
¼ tsp salt
½ tsp baking powder
2 tsp castor sugar
150 g butter
Cold water to mix
½ tsp vanilla essence

Filling:
20 g butter
300 g sugar
250 g walnuts roughly chopped
125 ml cream
1 egg yolk beaten

Add salt, baking powder and sugar to the flour. Rub in butter with your finger tips till the mixture resembles bread crumbs. Add the water and vanilla essence and knead to a quick, rough dough, handling as little as possible. Cover and chill for 30 minutes. Roll out two-third of the dough to the thickness of about ¼" and use it to line the base and sides of an 8" pie dish.

Filling:
Melt butter in a pan, add sugar and cook over low heat, stirring continuously till it caramelizes into a golden brown. Add walnuts, cream and turn up heat. Just as it reaches boiling point, remove from the heat. Let it cool and spread it into the pie shell.

Roll out remaining pastry dough to make a lid. Brush the overlapping edge of the pie base with a little egg yolk, press on the lid and seal the edges. Brush the top with egg yolk. Prick a design with a fork for the steam to escape while baking. Bake for 30–40 minutes at 180°C and serve warm with vanilla ice cream.

Mixed Fruit Pie

500 g apples
150 g dates
150 g raisins
150 g dry figs chopped
100 g dry apricots chopped
75 g cashew nuts chopped
50 g walnuts chopped
2–3 tbsp sugar
30 g butter
3 eggs
1 tbsp rum

Short crust pastry:
See walnut pie recipe

For the short crust pastry dough, use the same recipe as the walnut pie. Roll out three-fourths of the pastry dough and line an 8" pie dish. Prick the base and bake blind for 20 minutes. Sprinkle the pie base with 1 tsp semolina.

Filling:

Cook apples till dry and puree. Mix with the other ingredients of the filling and fill the pie base with this mixture. A pinch of cinnamon or nutmeg powder can be added to the fruit mixture. Roll out the remaining pastry dough, cover the pie. Seal the edges and prick a design on the top. Bake at 180°C till it turns golden brown. Serve with whipped cream.

Chocolate Espresso Sauce

1 tbsp instant coffee

175 ml boiling water

100 g castor sugar

110 g dark chocolate cut in pieces

Add boiling water to the coffee. Stir to blend. Add sugar and chocolate, and once it cools slightly, pulse it in a blender till smooth. Serve it hot or chilled. This sauce thickens when chilled and can be softened by standing the jug in a bowl of warm water.

Plum Sauce

425 g ripe dark plums

¼ cup castor sugar

1 cinnamon stick

¼ tsp grated lemon rind

1 tsp cornflour

¼ cup water

3 tsp Amaretto (optional)

Puree plums with the skin to let the colour seep into the sauce. Remove larger pieces of skin. Combine puree with sugar, cinnamon, lemon rind. Stir over high heat, adding cornflour when it begins to boil. Thicken, remove cinnamon, stir in liqueur if used. Serve chilled with a cheesecake, almond cake, or simply with vanilla ice cream.

Orange Sauce

1 tbsp water

½ cup castor sugar

1 cup orange juice

1 tbsp Grand Marnier

½ cup orange segments (bite sized)

1 tsp corn flour

Combine water and sugar in a saucepan. Stir over gentle heat till it caramelizes to a light golden brown. Remove from heat, stir in juice, liqueur, orange segments. Return to heat to thicken slightly with the cornflour. Serve chilled.

It's sweet nothings, really. Aman ambles into the lounge and sinks into the couch, to say to us, 'I'm tired.'

Dad says to him in turn, 'I'll give you four options why you are tired and sulky – a) you climbed the stairs twice today; b) you weren't given what you asked for; c) Mum made you drink nimbu pani instead of a banana milk shake; d) you asked to eat dinner out and you weren't allowed.'

Aman isn't amused and growls back, 'None of the above.'

Bunty implodes into the conversation vehemently, 'There are only four options for Aman – a) he is hungry; b) he is hungry; c) he is hungry; d) he is hungry.'

'Let's have dinner' is all Aman says, feigning a tired disinterest, which supposedly shows him to be intellectually superior to all of us who are laughing at him.

After dinner, it is my turn to sulk and mumble. 'Mujhe kuch meetha khana hai.' I am tired of pecking at overripe mangoes cut into irregular pieces, some almost pulpy and ready for cold storage. Bunny reels off choices from Link Road kulfi to gelato and kesar milk at M. I. Road, to Sodhani's ras malai... nothing works. 'Chalo, forget it, Rehan hasn't finished his homework, no point going out...' I say.

There is so much joy in tucking myself into bed with a bowl filled with three scoops of Butterscotch ice cream and watching a movie, its impact heightened by Bunny's snores, the cold touch of the spoon on my tongue, and the crunch of caramel folding into the creaminess of the ice cream. 'Bas, ab kuch nahin chahiye… as long as he doesn't wake up and ask to share my bowl of cold sin with him.' Each time I carry a snack to bed, Bunny *has* to wake up – he senses that I am eating even in deep sleep. 'I won't share my ice cream with you…' I mumble, and he turns and goes back to sleep, grunting his protest.

Sakshi wanders in with a face that looks as if she's been beaten up – one of those nights when she isn't her usual shrieking self. There are just two weeks left for her to leave for Minnesota and maybe that is troubling her. Maybe the reality that her life will never take her back to the same turn again is sinking in. Maybe the fear of living alone and having to go back to a dorm, instead of a cosy home, is gnawing at her insides.

She speaks with quiet determination. 'I've decided to do a BSc in child psychology, instead of the regular BA, and I was thinking that I'll work with an NGO for work experience before I do my post grad. I was also thinking, I won't come back next summer. I'll do the thirteen-week summer course there…'

I listen. Her eyes are dark and sombre, her voice soft. Is she looking for reassurance, a reaction maybe? I reply, 'You make up your mind and do what you think is best… but whatever you do, give it more than your hundred per cent…' Rehan blunders into the room with his racing car, saying 'vroom, vroom', and Sakshi sparks back into action. 'You stinky, sweaty fellow! You will not sleep in my room today.' She clicks her fingers at me. 'You heard that, woman. He will not sleep next to me – he stinks of his tennis sweat all night… I have a life. Remember, it's my room and I don't want him there.' I chuckle my way through the histrionics – it is a daily routine, which has to be gone through, like all clichés. She throws a couple of pillows at him and shuts the door decisively.

I protectively shepherd Rehan to Sakshi's room and keep ringing the giant ghungru that hangs at her door, until she opens up. 'Kya hai,' she snaps, looking at Rehan as if he were an alien from outer space. One heavy hand on his head, she pushes him towards her study table. 'You will sleep under the table in this corner. That's all the space you'll get. As it is, tum isi layak ho. Mum tumhe gutter se utha ke layi thi, you are her unwanted bhudape ki lathi.' Rehan and I have heard this line so often, we laugh and he cuddles into her duvet. For an eight-year-old, his sense of humour has matured beyond his age – a simple survival tactic for him, growing up with four elder siblings.

Every morning, the routine for me is to bang on Sakshi's door at 9.15 a.m. before I sit down to work. 'Sakshi, get up, move your butt, your breakfast (half a measly green apple) is still sitting here. You haven't even had any water. What is this, why do I have to do this jhik jhik every day with you? Why can't you be up and about? Have you got your address list for the US ready, and your medicine list? How will you survive on your own…' My usual torrent out, I step into the confines of my office. She grunts, just like Bunny, turns over, and goes back to sleep.

But, today, I have not woken her up. She comes in after a couple of hours, as if moon-walking. 'Arre, Mummy, you didn't come to wake me up today.'

I shake my head. 'You are incorrigible.'

My chair is swivelled around and she plonks herself on my lap. I feel a paralytic stroke numbing my legs. The tingling slowly subsides into a numbness, while she launches into her monologue of the day. 'Pata hai, Tushar called… and you know this guy…'

I counter with, 'We have to go to Kavita aunty's place tonight, it's her mom's memorial service. She specially asked for you to be there.'

Sakshi beams. 'It seems I am everyone's favourite, aren't I?'

I dread the silence that is going to engulf the house when she leaves.

'You are living in denial, aren't you?' I was asked a week before we left for Minneapolis to drop Sakshi. It had been hitting me in waves. The feeling of a vacuous emptiness would dig deep inside me and my eyelids would sting with a thousand needles.

Minneapolis is quiet when the university is closed and the students are away. Red brick buildings, neat roads and pruned flower beds led to the Mall, which has old colonial buildings that house the departments of technology, chemistry and physics, punctuated by towering trees with benches beneath them. We walked around exploring the campus, which we soon realized had to be bussed, since it was sprawling. We went down the river Mississippi with Sakshi while she trailed behind us – 'Why do we have to do this family shit of walking by the river? Dad, you don't have to pose like a tourist for pictures. Stop trying to embarrass me, I won't react.' Browsing around the Koffman Memorial students' bookstore, she figured out her MacBook Pro deal, and watching her choose her bag was fun. 'Ah, finally, she is doing things on her own.'

She went about her medicals and her international students' orientation while we lazed at coffee shops around town. Reading noticeboards was like facing my own college life, save that these kids seemed to know where they were going. Each board had the UM motto – 'Driven to Discover' – and I mocked Sakshi by saying, 'It will be a while before you learn the ropes of being driven to discover.' I continued browsing: 'Top Deals', 'Wanted a Male Room Mate', 'Researcher Wanted for Intercultural Communication Theory and Practice', 'Options, Advocates, Choices', 'Healing, Recovery, Renewal', 'A Safe You Is a Safe U'.

Just then, a lady rode her bike straight up to her office door, inside the building, and an old blonde manager rollerbladed smoothly into his cabin. We spent our waiting minutes musing, chuckling, and just soaking it all in. It was nice to get to know the town where I was leaving my child for the next four years of her life – the town that was going to shape her and the rest of her life.

We watched the students wheeling their bags down the road and off to Comstock Hall. For once, Bunny refrained from taking Sakshi's bags from her – it was time for her to know that Papa wouldn't be around to carry her baggage. Something came over her when we reached her room. She simply sat and watched me unpack. I prodded her, 'This is your stuff, your room, you should be emptying out your bags yourself. Why am I doing it?'

'I dunno, guess I'm kinda overwhelmed...'

'Yeah, right,' I said to myself, letting the magnanimous mom inside me take over for once. Every drawer was arranged, the clothes hung up and her stationary sorted, while she watched.

The next morning, she called. 'I can't find my clutcher, I couldn't find my pyjamas last night.'

'Too bad, kiddo.' I hung up.

'I'm going for dinner with my friends. We'll do our farewell dinner tomorrow, okay?'

It was Saturday. Buses ran at half-hour intervals from downtown. Lugging Sakshi's shopping around the theatre district, with her clothes hangers poking my sides, wasn't exactly my idea of an evening out. Crossing over to Fourth Avenue, South, we waved a cab down. The cabbie screeched to a halt just seconds before he could hit another car. The driver honked in protest and our cabbie, an Afro-American, cursed him loudly. Thankfully, the other driver zipped away, and I breathed again. The cabbie sensed my unease and said, 'Relax, ma'am, it's crazy when white men start acting like niggers...' I smiled, not wanting to continue the conversation.

We dropped Sakshi off at Koffman. It wasn't a happy feeling when I turned back to see her walking away from us. She was alone on the street and it was dark. As the cab moved away, she grew tinier. I had to grip my mind with a pair of steel tongs and shake some of the gelatinous grey matter inside – 'Stop this. You will drive yourself insane with fretting.'

With a resolution that drew upon all my strength, I grinned at Bunny. 'Let's go back to the Old Spaghetti Factory.' A fine bottle of rosé and a robust, homespun lasagne later, we were back on track – happily tipsy and well fed.

The last day in Minneapolis, we walked towards downtown via the old stone bridges, talking gibberish and jibing at each other. After a quiet lunch at the Loft – a literary centre and art gallery – we came upon a comic book store which was spilling over with comics and graphic novels. Sakshi and I went berserk, while Bunny indulged us patiently. Aimless wandering can be therapeutic.

For the family farewell dinner, we settled down at Masa, a Mexican restaurant. 'For the last minute parental burst,' as Sakshi said.

'You are going to get over with having that parent moment right here, Mommy, and when we go back to my room, you will depart in dignity, you get that?'

I wagged my finger at her and ordered the drinks. A peddling bar on a tram drove past, a bunch of people laughing as varying decibels left an echo down the road. I punctuated my dos and don'ts to her and she kept up a veneer of quiet patience.

We wandered over next door to my favourite joint in Minneapolis – Dakota jazz club and restaurant. We had spent an evening there, listening to the Kelly Rossum Quartet play. The entire club was swinging with music. Suzanne Vega had played there the night we landed in Minneapolis. Knowing that was enough to make me go crazy. The desserts had looked appealing, but we decided to leave. A last minute entry to listen to Ben Vereen playing would cost us $50 a head. The manager said, 'You can sit outside and listen in… no charge for that.'

We decided to splurge on the sweets instead. In came the prettiest looking dessert I had seen on this trip. The buttermilk panna cotta sat nimbly on a startlingly pink hibiscus soup and berry salad. A hibiscus, set under the glaze, shook delicately as I gently slid my spoon in, almost unwilling to disturb the perfect picture composition. This was a piece of art.

The Valrhona chocolate cake was served with blood orange segments and extra virgin olive oil. It was an orgasmic explosion on the tongue. Sakshi hadn't ordered dessert, but happily dug into our plates. 'I am telling you, you will miss someone stealing your food like I do.'

We were back in Sakshi's room to finally say goodbye. Bunny was brave. A simple hug and it was done with. I held her and felt as though I was pregnant again. My baby was still in my womb, how could she be out in the big world? It was as though she read my mind. I really didn't know who was holding whom. The blood in my veins was feeling the pulse of hers – in all these years, the reality of being a mother hadn't sunk in, as it did at that moment.

As I stepped into the lift, I questioned myself, 'Have I simply bumbled along, going through the routine of being a mom and somehow managed to do it? Why haven't I felt this sensation before?'

Shaking me out of my stupor was this burly man. 'We have to pack. Remember, we are off to Vegas in the morning?'

Acknowledgements

This book happened because Sakshi, Resham, Rehan, Tanay and Aman happened. It happened because Bunny threatened to write (and self-publish) a soft porn story and sell 75,000 copies of it from all the railway stations in the country. It happened because a friend once remarked, 'I guess Sakshi will finish writing your book for you once you are dead and gone.'

There are lots of people whom I have to thank for believing in and helping me along.

Mom and Dad – for always being there and bearing with all my eccentricities.

Ma and Papa – for making me what I am (whatever that is).

Atul and Smriti – for being the friends I need them to be.

Didi – for being my first teacher and more than a sister.

Preeti – for all the culinary chaos and entertainment and being a caring, concerned sister.

Sakshi – well, she knows why.

Resham – for constantly reminding me that I am the mom.

Rehan – for being so wise at all of ten years of age.

Tanay and Aman – they let me fatten them up.

Namita Gokhale – for believing in the very first draft and giving me the courage to go on.

Pramod – for pushing me along ever so gently and being the fine human being he is.

Mihir – for handling his 'luggage' (me) with care.

Jugal – for saying what he did about Sakshi finishing the book, and much more.